She turned around and froze.

A pair of hazel eyes bored into hers with such intensity that she suddenly felt flushed. Disheveled black hair hung in soft curls at the back of his collar as he gave her a familiar one-sided smile. "Hey, Bree."

"Tony?" Shakiness threatened to overwhelm her. Her heart pounded in her ears and she squeezed the box in her hands to hide their trembling. Seconds seemed to stretch into minutes as Sabrina fought to keep her composure. Years of anger, bitterness and betrayal fought against a ridiculous urge to throw herself into his arms. Her teeth worried her bottom lip as she struggled to find the words to say.

"I heard you were moving back. Are you here to stay?"

"I don't know yet." He was close. Too close. The sandalwood scent of his aftershave sent her heart into overdrive. She took a quick step backward and tripped over the cart. The breath rushed from her lungs as he caught her in his strong arms.

His face was close enough for her to make out a faint scar under his jaw, just below his left ear. The scar he'd gotten while defending her. Along with the bump on the bridge of his nose.

She pushed against his chest, struggling to right herself. Silence permeated the air between them and his gaze never left hers. Like a mouse caught in the hypnotic gaze of a cat, she couldn't move.

Breathe. You're not eighteen anymore.

Dear Reader,

As a public-school teacher, I've seen my share of defiant children walk in the door with a chip on their shoulder. I've come to believe the saying "Those that deserve love the least, need it the most." I'm not sure who penned that, but it's become my classroom motto. Oftentimes, all kids need is someone to believe in them, root for them and never give up. I know. I've seen it happen.

When I was fifteen years old, I spent many happy hours pecking away on an old typewriter I bought at a yard sale for a buck. Even back then, all my stories involved bad boys and the good girls who loved them. Because even my teenage mind reasoned that rebellious behavior was just a cover-up for some deep-rooted pain. All they needed was someone to believe in them.

That's when Tony was born. He was the perfect bad boy with a heart of gold. What he needed was a girl willing to give up everything for him. He had to wait almost thirty years for me to conjure Sabrina. She's a small-town girl with pride as big as Texas and a heart that's bigger. I finally had my perfectly flawed couple and they couldn't wait to tell me their story.

I hope you enjoy Tony and Sabrina's journey as much as I've enjoyed writing it. I'd love to hear from you! Please visit me leannebristow.com.

LeAnne

HEARTWARMING

Her Texas Rebel

———

LeAnne Bristow

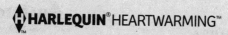

Recycling programs
for this product may
not exist in your area.

ISBN-13: 978-0-373-36830-3

Her Texas Rebel

Copyright © 2017 by Traci Rhodes

Printed in U.S.A.

LeAnne Bristow may have been born and raised in central Texas, but she's a desert rat at heart. She calls southeastern Arizona home, even though her husband wouldn't let her claim the title Arizonan until 2011, the year she'd officially lived in Arizona longer than Texas. When she's not arguing with the characters in her head, she enjoys hunting, camping and fishing with her family. Her day job is teaching kindergarten, but now that her three kids are grown, she's determined to teach her granddaughter how to catch lizards and love the desert as much as she does.

This is my first book and I feel like I've won an Oscar! There are so many people I'd like to acknowledge for helping me along this journey. First, I need to thank Janet Ferguson, Jackie Layton and Misty Beller for reading and rereading chapters and pushing me to be a better writer. Y'all are the best critique partners anyone could ever ask for. My wonderful agent, Scott Eagan, for never giving up on me, and my family and coworkers at Benson Primary School for cheering me on. I'd also like to thank Kaci Morrison for answering a million questions about the wonderful work that is done at the Cherokee Home for Children. This book is dedicated to all the people who work tirelessly to make a difference in the lives of children who don't have anyone else in their corner.

CHAPTER ONE

"YOU DON'T WANT to do this." Tony Montoya took a step forward, despite the gun pointing at his chest. His own weapon remained tucked in his holster. In eight years on the San Antonio police force, he'd only drawn it a handful of times.

The hand holding the gun shook, but the teen refused to lower the weapon. "Yes." The boy's chin lifted in defiance. "I do."

Adolfo wouldn't pull the trigger. He wasn't a bad kid; he was just trying to survive. Tony understood. How many times had he stolen food from a convenience store when he was a kid? But Adolfo wasn't trying to steal food for his family. The gun in the teenager's hand was evidence of that.

"What are you going to gain?" Tony took another step toward him. "You think if you bring Raul money you'll get moved from a peewee to a soldier?"

The boy's dark eyes widened at the mention of that name. "You don't know nothing, man."

"I know you ain't married yet." Tony nodded at the boy's right arm, bare of the bandanna marking him as a full-fledged member of the street gang.

A band tightened around his chest. Raul's gang suffered more deaths than any other in the area. If he failed Adolfo, how long would it be before the boy paid the ultimate price? Would a rival gang member end his life or would it be someone in his own unit? A heaviness settled over Tony's heart.

He'd seen too many young men ruined by the lure of gang life. Those losses far outweighed the people he'd managed to help leave the streets behind. Most of the boys, like Adolfo, weren't tempted by the money, drugs and women. It was family. A place to belong. Over half of them were on their own. Deserted by mothers too strung out on drugs to care where their children were anymore, or too stressed out trying to earn enough money to keep a roof over their heads. Whatever the reason, the result was the same.

Tony had one chance to talk Adolfo down. He had to remind the kid that he had a real family, a family that depended on him. Keeping his voice low, Tony said, "Raul will still have you jumped. How you gonna explain that to your *madre*?"

The boy's eyes flashed and Tony knew he'd struck a nerve. "How can you help her take care of your baby brother if you're dead or in jail? Your mama needs you."

"Leave my mama out of this." The gun shook even more, and Adolfo's eyes darted around the store.

Out of the corner of his eye, Tony spied the store clerk moving to the edge of the counter. He held a hand up to stop him. Mr. Chan kept a .22 rifle under the counter. *Please don't pull that gun out. Not now.* It might push the kid right over the edge.

Adolfo noticed, too. "Put your hands up where I can see them!"

"If I have to put my hands up, how am I supposed to get your money?" The old man looked bored. He'd experienced more than his share of robbery attempts.

Tension hung like a cloud of smoke as Adolfo and the clerk stared each other down. For the first time, Tony stepped away from Adolfo, putting himself between the boy and the old man.

"Move." Adolfo jerked the gun.

"No."

"Move. Or I'll shoot you." Adolfo waved the weapon again. His voice held a note of panic.

Tony remained in place. If he moved, Adolfo would see it as a victory and that would empower him even more. Tony looked the kid in the eye. "I'm not afraid to die. I know exactly where I'm going. But what about you? Where are you going when you leave this store? You got no place to go."

"I'll go to the club."

"No, you'll go to jail, if you're lucky."

"You don't understand."

"Try me." Tony knew the kid's life because it had once been his, too. "Your pop skipped out on you. Your mom works all day, so all you got is the streets. You're being challenged, *mijo*, and you're about to fail in the worst possible way."

Adolfo's shaking hands told Tony he still had a chance. If the shaking stopped, it would mean the boy had found his resolve and was lost. Tony edged farther between the counter and the waving gun. "Step up, bro. You're the man of the house now. Go home and take care of your brother. You want him to join a gang, too?"

"Shut up! You don't know nothin' about me." His voice cracked.

"I've known you for three years, *mijo*. I know your brother will follow you, and one of you will end up in a body bag." Tony's voice was hard now. "Maybe not right away, but you will."

"You're the one who's gonna be in a body bag!"

"Go ahead." Tony stepped forward now. His gun was within easy reach, but there was no way he'd pull it. He needed Adolfo's trust. "I told you, I'm not afraid to die. Not if my death will get you away from Raul."

"Stay back." Adolfo's voice was barely a whisper.

"The way I see it, you have two choices." Electricity swirled in the air between them. "One, you shoot me. You go to jail for manslaughter. It will break your mama's heart, but maybe it'll scare your brother enough to stay away from gangs. Two, you put down that gun and you come with me to the St. Paul's Mission and learn how a real man takes care of his family. I don't care either way, because in the end, you and your brother will be safe."

He paused, giving Adolfo time to think. "If

I were you, I'd take the second option. It's a lot less heartache for your mama."

"Yeah, right." Adolfo's face twisted with anger. "I walk out of here with you and you arrest me as soon as I'm out the door. No thanks."

"You walk out of here with me right now, and we'll pretend this never happened." He shot Mr. Chan a glance.

Mr. Chan nodded at him.

Time stood still as the young man considered his options. The tension in his thin frame melted and his trembling hands lowered the gun. The pressure around Tony's middle eased and he stepped to the side so Mr. Chan could see that Adolfo's weapon was lowered. As he stepped away, he held his hands in the air, so Adolfo wouldn't feel threatened.

A sudden movement from the clerk drew Tony's attention and made him realize his mistake. By stepping in front of Adolfo, he'd cut off Mr. Chan's view of the boy's hands. Now all Mr. Chan noticed were Tony's own hands in the air. He must've thought Adolfo had pointed the weapon at Tony.

"No!" Tony whirled around to face Mr. Chan and jumped in front of Adolfo, shielding him just as the clerk's gun went off. A searing pain ripped through his chest.

The room swayed and Tony sank to the ground. Adolfo tried to catch him, but Tony's weight was too much and they both ended up in a heap on the floor.

Adolfo stared as blood poured out of Tony's chest. "Oh, man! You're hit!"

"I'm okay," Tony muttered, the smell of rust and salt filling his nostrils. "I just need to sit for a minute."

In a flash, the boy rolled Tony off him and sprinted out the door. Mr. Chan rushed over. "Mr. Tony, I'm so sorry! The ambulance is coming! I'm so sorry!" The frantic man pushed a towel into Tony's wound. "I thought he was about to shoot."

Tony shook his head, trying to dispel the faintness quickly taking over. An image floated in front of his eyes. Long blond hair, so blond it was almost white. "Bree." Her dark brown eyes blinked and then she was gone.

SABRINA DAVIS KICKED the covers off and stretched. She opened her eyes and blinked. Bright morning light jolted her out of bed. If the sun was already up, she was late for work. Her pulse thundered in her ears and her gaze danced around the room. She let out a deep sigh and fell back on her pillow as she glanced at her bedside clock. Seven in the morning and for the first time in years, she didn't need to jump out of bed and race to work or get her son ready for school. The scent of honeysuckle drifted through the open window and she closed her eyes, reveling in the silence. No hum of Houston traffic, no horns blaring. Somewhere in the pasture behind the house, a meadowlark began to sing, and she couldn't stop the smile from spreading across her face. It was good to be home.

She rolled over in bed, listening for the crowing of the rooster that had been her alarm clock growing up. Nothing. What else had changed in the ten years she'd been gone?

Since a yelling match with her father had escalated into her storming off to live with her Aunt Patty and Uncle Troy in Houston.

At the time she'd thought her relationship with her father was beyond repair. Amazing what ten years and the love of a grandchild could do. It had been so late when she'd arrived at her father's the night before that she'd fallen into bed without even turning on the light. She propped herself up on her elbows and examined the room she'd grown up in.

Her breath caught. Everything was exactly the same. So much for change.

Her rose-colored bedspread, now faded to such a light pink it was almost white, lay clean and crisp on her double bed. The dresser across the room showcased her trophies and ribbons. Pictures of her high school activities and friends were still pinned on the corkboard next to the dresser.

Her bare feet didn't make a sound on the threadbare carpet as she padded across the room to the closet. She steeled herself and opened the door. The clothes she hadn't taken with her all those years ago were still on their hangers. Shoes lay scattered across the closet floor. With shaking hands, she reached up to the top shelf and her fingers brushed a small wooden box. She didn't need to lift the lid to know what was inside. As happy as she was to be home, some memories were just too painful. She left the box in its place and went to the kitchen to make coffee.

"Already made." Her father saw where she was headed and handed her a full mug.

"You should've woken me up. I don't normally sleep this late." She added sugar to her coffee.

"Figured you needed the rest." Dad took a

sip from his own cup. He nodded toward the alcove that had been added to the end of the large country kitchen. "What do you think of the addition?"

"It was so late when we got here, I didn't get a chance to see it. I still can't believe you finished it." The gesture had been the final straw in convincing her to come back to Salt Creek.

Her parents had dreamed of a big family, so her father had started building onto the small two-bedroom farmhouse when Sabrina was two years old. Four years and three miscarriages later, the cement foundation and wooden frame only served to remind Sabrina's mother of the family that would never be. When she hadn't been able to bear looking at the wood-framed walls another minute, Dad had taken a sledgehammer and torn it down, piece by piece.

"When did you start on it again?" It must have taken months for him to finish the addition all by himself, and goodness knew how much money. How long had he been hoping she would come home?

"I started working on it right after Patty decided to move to Florida."

Sabrina choked on her coffee. "That was seven years ago."

"Yeah, well, I thought maybe you'd want to move back home when she left."

Her heart leaped in her chest. "You never said anything."

"I was waiting for the right time."

She pushed down the butterflies swarming in her stomach. Her father cared much more than he ever said out loud. What was it her mother used to say? Actions spoke louder than words.

"I'll be out by the pond if you need me. Water pump broke again." He sat his cup in the sink. "We'll finish unloading your furniture as soon as I get done."

"Okay." She suppressed a smile. The farm came first. It always did. The 160-acre homestead had been granted to her great-grandfather over 150 years ago. Not large enough to be considered a ranch, it was just enough to sustain a family. How had he managed by himself for the past ten years?

"No rush. The only furniture I brought was Levi's bed and dresser. The rest of it is just boxes, and Levi and I can unload those."

She tiptoed across the kitchen and paused outside the finished addition. She swung the door open silently and looked for her son. Levi was curled up inside the sleeping bag her father had left out for him. He looked so peaceful, his curly brown hair framing his cherub face. She doubted his teachers would use the word *cherub* to describe Levi.

His less-than-angelic behavior had been what finally drove her to return home. Levi shared more than physical looks with his father. They had the same quick temper and nose for trouble. Despite her best efforts, he was becoming more like Tony every day. Levi tended to get bored quickly, and boredom led to trouble. For the second time in her life, she was putting college on hold for the good of her child.

Country life was ingrained in her bones, but even so, moving back to Salt Creek was hard. Almost like admitting that she was a failure—the valedictorian, National Honor Society president and Best All-Around Student returning home a single mother with no education and no job.

Two things gave her the courage to face her conservative hometown. The first was the knowledge that Levi needed a change of environment to keep him out of trouble and possibly out of juvie. Her son was way more important than her pride. The second was knowing that no one, not even her father, knew who Levi's father really was.

She topped up her coffee and carried it into the sparsely decorated living room. It was just large enough for a sofa and reclining chair, and her mother's throw pillows still adorned the leather furniture. The *Lampasas Dispatch* lay folded neatly on the coffee table and she picked it up. The small newspaper was delivered only on Sundays and Wednesdays. Did Salt Creek still have a small section on Wednesdays?

She flicked the newspaper open to the middle and settled back to read. A local high school girl was competing in the Miss Texas pageant. An engagement picture of a young couple. She frowned at the names. Was that the same little boy she used to babysit? Another break-in at a construction yard. It didn't take long to read the one-page section. She closed the paper to read from the beginning and her blood turned to ice.

The headline read "Hero Cop Has Roots in Lampasas County." One name jumped out at her and sent her heart into overdrive. Tony Montoya. It couldn't be. She scanned the article again.

Her hands shook and she laid the paper on the sofa. All the town had ever seen in Tony was a rebellious teenager looking for trouble. He'd certainly proven them wrong. A decorated police officer who put his life on the line by jumping in front of a bullet to save a young man's life in the middle of an attempted robbery?

According to the paper, he was at home with his grandparents, where he was recovering from a fractured rib and a bruised lung. He was expected to return to work by the end of June. How was she going to avoid running into him in a town of fewer than seven hundred people?

TONY RUBBED HIS EYES. There was someone standing next to his bed. His gaze finally focused as an imposing figure with gray hair hovered over him, making him jump. A sharp pain shot through his shoulder, jolting him back to reality. He wasn't at his apartment in San Antonio. He wasn't at the hospital. He was in the one place he'd sworn he'd never return to. Salt Creek.

"Papa. What are you doing? It's two in the morning." He rubbed a hand across his face.

"You were moaning in your sleep," his

grandfather said. "Your grandmother was worried."

Abuela wasn't the only one. Tony rolled his shoulder and winced. The nurses at the hospital had warned him that the pain would get worse. Still, he'd rather suffer a little than risk relying on medicine. He'd have to do a better job of masking the pain. The thought of his grandmother losing sleep over him pierced his heart.

Papa fumbled through Tony's things on the dresser. "Where are your pain pills? Didn't you take them before you went to bed?"

"I don't need them." Tony stood up, fighting a wave of lightheadedness.

Papa pulled the empty prescription bottle from the top drawer of the dresser. "Where are they?"

Guilt pricked him. Did his grandfather think he'd already taken them all? Was Papa worried he'd end up like his mother? Pain medication was the first of many drugs his mother had been hooked on.

"I flushed them down the toilet after Abuela brought them home from the pharmacy." Tony didn't voluntarily take narcotics of any kind. Not even the helpful ones. Ever.

The ones given to him immediately after his surgery didn't count.

"Why?"

Tony noticed the lines around Papa's eyes. He looked tired. He looked...old. "I've read that children of addicts are much more likely to become addicts themselves. I'm not willing to take that chance."

Papa stiffened. "So you didn't take the pain medicine?"

"No, Papa. I'll take some ibuprofen when it bothers me too much, but I won't take anything stronger than that. Please don't ask me to."

"You're not like your mother, *mijo*." Papa placed his hands on Tony's shoulders. "Abuela will make an icepack for that shoulder. Perhaps that'll help."

Papa walked out of the room and Tony sank back onto the edge of the bed. Where would he be today if social services hadn't discovered the grandparents he hadn't known existed? Would he have been holding up convenience stores and pushing drugs like Adolfo? No. Not drugs. Never that.

Before his mother died, he'd joined a small street gang in his neighborhood. Until he'd found out they were the ones pushing drugs at his school and his own mother was one of their best customers. Getting out had meant risking his life. The beating he'd taken would've been more than worth it if he could've saved his mom.

At the soft knock on the door, he gritted his teeth, determined not to let any pain show on his face. "Come in."

"I brought you some ice for that shoulder." Abuela placed the pack on the nightstand and sat next to him. "You will tell me if you need anything?"

"Of course," he lied. He'd been here one night and already he was interrupting their lives. "I'm sorry I woke you."

Abuela took one of his hands in hers, her calloused fingers running over his knuckles. "You try to get some sleep."

Outside the window, an owl hooted in the darkness. He peered out the window. He didn't feel at all tired, but he lay down on the bed, anyway. Placing the ice on his shoulder, he closed his eyes.

He'd spent much of his life trying to control the chaos around him. But here, in this small town, things moved at their own pace. His teenaged self had hated it. Now it was exactly what he needed. Too bad he couldn't stay.

The rattle of dishes woke him up. He didn't remember falling asleep. The rich aroma of warm bread drifted down the hall. Abuela must be making tortillas.

He slipped a pair of sweatpants on and made his way to the living room. Nothing had changed since the first time he saw it all those years ago. The flower pattern on the sofa had faded, but his grandmother's afghans and doilies covered up the worn places. Papa's recliner sat in the corner, facing the ancient cabinet television taking up most of the space on the far wall.

He smiled. "Does that thing still work?"

Papa looked up from the newspaper. "Yes. Do you want to watch something? We still only get the three channels."

No cable TV. No satellite. No cell phones. Yep. It was like he'd stepped back in history. If only he *could* go back in time. So many things would be different now. Starting with Sabrina.

"No, thanks." The crumpling sound of the newspaper page being turned drew his attention. And he froze. From across the room, he could clearly read the headline on the front page of the open paper. "Hero Cop Has Roots in Lampasas County."

"Can I see the paper for a minute?" Tony crossed the room and sat on the couch across from his grandfather.

Without waiting for a reply, he took the paper and scanned through the article. His name jumped out at him, followed by a story hailing him as a hero for jumping in front of a bullet to save a young man's life. It failed to mention that the young man he'd taken a bullet for was the same one trying to rob the store. "How did the newspaper get this information?"

Abuela appeared, wiping her hands on a dish towel. "Me. A reporter came by and wanted to know if you were the cop."

"So you gave them a story?" He rubbed his hands on his legs. "You shouldn't have done that."

"Why not?" She lifted her chin. "I'm proud of my grandson and I don't care who knows it."

He pinched the bridge of his nose. It wasn't her fault. The last thing he wanted to do was worry her, but she had to know. "Abuela, sometimes I work with dangerous people. If they ever wanted to retaliate for any reason, this article could lead them right to you two."

Her mouth opened but nothing came out.

After a moment, she turned to her husband. "Did you know about this, Antonio?"

Papa shrugged and stood up. "No. Not until I got to San Antonio and talked to his captain."

"How dangerous?" Her eyes darted back and forth between Papa and Tony. "Should we be worried?"

This was exactly what Tony wanted to avoid. He set the paper down. "I chase drug dealers and I work with kids from gangs. All small, local operations and I've managed to stay under the radar, but if I get promoted to detective, it may not stay that way."

Abuela's brow creased. She pressed her lips together and turned to her husband. "You call his captain and tell him he's not coming back. He's staying here."

"You can't protect him from everything, Elaina. He's a grown man and makes his own decisions."

"That's what you said about Teresa and look how that turned out." Her voice had risen an octave.

Tony held his breath at the mention of his mother's name, waiting for the explosion. He'd lived with his grandparents for four years in his late teens, but it had only taken a few months to learn not to ignite Abuela's anger.

Papa pulled her into his arms and pressed a kiss to the top of her head, immediately defusing the tiny woman's temper. Only Papa could calm her down as fast as she riled up.

Tony swallowed. He'd once had someone who affected him the same way. How much trouble had he avoided because Sabrina had talked sense into him? He'd believed they would be as happy as his grandparents.

Until she'd ruined it by believing in him enough to sacrifice her future.

CHAPTER TWO

FOR OVER A WEEK, Tony stalked his grandparents' house, looking for something to keep himself busy. How was he going to make it six weeks without going nuts? Or driving everyone around him nuts? More than once Abuela scolded him for moving around too much.

Tony decided that when Papa came home for lunch, he'd insist on returning to the hardware store with him for the afternoon. Papa was probably still using the same old cash register he'd had when Tony was in high school. Abuela couldn't complain about him sitting on a stool and checking people out. It's not as if the tiny store would be swamped with customers.

The thought of getting out of the house for a while lightened his dark mood. He stuck his head into the kitchen. "Can I set the table?"

Abuela flipped some frying potatoes. "That'd be just fine."

Tony slipped behind her and gathered plates from the cabinet. When he'd first come to live with his grandparents, he thought it was odd that Abuela cooked her biggest meal at noon. The evening meal was lighter, usually leftovers.

He'd just finished placing the condiments on the table when Papa came in. Like clockwork, he closed the store every day at noon to come home and eat what his grandparents called dinner. Breakfast. Dinner. Supper.

"How are things going at the store?" Tony waited for Papa to sit down before pulling his own chair out.

"Good." Papa never elaborated on work. "Robert Davis came in this morning."

Tony almost dropped his fork. Sabrina's dad. His heart kicked into overdrive. "Why're you telling me?"

"He heard you was in town and he doesn't want you getting any ideas about going out there and bothering Sabrina." Papa's words were clipped.

That meant Sabrina was in town. Her memory had haunted him for ten years. No way he was going to pass up an opportunity to make things right. He swallowed. "Nice to see Robert's opinion of me hasn't changed much."

The platter Papa was holding hit the table with a thud. His eyes were hard as flint. "It's got nothing to do with you. Or Robert. Sabrina hasn't had it easy. Her fiancé was killed in Afghanistan, leaving her to raise her son alone. Robert only just convinced her to move back home where he could help her."

Fiancé? Son? His racing heart plummeted. She'd moved on with her life, just like he'd wanted her to. So why did it bother him so much? "He told you all this today?"

Abuela piped up. "We heard about Sabrina's fiancé years ago."

"Years? When did this happen?" And more importantly, why hadn't they told him?

"Let me think." She pressed her lips together. "I guess it was about the same time you started at the police academy."

Tony leaned back. Eighteen months. It'd taken her all of eighteen months to get over him and love someone else.

He had hurt her. On purpose. It was the only way to keep her from giving up her scholarship to follow him to Louisiana. The kicker was that he'd only accepted a job out of state so he could earn enough money to follow her to the university in Houston. But when he got to Houston, he couldn't find her.

She wasn't in any of the student directories and none of their mutual friends knew where she was. If they did, they wouldn't tell him. Now he knew why.

He shot a glance at Papa. "Why did Robert feel it necessary to send me a warning?"

"You know why."

Silence filled the room. Yes, he knew why. Until he came along, Sabrina Davis had been Salt Creek's brightest star. And he'd tarnished her.

Papa stood up. "Might as well come to the store with me. I need to get some inventory done if we have to go to Lampasas tomorrow morning."

"Yes, sir." Tony picked up his plate along with Papa's and carried them to the sink.

The ten-minute ride to town was quiet. Tony expected another lecture from Papa about staying away from Sabrina, but nothing was said. His cell phone chimed as Papa parked his small truck in front of the hardware store he'd owned for decades.

Tony looked at the number and grinned as he answered. "Hello, David."

"Are you still playing sick?"

"You're just jealous."

"Six weeks paid leave? Who wouldn't be?"

David laughed. "How close are you to Lampasas?"

"Twenty-two miles. Why?"

"Ashley's dad is turning sixty-five this weekend. We're heading to Hamilton tomorrow and have to go right through Lampasas."

"Okay…" Did David want to stop by and see him?

"I thought I'd bring your SUV to you."

Having his Dodge Durango would give him some measure of freedom. "That'd be great. I have a doctor's appointment at ten in the morning, so I'll already be in town. What time should I meet you?"

SABRINA WAS DUSTING THE mantel over the large fireplace again. She'd spent the better part of the last week deep-cleaning Dad's house. There wasn't much more to be done. She picked up one of the photographs perched on the ledge. A smiling woman with blond hair and laughing brown eyes grinned at her.

The screen door slammed shut as Levi tromped in from outside. "Who's that?"

She traced the picture lightly as Levi came to stand beside her. "My mom."

"She looks like you." He took the picture from her. After staring at it for a moment, he let out a sigh. "I bet it would've been nice to have a grandma."

The admission caught her off guard. She'd never thought about how much Levi had missed out on. "She would've been the best grandma ever." She ran a hand over his back. "I really miss her."

"She died when you were twelve?"

"Yes. She had breast cancer."

He frowned. "At least you had two parents for twelve years."

She sucked in her breath. She'd told him this one lie his whole life. What choice did she have? "I never thought about it like that. I guess I was lucky, in a way. But knowing her for twelve years makes me miss her that much more."

Levi shoved the picture back at her. "What you're really saying is it's a good thing my dad died before I was born. Since I never knew him, it shouldn't bother me, right?"

"That's not what I meant at all." She rubbed her temples. Constantly walking on eggshells around him was exhausting. Would he ever get rid of the chip on his shoulder?

His left dimple deepened as he pressed his lips together. Sabrina knew that look. He was deciding if he wanted to go into battle. His gaze darted around the room and stopped on the picture she still clutched in her hands.

Levi's breath escaped like a deflated balloon. "Grandpa wants to know if you're ready to go."

She sighed in relief. His acts of defiance had diminished in the last couple of weeks. Especially when her dad was in the room. Looked like the school counselor was right— all Levi needed was a positive male role model. Why couldn't she be enough?

"Run out to the barn and tell Grandpa I'll be ready in five minutes." They needed groceries, and at least Lampasas, twenty-two miles from Salt Creek, was big enough that she probably wouldn't see anyone she knew. And by anyone, she meant Tony.

In a flash, her son bolted down the worn dirt path to the barn. A few minutes later, Levi and her dad ambled back to the house.

"Ready?" she asked.

"Let's take the truck," Dad said. "I need to run by the feed store."

Lampasas was the county seat and a hub of activity. The small stores in Salt Creek only carried the basics, so most people drove to Lampasas every few weeks to stock up on supplies. The drive didn't take long, and Sabrina pointed out the local landmarks to Levi as they drove—the show barn, where stock shows were held each January, the river walk and, of course, Storm's Drive-In, home to the world's best burgers.

"What's going on?" Levi pointed to the bucket trucks parked along the side of the road. A large banner hung from the side of one bucket.

"They're hanging signs across the street." Dad slowed down so Levi could have a better look. "Spring Ho is in a few weeks, so they're getting ready for it."

"What's Spring Ho?"

"It's like a big fair. They'll have a carnival, booths set up along the river, a parade, and one night they'll have fireworks and a street dance over by the court house."

Levi wrinkled his nose. "But it's summer."

Sabrina laughed. Having grown up in the area, it'd never occurred to her that the term might be confusing to people. "The town of Lampasas is home to a lot of natural springs, so the festival is named after their water source, not the season."

The big Ford truck slowed to a crawl as Dad shifted gears and pulled into the parking lot of the H-E-B grocery store.

Robert waved at her as she jumped out. "I'll pick you up after we're done at the feed store."

It wasn't even noon yet, but already the sweltering humidity was unbearable. The grocery store's air-conditioning was a welcome relief. Sabrina grabbed a shopping cart and in no time had everything on her list. Colorful boxes beckoned her as she passed the cereal aisle. She whipped her cart around. How could she forget Levi's cereal?

She stopped her cart and frowned. The cereal she wanted for herself sat on the top shelf, just out of her reach. Just as she started to use the bottom shelf as a step, an arm reached over her and handed her the box.

"Thank you." She turned around and froze. A pair of hazel eyes bored into hers with such intensity that she felt herself flush.

Disheveled black hair hung in soft curls at the back of his collar as he gave her a familiar one-sided smile. "Hey, Bree."

"Tony?" Shakiness threatened to overwhelm her. Her heart pounded in her ears and she squeezed the box in her hands to hide their trembling. Seconds seemed to stretch into minutes as Sabrina fought to keep her composure. Years of anger, bitterness and betrayal warred against a ridiculous urge to throw herself into his arms. Her teeth worried her bottom lip as she struggled to speak.

He shoved his hands into his jeans pockets, the muscles in his arms stretching the sleeves of his T-shirt. "My grandfather mentioned you were moving back."

Could he hear her heart pounding? "Good news travels fast. I read the article about you in the paper. You're a hero."

Silence permeated the air between them and his eyes never left hers. Like a mouse caught in the hypnotic gaze of a cat, she couldn't move. *Breathe. You're not eighteen anymore.*

The smile faded. He shook his head. "No. Just doing my job."

Exactly what she'd expect a hero to say. "I'm sure your grandparents are thrilled to have you home for a while."

"You should stop by and see them sometime. Abuela misses you." He held her gaze. "How are you?"

Was he really trying to make small talk? She clasped her hands together. "I'm fine."

The way his gaze swept over her gave her the impression that he was taking a mental inventory. She straightened the wrinkled T-shirt she'd thrown on in her rush to get out of the house.

The dimple under his left eye deepened. "I'd really like to get together while I'm still in town. Catch up. Could I take you to dinner sometime?"

He was close. Too close. Close enough for her to make out a faint scar under his jaw, just below his left ear. The scar—along with the bump on the bridge of his nose—that he'd gotten while defending her. She swallowed.

The sandalwood scent of his aftershave sent her heart into overdrive. She took a quick step backward and bumped into the cart. Strong arms caught her inches from hitting the floor.

His muscles tightened, and something flashed in his eyes. Before she could decipher it, thick black lashes blinked, and the mask she'd seen every time he wanted to hide his feelings returned. She pushed against his chest, struggling to right herself.

"Are you okay?" His husky voice sent shivers along her skin.

"I'm fine." She took a breath in an effort to calm her galloping pulse.

Her knees almost buckled and she reached for the grocery cart. Leaning on it for support, she pushed it between them, forcing him to step back. A flicker of pain crossed his face. "You're still injured. Are you okay?"

"I'm fine. It was only a flesh wound. What do you say? About dinner?"

"It was a long time ago. No need to rehash the past. Goodbye, Tony." She pushed her cart past him and hurried to the checkout line.

She flinched as she slammed the groceries onto the moving belt. She kept her eyes trained on the items in her cart. *Don't look around for him. Don't give him that satisfaction.* How long had he said he was going to be in town?

The beeping noises from the cashier were drowned out by the pulse thundering in her ears. She paid as quickly as she could and pushed the cart outside just as her father's beat-up Ford pulled into the parking lot. She scanned the area once more for any sign of Tony before making a beeline to the truck.

What was she afraid of? That Tony would be waiting to ambush her in the parking lot? What would he do if he found out the truth? Would he even care?

Her lie had never bothered her before. It was simply a means to an end. She'd done everything she could to get Tony to stay and he still refused. He'd been long gone by the time she found out she was pregnant. If he was that desperate to be rid of her, she wasn't about to use a baby to blackmail him into coming back. Especially when he'd made it clear he didn't want a family.

She pasted a smile on her face and opened the truck door. "How was the feed store?"

"Levi was a big help loading the sacks," her father said. "He's pretty strong for a nine-year-old."

On the seat between them, Levi puffed his chest out. Sabrina let out a sigh of relief.

What would happen if the truth came out? No. She wouldn't let that happen.

TONY STOOD INSIDE the store, waiting for Sabrina to leave. The pain in her eyes cut him to the core. What had he expected? For her to fall into his arms? The engagement ring she still wore on her finger was proof that she'd moved on. If he needed further evidence, all he had to do was look at the little boy who hopped out of Robert's truck to help her load up the groceries.

David's offer to deliver Tony's SUV to Lampasas had been a godsend, and he'd given David directions to the H-E-B, right off the main road. His grandfather had dropped him off after his doctor's appointment. What were the chances that Sabrina would be shopping there at the same time?

Here. Where are you?

Tony texted David back. Be right there. He stepped outside, looking for his Dodge Durango.

A horn honked and Tony saw a short, stocky man waving at him from across the parking lot. Grinning, he hurried over to shake his partner's hand.

"How're ya feeling, man?" David pulled Tony in for a quick hug.

For the next few minutes, Tony and David discussed doctors, the kids from St. Paul's Mission and the weather, all the while ignoring the one thing Tony wanted to know the most.

Finally, he couldn't stand it any longer. "Is Captain Rodriguez still pissed?"

David's brow furrowed. "It's not him you need to worry about. You screwed the mayor out of an opportunity to prove his anti-gang initiative is working. He's the one gunning for you."

"But it's *not* working." The only way to

combat gangs was to get to the kids before they joined up. But the results took longer than most politicians had in office. None of them had that much time or dedication. "So I guess I'm still exiled."

David shrugged. "It's for your own good, you know. What would you be doing in San Antonio right now? Hanging out with the kids at St. Paul's Mission? Tell me I'm wrong."

"I can't." Tony lifted his chin. "I've put a lot of time in with those kids. You can't expect me to abandon them just because Captain Rodriguez doesn't think I should be seen there."

"Most of those kids are known gang-bangers and Cap is trying to keep you from being brought up on charges of hindering an investigation."

"But I didn't do anything wrong." It wouldn't matter. Tony had seen it too many times. Once a political witch hunt started, it didn't end until someone went down. So in the meantime, he'd been banished to Salt Creek.

"You asked Mr. Chan not to press charges, so technically you did."

Tony curled his fists. David was right. He'd let his own emotions get the better of him and he'd made a huge error in judgment. Stupid.

Stupid. Stupid. Pain shot through his chest wound. "I guess I can kiss that promotion goodbye."

"Captain Rodriguez is convinced the mayor is just blowing smoke. Hang tight and stay out of trouble. It'll all work out."

"Thanks, David. Keep me posted."

"Will do, brother. Will do."

A horn honked and then David's wife pulled into the parking spot next to them.

"How are you doing, Tony?" Ashley asked through the open window.

"Good. Anxious to get back to work."

"Well, hurry up. Without you around, David thinks he has to try out all his new jokes on me."

David waved and jumped into the car. Tony waited for the two of them to pull away before climbing into his SUV. If he hadn't blown it with Sabrina, would his life be more like David's?

"CAN YOU STOP at the nursing home so I can pick up a job application?" Sabrina pointed the road out to her father.

Robert shot a look at her over Levi's head. "Why do you want to do that?"

"I need a job, Dad. How else will I pay my

half of the bills? And I want to try to get into the nursing program at Central Texas College. I need money for tuition."

"Hmph. I managed to pay the bills before you got here. I reckon I can keep paying for them. All you need to do is worry about that boy of yours. Ain't that the reason you moved here?"

"Yes, but I won't let you pay for my school. If you don't want to stop now, I'll just come back and apply later."

"Suit yourself." He whipped into the turn lane. "You always do."

It was on the tip of her tongue to remind her father where her stubbornness came from, but she clamped her mouth shut. She loved her father, but sometimes he was a hard man to get along with.

After her mother's death, he'd retreated into a shell, cutting off everyone. Including his twelve-year-old daughter, who'd desperately needed to know someone still loved her.

Sabrina had tried to fill the void left in the house. She cooked, cleaned, shopped for groceries and paid the bills. Her father never seemed to notice. After a while, Sabrina had stopped caring if he appreciated her or not.

Instead, she'd found acceptance by excelling at school. She participated in every sport, organization and club her small high school offered. Most people saw her as an over-achiever. Only Tony had understood.

Dad pulled up in front of the large brick building that housed the nursing home and parked without even glancing at her. She reached out to touch his arm. "I'm not try-ing to be stubborn, Dad. I want to contribute my fair share."

She was proud of the fact that she'd been able to support herself ever since Aunt Patty moved to a retirement community in Florida. She refused to be a burden to her dad's lim-ited finances.

She returned just a few minutes later. Dad shifted into Drive and pulled out of the park-ing lot before saying, "They aren't hiring right now."

Sabrina stared at him. "How did you know that?"

He shrugged. "I called last week."

He'd called on her behalf?

"Never could figure out why you always worked in nursing homes."

"The only thing I have going for me is my CNA certificate. I don't understand. Nursing homes are always hiring." Now what was she going to do?

"They don't pay much anymore, anyway. Ever since the high schools started letting kids earn college credits and certifications through them, the market is flooded. CNAs are a dime a dozen around here." He turned onto the main road that would lead them back to Salt Creek.

"How do you know so much about it?"

His eyes never left the road. "I've been watching for CNA jobs ever since Patty moved to Florida."

Sabrina's hand came up to her throat. The same time he'd started rebuilding the addition to the house. She swallowed hard. "Thanks, Dad."

"Something'll come up. Don't worry."

The ride back to Salt Creek was made in relative silence. Only the drone of country music blaring from the radio filled the void. The highway ahead split and Dad took the left lane, bypassing the little town of Salt Creek. A few minutes later, he turned off onto a farm-to-market road before taking the long stretch of dirt laneway that led to the farm.

After crossing a cattle guard, the truck topped a hill and it felt as if Sabrina's heart broke into song. Waving grassland stretched for miles. The red flagstone farmhouse stood out against the blue Texas sky, a testament to old-fashioned ingenuity. It was a sight she'd never get tired of. Funny how she didn't know how much she missed it until she came back.

Taking refuge in Houston with her dad's sister, she hadn't planned to stay gone long. Just long enough to figure out how to juggle college and a newborn. Then her uncle Troy had suffered a stroke. Aunt Patty had had her hands full working enough hours to keep her insurance and find a home health aide to care for her beloved husband.

The Certified Nursing Assistant certificate Sabrina earned in high school had been intended to give her an advantage over other nursing program applicants. Luckily, it also gave her the qualifications required by Aunt Patty's insurance company—and a convenient excuse to stay away from Salt Creek.

Aunt Patty was the only one who knew who Levi's real father was. When Sabrina's letters to Tony were returned unopened, it was Patty's idea to create a fictional relationship with her GI friend to place the blame on. At the time, Sabrina had been too distraught and heartbroken to care. After a couple of years, the lie became easier and easier to live with.

Did anyone else suspect the truth? Her father had run Tony off the farm enough times to know there was more going on than homework. Certainly her friends and half the town knew about the secret relationship that wasn't much of a secret. Would anyone even care enough ten years later to put the pieces together?

The truck jolted to a stop as her father pulled up in front of the house. Before Sabrina could unfasten her seat belt, Levi barreled out of the cab and grabbed two plastic grocery bags.

She smiled. "Wow. I didn't even have to ask. You're good for him."

Dad reached over the bed of the truck and scooped up several bags himself. "I saw Antonio pulling out when I dropped you off. Did you run into Tony in H-E-B?"

"I did. He stopped and said hi." She kept her voice light.

He looked her straight in the eye. "Stay away from him."

CHAPTER THREE

TONY'S AFTERNOON HAD been filled with more doctor appointments and medical tests. All the way back to Salt Creek, his knuckles had been white from gripping the steering wheel. The tightness in his chest had nothing to do with his injury and everything to do with the woman who'd walked away from him in the grocery store that morning. He stretched his fingers, but it did little to relieve the tension, or the ache in his jaw from gritting his teeth.

Why was it that the pending investigation at his department didn't bother him nearly as much as seeing Sabrina? As a police officer, he was accustomed to noticing details others missed. Sabrina's appearance screamed at him. Her faded jeans, thin from so many washes. Shoes with soles worn down to nothing. She even carried herself differently. Shoulders slumped, as if she had given up on the world. He'd never wanted to see her like that. Dejected. Sad.

When Tony pulled up to his grandparents' house, he saw Papa sitting in an old rocking chair on the porch, holding a chunk of wood.

Tony gingerly climbed the weather-beaten steps.

"Hello, *mijo*." The old man didn't look up. He opened his pocketknife and began to whittle. "How was your visit with your friend?"

"Fine." Sitting next to his grandfather's chair, he let his legs dangle over the edge of the porch. Tony watched with fascination as wood shavings began to fall to the ground. "I wish I'd learned to do that when I was a boy."

"You can still learn." Pausing from his work, the older man reached into a bucket next to him and brought out a scrap piece of wood. "Here. Whittling is good for clearing your mind." He looked Tony over with his sharp eyes. "You may need a bigger piece. You saw her today, didn't you?"

"Am I that obvious?"

Neither had to say her name. Papa leaned back in the chair, his hands a blur as he carved.

"Yes." Tony's hands twisted the wood around and around, wondering what he was supposed to see in it.

"Hmph."

"She isn't doing well. What if it's my fault?"

"We all make our own choices in life. Fault lies within ourselves."

"Sometimes choices are made for you." By leaving, what choices had he forced her to make?

Ten years ago Sabrina had had a bright future and he'd had nothing to offer: no job, no home, no money, no hope. When he got a job offer working for a construction company in Louisiana, it was for more money than he'd ever made in his life. But she'd wanted to put college on hold and go with him.

So he made the decision for both of them and broken up with her.

"She hates me."

"Maybe." Papa paused from his whittling. "Emotions are like that block of wood. You can look at, examine it, think about it. But until you cut into it, it can never reach its potential. You might cut yourself. You might bleed. But until you cut, you can never shape it into what it could be." Standing up, he handed his wood to Tony and walked into the house.

Tony stared at a perfectly carved bear.

After a few stabs at his own wood with his pocketknife, he gave up.

Sabrina deserved to know the truth. But which truth? That he'd never gotten over her? That not a day went by that he didn't wish he could take back what he'd said to her?

Sabrina might hate him even more when she heard the truth, but until he could sit down and explain the real reason he'd left, he'd never be able to move on.

SABRINA'S GUT TWISTED as she hung up the phone. How naive of her to think that moving here would give Levi a chance to start over.

"What was that about?" Dad took his hat off the deer antlers mounted on the wall.

"Nancy Beal."

He turned from the door to face her. "The principal? What did she want?"

"To let me know that the school had received Levi's records and they have some concerns about him attending a regular class." Tears welled in her eyes.

Dad hung his hat back on the wall. "What else is there besides a regular class? He doesn't need special education."

"She thinks I should consider the alternative school." Her breath caught in her chest. "How am I going to tell my son that he's not wanted here, either?"

Dad pulled her in for a hug. "They can't do that. We'll go to the school board if we have to."

Levi was already convinced the world was against him. She only hoped this didn't push him over the edge.

"Where is he, anyway? I haven't seen him since he fed the pigs this morning."

"He went fishing at the pond." Sabrina glanced at the clock on the wall. "I'm going to town to talk to Mrs. Beal in person. Maybe I can change her mind."

"Want me to come with you?"

Her father stood poised for battle. He wasn't known to have a quick temper, but once he was riled…

"Thanks, Dad, but this is something I should do on my own. Can you keep an eye on Levi? I don't want him to know what's going on. Not yet."

He nodded. "I think I'll grab my pole and join him at the pond." Whistling, her dad put his hat on and strolled out the door.

She watched him heading to the barn. When was the last time she'd heard him whistling? Probably before her mother died. Was he finally getting over his grief, or were she and Levi bringing him out of his shell? She'd moved home because it was what her son needed. She'd never expected her dad might have needed it, too.

THE MEETING TOOK less than an hour and although Sabrina couldn't claim victory yet, there was a glimmer of hope. All she had to do was enroll Levi in some counseling sessions and have the therapists evaluate him for anger issues.

Simple. Ha. Try explaining that to Levi. Slamming the door of her old Toyota Camry, she paused at the gate to the front yard. She could hear the faint drone of another vehicle approaching. Her heart caught in her throat. Could it be Tony? He'd never been good at taking no for an answer.

When a shiny, red Lexus came into view, she relaxed. She didn't know what kind of vehicle Tony drove, but the fancy sports car didn't suit him at all. She waited by the gate for the car to come to a stop behind her own.

A tall, slender woman got out and straightened her pencil tight skirt. "Hi, Sabrina."

Sabrina took in the professionally dressed woman. She was older than Sabrina, but not by much. The woman waited, tapping her toes in three inch heels. "Marissa? Marissa Porter?"

Marissa was a couple of years older than Sabrina, but they'd become friends in high school, only to lose track of each other after Marissa went away to college.

"I knew you couldn't forget me," Marissa said. Reaching over the gate, she enveloped Sabrina in a giant hug.

"What are you doing here? How are your parents?" Sabrina hadn't attempted to contact any of her childhood friends since moving home.

"They're good. Dad retired and drives Mom crazy." She wiggled her left hand in front of Sabrina, showing off the shiny diamond. "I'm Marissa Butler now. My husband, Jarrod, is a county deputy. We moved back a few years ago. I know, I swore I was never moving back to a small town…but here I am!" The slamming of her car door interrupted them.

Sabrina looked behind her to see a young boy about Levi's age.

Marissa beckoned the boy. "Come on, Bradley, I want you to meet a friend of mine from high school." The boy shuffled his way around the car. "Sabrina, this is my son, Bradley."

"Pleased to meet you." The boy reached out to shake her hand.

"Likewise, I'm sure." Amusement tugged at her lips. She glanced at Marissa.

"Don't let his manners fool you," Marissa whispered, reading her thoughts. "Wait till he gets to know you. He really lets loose."

"Mom," the boy protested.

Levi ran around the back corner of the house. "Mom, where does Grandpa keep his trowel? We need to dig up more worms." He stopped short when he saw their visitors. "Oh. Hi."

"Levi, this is Mrs. Butler and her son, Bradley. This is my son, Levi."

Marissa's brow crinkled and she gazed from Levi to Sabrina and back.

Bradley didn't seem to notice his mother's silence. "Are you digging worms for fishing?"

Levi grinned. "Yeah. Wanna help? I have an extra pole you can use."

Bradley looked at his mother. "Please?"

Marissa nodded. "Only if it's okay with his mom."

"The trowel's hanging on the wall of the shed, to the right of the door," Sabrina said.

"Thanks, Mom." Levi took off like a shot with Bradley on his heels.

Shaking her head, she opened the gate. "It looks like the boys didn't need any introductions. Would you like to come in and have a glass of tea?"

"I would love that." Marissa's high heels clicked across the stone sidewalk as she followed Sabrina inside. "How old is your son?"

Sabrina lifted her chin. There was no sense in lying. "He's nine."

She motioned for Marissa to sit at the kitchen table as she poured the tea. "What are you doing here? Don't get me wrong, it's nice to see you again, but how did you know I was here?"

Marissa grinned. "Your dad has been telling everyone at the café for weeks that you were moving back. He's your biggest fan. How long have you been home?"

Ah. The Eagle's Nest Café. Every morning farmers and ranchers met at the café to drink coffee and solve the problems of the world. "About two weeks."

"Are you still a CNA? Do you have a job yet?"

"How did you know I was a CNA?"

"Did the big city affect your memory?" The other woman reached over to squeeze her hand. "We did go to high school together. We were in CNA classes at the same time."

Sabrina repressed a grin. Marissa had been the first one to faint at the sight of blood.

She'd quit after the second week. "Yes, I still have my license."

"Good. That's partly why I'm here." Marissa fished into her purse and slid a business card across the table.

Sabrina read it. "Independent healthcare contractor?"

"Yes." Marissa nodded. "I work for Crestview Health Care Contracting."

Sabrina leaned back in her chair. "Are you offering me a job?"

Marissa arched one delicately shaped eyebrow. "Well, technically, I can't offer you a job until you apply for it. Interested?"

Sabrina's throat tightened. "Absolutely. What is it?"

"On-site medical assistant for the alternative school in town."

That was the second time today she'd heard the alternative school mentioned. "What exactly is an alternative school and why do they need someone in the summer? Isn't school out right now?"

Marissa took a long drink of tea. "Most of the students come from Little Mountain Children's Home. The home hires staff in the summer while house parents get some leave time."

"House parents?"

"They want the kids to feel like they're home, not in a facility, so children live in homes with a couple that serves as their foster parents. During the summer, the couples recharge, so they need a medical assistant on-site to help handle any issues that come up."

Sabrina's mind raced back to the times she traveled with her church youth group to volunteer at the children's home in Cherokee. "Do I have to stay on-site? Overnights, I mean."

"No," Marissa said. "The kids double up with other house parents at night, but they like to have one person who is aware of the medical needs of all the students. You know, one constant among the change."

Sabrina bit her bottom lip. Although she couldn't remember specific faces from so long ago, there was one thing she did remember about the kids. How eager they were to love. And be loved. "I imagine some of those kids have seen too much change."

"So, you'll come to my office tomorrow and apply for the job?"

"Yes. But why me? According to my dad, there are tons of CNAs in the area."

Marissa pressed her lips together. "The truth? The kids can be a little rough and some of them have some serious issues. So far, no one's been able to last more than a month."

"What makes you think I'll be any different?"

"When we were growing up, you took in every stray animal and every outcast that moved to town. I'm willing to bet some things haven't changed."

"I also let people use me as their doormat and take advantage of me. That'll never happen again."

"I always knew there was a tough nut under that soft exterior. Are you in?"

Sabrina paused. If she was going to get Levi the counseling he needed, she had to have an income. Maybe working with troubled youth would give her some insight into helping her own son.

Wait. She straightened up. "Do the residents at Little Mountain receive any kind of counseling?"

"They have group sessions every Thursday and a few of the older ones receive one-on-one counseling. Why?"

"I'll take the job if Levi can participate."

"Deal." Marissa grinned. "By the way, does Tony know he has a son?"

CHAPTER FOUR

TONY STARED AT the television, but had no idea what he'd just watched. He stood up and paced around the living room. He'd finished the breathing treatments the doctor had ordered and was given the okay to start exercising. Lightly. *Right*. Tony didn't understand the meaning of light exercise. What good was it if it didn't make him sweat and leave him tired?

The phone in the kitchen rang and his grandmother answered. "Tony, it's for you."

Who would call him here? Most people called his cell. "Hello?"

"Tony Montoya?" an unfamiliar voice greeted him. "My name is Jarrod Butler. I work with the Lampasas County Sheriff's Department."

"Hello, Jarrod. What can I do for you?"

"I was wondering if you could meet me for coffee. I'd like to discuss some things with you."

What did someone from the sheriff's department want with him? "Yeah, sure. What time?"

"I have time right now. How about meeting me at The Eagle's Nest in about twenty minutes? I'll buy lunch."

The Eagle's Nest. Any place but there. His first instinct was to insist on discussing this on the phone, but curiosity got the better of him. "Sure. See you in a few minutes."

He'd been through town several times in the weeks since his return, but this was the first time that he paid attention to his surroundings. It looked the same as it had… well…almost. A few more of the old buildings were boarded up. The drought that had racked the area over the past few years had taken a toll on the small ranching community and many of the smaller mom-and-pop shops had closed. How much longer would the place be able to survive?

When he paused at the town's only intersection, next to what used to be a dry-goods store, Tony scanned the graffiti on the weathered lumber across the window. A force of habit. There were no gang signs or hidden warnings in the scribbles on the warped wood. Just kids looking for something to do.

The gravel crunched under his tires as he pulled into the café parking lot. He recognized many of the vehicles. More proof that small towns were reluctant to change. Might as well get this over with.

Pausing at the café's entrance, he tried to shake off the feeling that he truly was about to walk through time. A small bell rang when he opened the door. He scanned the dining area but didn't see a uniformed officer anywhere.

Nostalgia punched him in the gut as he slid into a booth to wait for Jarrod to arrive. How many hours had he sat in the exact same booth, waiting for Sabrina to finish her shift as a waitress here? He shook his head, warding off the memories.

"Tony? I'm Jarrod Butler, I'm an investigator with the Lampasas County Sheriff's Department." He looked up to see a redheaded man with freckles.

Standing up, he shook the man's hand. "Nice to meet you." He followed Jarrod to a secluded area at the back of the café.

The waitress greeted them. Makeup pancaked her face in an attempt to cover the wrinkles. "What can I get for y'all?"

The aroma of fried chicken overpowered his resolve to find out what Jarrod wanted and leave. "Give me the special and a glass of sweet tea."

Jarrod placed his order and then they were alone. He swirled his water glass, watching Tony carefully. "I read the article in the paper about you. Impressive."

"I was just doing my job."

"I talked to your captain." Jarrod leaned his forearms on the table. "He says you've got quite a gift for working with troubled kids."

Jarrod had talked to his captain? Why? He gave the man a level stare. "It's not a gift. It's experience. I've been where those boys have been. I understand what they're going through."

"He says you've helped more boys get out of gangs than the rest of his staff combined. Sounds like a gift to me."

"I like to think I'm using my rebelliousness to allow me to connect with the kids no one else wants to deal with." Was Jarrod aware of Tony's teenage reputation in this town?

"While you're here, I wondered if you would be willing to put your experience to use."

"Surely you're not having gang trouble in Salt Creek?"

"No." Jarrod shrugged one shoulder. "At least, not yet. But we are experiencing some issues."

"Issues?"

"Vandalism, theft."

Tony shook his head. "Sounds like typical teenagers."

"I thought so at first. But we've received reports of drug activity in the area. Maybe linked with a group home here in town." Jarrod leaned back in his chair. "Some of the teenage boys have suspected gang ties."

"So what do you want from me?" Bitterness soured his sweet tea. Was Jarrod looking for someone to tell him it was okay to send the kids away? Pack them up and ship them out. That's how everyone wanted to deal with kids in the foster care system.

Jarrod reached into his shirt pocket and pulled out a piece of paper. He slid it across the table. "I want to help them. But I don't know how. I've tried to get to know these boys but—"

"You were shot down." Boys like that didn't trust easily. Especially a deputy sheriff. Tony studied the list of names, complete with ages and where they were from.

The platinum blonde waitress appeared with their order. "Can I get you anything else?"

"No, thank you," Jarrod and Tony said in unison.

She started to walk away, then stopped and turned back toward Tony. "Don't I know you? You look real familiar."

He narrowed his eyes as he tried to place the woman. "Could be. I lived here for a few years."

She studied him for a moment before a toothy smile brightened up her chubby face. "You're Antonio Montoya's grandson, ain't ya?"

She set the coffeepot down and grabbed him by both arms. "Stand up, boy, let me get a look at ya." She clicked her tongue. "I guess I just lost a bet."

Betty. She'd been best friends with Sabrina's mom and had taken Sabrina under her wing when her mom died. "What bet?"

"I figured you'd end up in jail 'fore you were twenty-one, but Sabrina always said you'd come back here one day and prove everybody wrong."

"If it wasn't for her, I probably *would* be in jail," he told her honestly.

"When Sabrina lit out right after you, we was sure you two had run off together."

His gut wrenched. No way had she tried to follow him. He'd made sure she wanted nothing to do with him. From her reaction yesterday, he had done a good job.

A customer across the café called her name and Betty gave him one last bear hug before leaving.

"You okay?" Jarrod's face was one of concern. "You look like you just saw a ghost."

"This town is full of ghosts." He slipped the list into his shirt pocket. "Thanks for the lunch, Jarrod. Can we talk tomorrow?"

THE WARM SUMMER breeze flowed through the windows of Tony's SUV. For the last two hours, he'd been touring the back roads of Salt Creek. His own trip down memory lane. But more recent events were troubling him. It'd been almost a week since he'd seen Sabrina. Why didn't she ever come into town?

The setting sun bathed the cab of his truck in an orange glow, and his stomach growled. Time to head home. He slowed down as he approached the outskirts of town. The large brick school that housed kindergarten through twelfth grade looked the same, but the area surrounding the school had changed. The residential houses across the street had been replaced by mobiles. A sign identified one of the buildings as an alternative school.

Code for the place where the troubled kids had to go.

Was that where they would've sent him? A small dirt road branched off the main one and disappeared over the top of a hill. One more stop down memory lane. Tony turned his SUV onto the gravel and followed it to the end. Little Mountain. The namesake of the children's home.

Tony got out of his vehicle and climbed onto the warm hood. Leaning against the windshield, he listened to the wind rustling through the tall oak trees surrounding the area. The stars twinkled as the heat from the day began to ebb.

This was the first place that he'd been alone with Sabrina. He had done nothing but complain about Salt Creek and she'd been desperate to make him see the beauty of small-town life. So she brought him to Little Mountain. After a brief history lesson on the town, she'd spread a blanket out in the back of his old pickup truck. They were there for hours. Just talking. He never even held her hand, but it was the closest Tony had felt to anyone in his entire life.

Now, as he lay against the windshield and searched for the constellations she'd loved to point out, a sense of peace washed over him. How long had it been since he'd taken the time to look at the night sky? Too long. It was almost impossible to see stars through the glare of city lights.

His time in Salt Creek was slipping away. It was the middle of June. Half of his six-week sentence was over and he didn't want it to end. He took a deep breath, and the smell of cedar trees, wildflowers and mesquite enveloped him. By the time he got back in his truck and headed slowly down the hill, lightning bugs were dancing in the tall grass.

As he approached the school, the lights on the outside basketball courts drew his attention. A group of boys tossed a ball around on the center court. He pulled into the parking lot and shut off the engine. Jarrod wanted him to get to know the boys in town. The best way to learn about someone was to watch them when they didn't know they were being watched.

The group home was just on the other side of Little Mountain. How many of the boys on the court were from the home? And were they here unsupervised?

A few scantily clad teen girls chatted on the benches while watching the game. Another group of boys huddled together in the far corner of the parking lot.

One shadowed figure straightened up and turned toward Tony's vehicle. His companions followed suit. When three of the boys broke off from the group and headed to him, Tony pulled out his smartphone and pretended to be sending a text.

Aware of every move made close to his truck, Tony didn't look up from his phone until he heard a sharp rap on the window.

"You lookin' for somebody?" Long brown hair fell in the young man's face.

"A place, actually." Tony looked down at his phone. "Little Mountain Group Home. Ever heard of it?"

"I've heard of it. Nothing there but a bunch of losers."

Yep. This kid was definitely trouble. It was in the way he moved and talked. Tony recognized it because he'd been like that once. "I'm supposed to start volunteering there tomorrow morning and I want to be sure I know where I'm going."

The boy placed one hand on the roof of Tony's Durango. "Why would you do that?"

Tony shrugged. "I have to."

He was purposely vague. Someone used to

trouble would assume he'd been ordered to do some type of community service.

"Kyle," one of the boys on the court shouted at a kid walking away. "Where you going? We need you."

Tony remembered seeing a Kyle on the list Jarrod had given him and looked up to see a lanky kid strutting across the concrete. He stopped next to Tony's truck.

"Wassup, Nick?" The kids bumped fists.

Nick nodded toward Tony. "This guy wants to know where the home is. Says he's supposed to start work there tomorrow."

Kyle turned his head to spit on the ground. "Just follow the road around the mountain and follow the signs out of town. Can't miss it."

Tony frowned. Well, that had backfired. Now he had no choice but to leave. Unless he wanted to look suspicious. He fell back on his training. Keep 'em talking. "What's there to do around here?"

"Not much. Where you from?" Kyle stepped between the truck and Nick.

Something about the way Kyle stood put Tony on edge. He hovered around the truck, his eyes darting back and forth from the dark alley next to the basketball courts to Nick.

"San Antonio."

Kyle grinned. "No way. I'm from San Marcos."

"I've been there. My buddies and I like to tube the Guadalupe River down to New Braunfels."

"Yeah? We did that a few times, too."

Nick slapped Kyle on the shoulder. "The guys are ready. You coming?"

"Yeah. I'll be right there." Kyle leaned against the truck, clearly in no hurry.

"I take it you're from the home. What about him?" Tony nodded toward the retreating kid.

"Nah." Kyle glanced over his shoulder. "His grandpa donated the building the state turned into the home, and his dad's some big shot who inspects all the group homes in the area."

"Sounds like the kid's got it made."

"Yeah."

"Guess I'll see you tomorrow." Tony watched the teen head back to the others.

Kyle took his time getting to Nick's group. He stopped and talked to a girl watching the game and another boy coming off the court. Tony smiled. Nick liked to run the show and Kyle was making it known that he wasn't going to jump through the kid's hoops.

Tony looked around the area. How many of

the teens were from the home? He was pretty sure they were supposed to have adult supervision at all times. Wherever the chaperone was, they weren't paying much attention to the boys on the courts. Kyle got in a truck with Nick and a few others and left without saying a word to anyone else. Was Nick one of the long-time residents of Salt Creek? Was he a transfer from the city?

Most people who grew up in the small town couldn't wait to get out. Then, as they got older, they tired of the hustle and bustle of city life and recalled an idealistic childhood. When their teenage children became belligerent, the parents' solution was to ship them to the grandparents, convinced life in small-town America would cure them. Sometimes it worked, like with him. Sometimes it didn't. Too bad those parents didn't realize it was the first decade of their life that counted the most. Was Nick one of those kids?

SABRINA SCRAMBLED EGGS while listening for Marissa's car. She rolled her shoulders. Lack of sleep over the past week had given her a dull headache and an aching back.

She had no reason to be so worried. Marissa had promised to keep her secret but if

Marissa had guessed that Levi was Tony's son, how long would it take for others to figure it out? After almost an hour of questions, she'd managed to convince Marissa that she didn't intentionally lie to Tony. She doubted others would be as forgiving. Especially Tony.

Her own sense of morality was the cause of most of her uneasiness. Would things be different today if he'd opened the last letter she'd sent? More than once he'd declared that he never wanted a family but deep down she knew he'd never abandon his child the way his father had abandoned him. And that was the crux of her dilemma.

Aunt Patty told her not to feel guilty because every effort had been made to notify Tony about Levi's birth. After hearing her story, even Marissa agreed that Sabrina had done everything she could. Back then. But what about now?

Her son was finally returning to the happy, carefree boy she knew. If she told the truth, would it help her son or make him worse?

"Levi," she called, scooping the eggs onto a plate. "Breakfast is ready."

"Is Bradley here?" He came out of his room, already dressed.

"Not yet, but any minute now." She poured him a glass of milk.

"I hear them." Levi shoved the scrambled eggs into his mouth and jumped up from the table.

By the time Sabrina met Marissa at the door, the two boys had taken off to the barn in search of her father.

Marissa watched the boys from the porch. "I take it that Levi's as excited about this fishing trip as Bradley."

Sabrina laughed and held the door open for her. "I don't think either of them are as excited as Dad. He's been packing things all week."

Marissa's easy laugh put Sabrina at ease. It was clear Marissa wasn't going to judge her for the sins of her past. As soon as she signed the paperwork in Marissa's briefcase, she'd officially have a job. And better yet, Levi would get the counseling required to get him back into school. Little Mountain even promised a bonus after six months of employment. A bonus that was large enough to pay the first semester's tuition for the nursing program.

By the time she'd poured Marissa a cup of coffee, Marissa had papers scattered across the dining table.

She handed the cup to her friend and sat down to look over the forms. "Thanks for bringing these over. I hope it wasn't too much trouble."

Marissa sipped her coffee. "No sense in you having to drive to Lampasas to sign papers and turn around and come back. Especially if you want to start today. Besides, it gave me an excuse to go into the office late this morning. And Bradley was going nuts waiting for Levi. This was the fastest way to get him out of my hair."

A thrill ran through her as she signed the last form. "How are you involved with Little Mountain? I'm going to be working for them, not Crestview, correct?"

Marissa stacked the papers together. "Yes. We're a contracting company and just assist with the hiring process. They tell us what they need, we find them the best applicants for the job. Once hired, you're all theirs."

Sabrina nodded. Her dad was less than thrilled to hear she'd be working at the children's home. Maybe they were rougher than what she'd been led to believe. "Any advice on working with these kids?"

Marissa nodded. "I understand your concern, but we've never had any major problems with them. They're troubled, yes, but most of them are just kids who need someone to care about them. The state puts those who have a violent history in a different facility. This one only takes fifteen to thirty children at a time, and the ages range from seven to eighteen.

"A couple of the kids have diabetes and need glucose monitoring and shots occasionally. And several of them have asthma. The entire staff is CPR certified, but the state requires someone with more medical training during the day. At least while the kids are out of school for the summer."

She relaxed. That didn't sound too bad.

"The home is in the old Johnson house, outside of town. Do you remember where that is?"

Sabrina nodded. She knew the house where the home was located well. Once considered a model home in the county, years of neglect had taken its toll. Sabrina and Tony had gone into the abandoned house one night. Not one ghost jumped out to scare them, much to their disappointment.

It was a large home, but not large enough for thirty children plus all the adults it took to supervise them. "Where do they fit that many kids?"

"The younger children stay in the main home, but they built cabins on the ten-acre property for the teens. The boys and girls are separated, of course, and each cabin has a married couple who lives with them."

Thirty minutes later, Sabrina stood in front of the double wooden doors of the main house. It looked like the property had been a good investment. The State of Texas had probably bought it for next to nothing, which made the obvious repairs on the home that much more affordable.

The door was unlocked, so she stepped inside. Chimes echoed, alerting anyone in the building someone had entered. Where was everyone? A small girl ran across her path and stopped short when she saw Sabrina. Her dark brown eyes opened wide. "Are you a wobber?"

"A what?" Sabrina squatted down so she could understand her better.

"A wobber," the girl said slowly, then smiled, revealing her missing front teeth.

Sabrina smiled. "No. I'm not a robber. I'm a medical assistant. Is there an adult around here?"

"Ms. Paula!" the little girl yelled, and ran down the hall.

The hallway ended in a large playroom. Several children, boys and girls who all looked to be under the age of ten, were sprawled across the floor, engaged in different activities. A woman with short, spiky hair sat cross-legged, reading a story to a small group.

She jumped to her feet when she noticed Sabrina. "Can I help you?"

"I'm looking for Karen?"

"Down the hall and to the right."

Sabrina followed her direction and almost ran into a robust woman in a hot pink dress decorated with ducks. "I'm looking for Karen."

"You found her." The woman smiled and reached out to shake hands with her. "From the scrubs you're wearing, you must be our new medical assistant."

"Yes. I'm Sab—"

The back door burst open and a young man in his early twenties shouted, "Miss Karen! Help!"

Karen rushed to him, with Sabrina right behind her. The man carried a boy down the hall. Blood dripped from under the hand he had pressed to the child's scrawny arm.

"Bring him in here." Karen held a door open.

Sabrina followed closely, recognizing the room as the medical office. She snatched some alcohol wipes and gloves off the shelf next to the exam table. Karen stepped back to let Sabrina examine the wound.

"What happened?" Sabrina removed the man's hand from the cut.

"We were on a nature walk when Jake decided to run again. He tried to climb the fence and cut his arm."

Jake, the boy in question, winced as Sabrina dabbed an alcohol wipe over the cut. When she asked him questions, he turned his head, refusing to talk. A current of anger ran through the boy. He was about the same age as Levi. What could cause so much rage in such a young kid?

"What a day for you to show up." Karen handed Sabrina a box filled with different sized bandages. "It's usually not this exciting."

The ringing of the doorbell was followed by a man calling out, "Hello? Anyone here?"

Sabrina didn't need to look up from the butterfly bandages she was applying to Jake's arm to know who was in the hallway.

"That must be the new volunteer," Karen said. "Travis Anderson, our campus director, is out of town for a few days, so I'm holding down the fort. Be right back."

A few minutes later, Jake was bandaged up

and sound asleep on the cot in the corner of the room. Sabrina held her breath. Was Tony gone? Was it safe to come out?

The half-open door swung open all the way and Tony leaned against the frame. "I thought that looked like you in here. Everything okay?" The dimple on one cheek deepened.

"Fine. Thanks." She kept her voice calm.

"I didn't know you worked here." He ran a hand through his dark hair, pushing the curls out of his face. He nodded toward the sleeping figure. "The kid going to be okay?"

"He'll be fine. And today is my first day. What are you doing here?" She pretended to organize items inside the desk.

"I work with an outreach program to try to keep kids out of gangs back in San Antonio, so I stopped by to see if I could hang out with the kids here."

She looked up at him. "I thought you were a police officer."

He cocked his head to the side. "I am. I volunteer at St. Paul's."

"Does it work?"

"What?"

She sighed. "The outreach program. Does it keep kids out of gangs?"

"Sometimes." He looked squarely at her.

"We do what we can, but not every kid wants to be saved."

She chuckled. "Seems like someone told me the same thing about animals once."

He reached over and took her hand. His fingers traced the deep scar running across her palm. "I was right, but you had to learn the hard way."

His featherlight touch sent chills up her arm. She snatched her hand away from him. "It may take me a while, but once I learn something, I never forget."

The last thing she wanted was to be reminded of his gentle side.

"I have scars from that night, too." He held up his own hand to reveal a matching mark.

Sabrina looked down at the sleeping child on the cot. "Funny thing about scars. The worst ones are the ones people can't see."

A SHARP PAIN twisted Tony's gut. Sabrina was looking at the little boy curled up on the cot, but he had the feeling she was talking about herself. The last ten years hadn't been easy for her. He could tell without asking. She was still beautiful, despite being much thinner than she'd been in high school. Her long blond hair was wrapped in a tight bun, making her high cheekbones stand out.

He'd thought he made the right choice so long ago. Or, rather, that he'd forced her to make the right choice. But looking at her now, it was easy to see that she carried a heavy burden.

"Bree." He swallowed. Where to begin? "I heard about your fiancé. I'm sorry."

She crossed her arms. "Thank you."

"It must be hard being a single mom. I'm sure his family helps you a lot."

Sabrina found a supply chart inside the desk and pulled it out. "No. They aren't involved."

"Why?"

"Levi's father didn't know I was pregnant when he left." She placed the clipboard on the desk. "I'm really not comfortable talking about this. Especially here. Do you want something?"

Something was wrong. Her voice was missing the bitterness and pain he would've expected from a woman in her situation. She couldn't even look at him.

First she'd been abandoned by him. Then she'd lost her son's father.

The boy on the cot stirred and he knew

the conversation he wanted to have with her would have to wait.

"Sorry about that." Karen breezed back into the room. She stopped three steps inside the door. She looked back and forth between Tony and Sabrina. "Everything all right?"

"Yes," Tony said. "I'd better be going. I only wanted to stop by and introduce myself."

"Come on back to my office," Karen said, "and I can go over the schedule with you."

He nodded. "I'll be right there."

Karen waited at the door for a moment. Tony crossed his arms. She pressed her lips together. "I'll just go get the schedule for you."

He waited for her to leave and turned back to Sabrina. "I don't want things to be like this. Can we get together sometime and talk? Please."

"What do you want?" Her eyes were red. Was she holding back tears?

His mouth dropped open. "I need to know you're okay. That my leaving didn't force you into a doomed relationship with a guy that was no good for you. That you won't hate me forever."

She lifted her chin. "I know you're only going to be in town a few more weeks, so

I'd appreciate it if you'd stay away from me while you're here."

There was the pain and bitterness he'd expected. Aimed at him. Of course. She couldn't be angry with a dead man. It was easier to be mad at him. She'd confirmed his fear. Her life hadn't turned out as planned and it was his fault. He couldn't go back to San Antonio without setting things right. But where did he start? "I need you to know that leaving you was the hardest thing I've ever done in my life."

"Good." Sabrina turned her back to him and opened a supply cabinet at the back of the room.

AFTER HIS BRIEF meeting with Karen, the assistant director, Tony decided to stay for rest of the day. The kids at Little Mountain were a different kind of intense than the ones at St. Paul's Mission. He could see a little of himself in the eyes of the children at both places.

He was signing out at the front desk when Sabrina closed and locked the medical office. For a brief moment, their eyes met.

He caught a whiff of honeysuckle as she whisked by.

Taking his visitor badge off and setting it

on the counter, he nodded at the woman behind the desk. "Thanks. See you tomorrow."

Without waiting for a response, he turned and almost ran to the parking lot. He stopped short when he saw her open the door of a beat up gray Toyota. At least he thought it was gray. Wasn't that the same car she drove in high school? It'd been on its last leg back then. How had it lasted this long?

Catching up to her, he cleared his throat.

"I'm in a hurry, Tony." She kept her back to him and opened the door.

"Please. I need to get this off my chest."

She tossed her purse on the seat. "You've got two minutes."

Tony rubbed his palms on his jeans. She wasn't going to make this easy. "I am so sorry for the way I treated you. And the way I left. I never meant what I said that night."

"Yes, you did. Otherwise, you wouldn't have said it."

"That's just it. You ruined your reputation by vouching for me the night I was accused of robbing that store, so I couldn't let you take any more chances on me until…" He paused. "Until I could deserve you."

Sabrina shrugged and looked down at her feet. "It doesn't matter anymore. We were young. I'm over it. I went on with my life, just like you."

"Is that what you think I did? Just went on with my life like nothing happened?" He pointed to the diamond on her left hand. "Looks like you didn't have a hard time moving on."

She whipped her head up to look at him. Anger flashed in her eyes. "You're the one who left me. You have no right to judge me for the decisions I made when you left."

Is that what he was doing? Judging her? The truth was, he was jealous of the man she'd loved enough to have a family with. Angry, even. "I only left because I thought it would make things easier on you."

She threw her hands in the air. "How was leaving me when I needed you the most supposed to make things easier for me?"

"When I heard you tell Adalie you wanted to put college off for at least a year so you could go to Louisiana with me, I panicked. Without me around stirring up trouble, I thought the town would forget about me, and you would go to college like you were supposed to."

"Well, guess what? It didn't work."

"If I'd stayed, you'd never have become a nurse. We'd both be stuck in this little town forever."

Her hands curled into fists. "Here's a news-flash for you. I'm not a nurse. I still haven't finished college and I *like* this little town."

Tony sucked in a breath. "Your scholar-ship—"

"Got yanked right after you left." She pulled herself up tall. "And thanks to your disappear-ing act, people just shook their heads when they saw me. So I pulled a page from your book and ran away, too."

"I didn't know." Stepping over to her, he took her face in his hands. How had things gone so wrong? "Everything was planned. You were going to finish school and become a nurse."

"No, we *had* everything planned. Then *you* decide to leave. I have the same CNA certi-fication I had when I graduated high school. That's how perfect our plan worked out."

The words slapped him in the face. He had hurt her. On purpose. And it killed him. Had he done it for nothing? "I'm sorry."

"I don't care. Not anymore." Sabrina slid into the car and slammed the door.

CHAPTER FIVE

SABRINA SNUGGLED DEEPER into her pillows. It was Sunday afternoon and she wasn't moving until she finished the book she was reading. She caught a whiff of honeysuckle and listened to the bees humming a steady rhythm as they gathered sweet nectar from the rose bushes growing along the rock wall.

How long had it been since she'd had the time to read a book? In Houston, what little time she had between two jobs and Levi was spent taking classes at the local junior college. Simple things like reading for pleasure were luxuries she hadn't been able to afford for a long time. Especially in the middle of the afternoon.

"Don't you look like the cat that ate the canary." Her dad stood in the hallway and grinned.

Sabrina closed the book and stretched out across her bed. "That's how I feel."

"Are you sorry you came home?"

The question surprised her. She'd been too

ashamed to visit after Levi was born, but Salt Creek would always be home. What would people think of her now? After all, she'd found acceptance by excelling at school.

"No, Dad, I'm not." She got up and padded across the carpet to brush a kiss against her father's cheek. "It's one of the few decisions I got right."

Dad wrapped an arm around her and hugged her. Not one to show emotions, he stepped back quickly. "I got to run to San Saba."

"I guess Levi's going with you." She was glad that her father and Levi had bonded so well. But her father was used to doing things by himself. She didn't want Levi to become a pest.

"No. Levi's out at the barn trying to build a hutch."

"A hutch?"

"He found some baby rabbits and he's convinced he can take care of them."

Sabrina slipped her shoes on. "I better go help."

"I told him no one knew more about taking care of orphaned animals than you." Dad shuffled down the hall.

By the time she trotted down the path to the barn, sweat soaked her T-shirt and caused it to cling to her back and chest. She pulled the shirt away from her skin. Not a blade of grass waved underneath the bright blue sky.

The shade of the barn offered little relief without a breeze. Levi sat next to a cardboard box, boards and pieces of plywood littering the ground behind him.

"Whatcha got there?"

"Bunnies." Levi tilted the box so she could see the three tiny animals.

"Where did you find them?"

Levi pointed toward the stock pond. "I was trying to build a hutch for them, but I can't find the right-sized pieces."

Sabrina sank to the ground next to him. "Honey, I think you need to take them back where you got them. Their momma is going to be looking for them."

"But they don't have a momma. I looked and looked and I couldn't find her anywhere. Maybe a coyote got her." His hazel eyes were wide with concern.

"That's how they protect them." Sabrina carefully picked up each kit and examined it for injuries. "These babies are fat and healthy, which means they have a good mother who knows the best way to keep her babies safe is to not draw attention to her nest."

Levi wrinkled his nose. "She protects them by leaving? That doesn't make sense."

"Come on." Sabrina stood up with the box. "I'll explain it while you show me where the nest is."

They walked through the pasture, talking about different animals and their habits. Once they found the grassy area where the rabbits had been, Sabrina assured Levi the mother would be back. "We'll come check tomorrow, to make sure."

"But if she doesn't, you'll help me take care of them?"

"I'll even help you build a hutch." It was nice to see that Levi had inherited her love of animals. Most of the time, he was so much like Tony she wondered if she'd had any influence on him at all.

When they got back to the house, Levi plopped on the couch and flipped on the television. That wouldn't last long. Dad only got three channels with the antenna. Would Dad let her order satellite television? Now that she had a job, she could pay for it herself.

After a few minutes, he turned the television off. "Does Grandpa have any board games?"

"I bet I still have some in my bedroom."

Levi followed her down the hall and settled on her bed as she opened the closet. Reaching up to the top shelf, she removed a board game and accidentally knocked the wooden box from the shelf. It landed on the floor with a thump.

"What's that?" Levi jumped off the bed and scooped it up.

Her hands shook. "My treasure box."

"A treasure box?" His eyes opened wide. "What's in it?"

All the things near to her heart. She ran her fingers over the polished wood. Dad had made it for her when she was five years old. She'd been convinced that every rock and broken piece of pottery she found held some sort of magical secret. As she grew, the treasures changed. The things she'd put in it later still had the power to tear her heart out. She lifted the lid.

Levi watched her carefully pick up each item from the box and show it to him. The arrowheads she'd found while hiking with Dad. She swallowed a lump and touched the newspaper clipping of her mother's obituary. A faded ticket stub from the first movie Tony had taken her to see fell on the bed. She replaced it in the box.

"What's in here?" Levi held up a small manila envelope. She plucked it from his hand. "Photos. Let me find the ones of my mom."

She shuffled the pictures of Tony to the back and laid out some family pictures on the bed, instead. "I never met any of my grandparents." She pointed out the picture of her dad's family.

"Why not?"

"Dad's parents both died before I was born."

"Like my dad's parents?" Levi nodded. "That's why he joined the Army. 'Cause he didn't have any family left."

Guilt slammed into her like a wrecking ball. Her throat tightened as Levi looked at the picture of his great-grandparents. She'd always thought she was protecting him by letting him think his father was dead. But she'd taken away an entire family from him. Family who would've welcomed him with open arms.

"What about your mom's parents?" Levi sorted through the photographs. "Where are they?"

"They disowned my mom when she married my dad. So I've never met them."

"Really? Why would they do that? Grandpa's great."

She pointed to a picture of her mother as a

child. "She was a dancer. A very good one. She gave up an invitation to join a ballet company to marry Grandpa. Her parents thought she was throwing away her future on a farm boy."

"Wow." Levi looked at the picture with renewed interest.

She straightened all the pictures and replaced them in the envelope. The only contact she'd ever had from her mother's parents never made it to the treasure box. The card she'd received in the mail after her mother died. Unfamiliar handwriting introduced the sender as Sabrina's grandmother. It ended with an invitation to come live with them. Sabrina had taken great pleasure in burning the card and she never told her dad.

IT WAS LATER than usual when Tony finally got out of bed Monday morning. Hanging out at Little Mountain the last couple of days had left him exhausted, but how could his muscles ache when he hadn't done anything physical? It was going to take him forever to get back into shape. He pulled a T-shirt over his head and followed his nose to the kitchen.

Papa sat at the dining room table. "Morning." He eyed Tony over the top of his newspaper.

"Have I gotten any phone calls?" The wooden chair scraped against the tile as Tony slid it out to sit down. He'd been hanging out at the group home for the past week, but he needed permission from the director to do anything outside of the home. Anderson was supposed to be returning this weekend.

"No." Abuela slid a fried egg onto his plate.

Papa probably knew as much about the boys as anyone. He knew everything that happened in Salt Creek. "What do you know about the boys causing trouble in town?"

"They're not the problem." Papa folded his newspaper. "Anderson is."

"Travis Anderson? The director?"

"It's not good to talk about others, Papa." Abuela set a glass of orange juice in front of Tony.

Papa waved her away. "I can when it's the truth. He's greedy. He's not interested in those kids, just the check the state gives him each month."

Great. Tony's specialty was troubled teens. Adults were an entirely different matter. "Most of the boys are good kids," Abuela said. "They just need guidance."

"What kind of trouble have they been causing?"

Papa put his fork down. "A few of them snuck out and broke into the high school. Stole some things. Even took one of the buses on a joyride."

"Hmph," Abuela snorted. "If you ask me, the ringleader isn't even from the home. It's Nick Johnson. He's no good."

"Johnson?" Tony stopped midchew.

Abuela sighed. "Yes, *mijo*. The same family."

Tony pinched the bridge of his nose. He hadn't thought about the Johnsons in years. Their patriarch was as wily as a snake charmer. Monroe Johnson had been the mayor of Salt Creek for as long as Tony could remember. How a weasel like that kept getting elected, he'd never know. His boys weren't much better. Acid churned his stomach.

"How is Nick related?"

"Nick is Monroe's youngest grandson. He was just in elementary school when you lived here."

The chair groaned as Tony leaned back. He'd gone to school with the two oldest boys, Kurt and Allen. Both of them hated him with a passion. "Anything else I need to know?"

"Yes." Papa cleared his throat. "Anderson's

the campus director. But Allen Johnson is the executive director for all group homes in more than three counties."

"How'd he get that job?"

Abuela shrugged. "Allen got the job when his daddy donated the old ranch to the state to turn it into a group home."

Tony scrubbed his hand over his face. "No wonder nothing's been done. The director of the home has to report all problems to the regional manager. Who is sweeping all the trouble under the rug? Anderson or Johnson?"

"My bet is Johnson," Papa said. "Too much trouble would cause the home to lose their license and that would make the family look bad."

At least his questions about Nick had been answered. "I met Nick at the basketball courts last week."

How was he supposed to help the kids if the real trouble began from outside the home? Would his involvement be welcome? He knew it shouldn't matter—after all, he'd be returning to San Antonio in two weeks. But the chance to be a thorn in the Johnsons' side made him all the more determined to find out what was really going on at the home.

"Why are you asking about Little Mountain?"

"Deputy Butler asked me to try to get to know some of the kids from the home. He thinks there's more to the trouble than just boys getting rowdy."

"What do you mean more?" Papa's face was somber.

Tony didn't want to point any fingers. Not yet. But it wouldn't be the first time someone had used a group facility like Little Mountain Children's Home as a cover for other things. Drugs. Burglary. Chop shops. The list got worse. "I'm not sure. But if I can gain their trust, I might be able to find out."

"Mondays are always busy. I better get going. You coming by the hardware store later?" Papa stood up.

"Yes. I'm heading to the group home first and I'll meet you at the store in a while." What would Allen do when he found out he was the volunteer Jarrod Butler had sent to work with the boys? He had two weeks to find out what was really happening at the group home. And two weeks to make amends with Sabrina. Would it be enough time?

His phone vibrated on the table. He frowned at the unfamiliar number. "Hello?"

"Morning. My name is Travis Anderson and I'm the director of Little Mountain Children's Home."

Took him long enough. Karen had assured him that once Travis was back in town, they could discuss some of Tony's ideas. She must have given him the message. "Thanks for calling."

"I'm sorry I wasn't around when you started. Karen speaks highly of you. What did you want to talk to me about?"

"Well, sir, I'm looking to find a ways to get the boys more involved in the community."

"I'd appreciate that. Some of these boys are a little rougher than we anticipated. What'd you have in mind?" At least the gruff voice on the other end of the line seemed eager.

"Who's the best mechanic of the bunch?" Tony already knew the answer. He'd spent the last week with the boys, and the grease underneath Kyle's fingernails was a dead giveaway.

"Um…that'd probably be Kyle. His daddy was a mechanic. Owned his own shop."

His dad? Tony's brows drew together. "I'm sorry, Mr. Anderson. I'm confused. How did a boy with a family end up in a children's home? I thought spots were reserved for wards of the state without family."

"His dad died and no one knows what happened to his mama. So I have him."

Tony suspected that there was much more to the story, but knew Anderson was legally prohibited from telling him. "I'd like to give Kyle a job. Would you be opposed to that?"

"No, that'd be fine." Silence filled the line for a moment. "Residents of the home aren't allowed but a certain amount of money at a time, so you'll give his paychecks directly to me."

Sure I will. "The work I'm offering won't be drawing a paycheck. More of a community service project."

"Oh." The disappointment in the man's voice was too evident. Tony's nostrils flared. Papa claimed the man had more interest in the money than the kids. Was he right? How did a man like that become the director of a state-run home for troubled kids?

"Can Kyle meet me at my grandfather's hardware store this afternoon?"

"Sure. I'll send him over there after lunch."

Hanging up the phone, his mind whirled with ideas. Maybe there was a better way to help teens than pounding the city streets. He glanced at his watch. Papa hadn't left to open the hardware store yet. Better go talk to him first. This wouldn't work without Papa's support.

"THE CUTS ARE looking good, Jake." Sabrina applied ointment to the healing wounds. "Promise me you won't climb any more fences."

Jake shrugged. Not once had the little boy spoken to her. She was lucky if he even looked her in the eye.

"Hello, Jake." Tony knocked at the door and then sauntered inside. "I've been looking for you."

At five foot nine, Tony wasn't a tall man, but he had a big presence. His arms looked like tree trunks, the muscles stretching the sleeves of his black T-shirt. The football coach in high school had taken one look at him and declared that Tony was built like a tank. Too bad his mouth and attitude got him kicked off the football team before the first game. When he walked into the exam room, the walls seemed to shrink.

Sabrina kept her eyes on Jake. It was safer than looking at Tony. Her heart did funny things when she saw him.

True to form, Jake acknowledged Tony with a nod.

"I'm building a playhouse in the backyard. I could sure use some help." Tony sat on the edge of the exam table. "I have my frame up, but I'm having a hard time getting those triangle thingies in place."

What was Tony doing? He'd worked construction all through high school. She'd never heard him refer to anything as a "thingy."

He winked at her and then turned his attention back to Jake. "I've got one triangle at the front and one at the back, but somehow I can't get it to look right."

Jake stared at the floor.

"If you change your mind, you know where I'll be." Tony patted the boy's shoulder and turned to go. "Sabrina, could you help me hold one of the triangle thingies is place?"

"Trusses." Jake rolled his eyes and hopped off the table. "They're called trusses. And you can't just hold them in place."

"Where are you going?" Tony asked the boy as he stormed past him.

"To get my level and meet you in the backyard."

Sabrina covered her mouth to keep from laughing. "How did you know?"

Tony's hazel eyes bored into hers. "You learn a lot about a person if you take the time to really listen. Even when they're not saying anything."

She raised one eyebrow.

Tony glanced at the door. "It also helps if you notice the only thing he checks out of the library are books about construction."

"Did you know this when you decided to build a playhouse or was it just a happy co-incidence?"

"Building projects can be good therapy. So I guess it was a happy coincidence. I better get going."

Sabrina felt a prick of disappointment when he left. Had he stopped by her office to see Jake? Or her? Last week she'd told him to stay away from her. But he hadn't. He stopped by every morning to tell her hello. Just before lunch he stopped again to say goodbye. To be fair, he did the same with Karen.

This Tony was vastly different from the one she'd known all those years ago. And yet he was also the same. She tried to picture Tony walking through the hallway of Salt Creek High School, stopping to talk to everyone, but that wasn't how it had been. He'd kept to himself. She'd caught glimpses of the true Tony. But every time he'd come out of his shell, something, or someone, had caused him to go back in.

Had she played a part in creating the confident man who had just left her office? Had she helped him tear down the walls that kept him from taking a chance with people? The weight of the engagement ring around her finger mocked her. Aunt Patty had bought it at a pawn store to make her story more credible. She wore the ring as a symbol of the wall around her own heart. A reminder that it was too painful to love anyone again. She twisted the ring around her finger.

Panic clawed her chest. She was going to have to tell him. Ten years ago she'd had valid reasons for hiding the truth. Those reasons didn't seem as important now. After looking at those family photos with Levi, she knew she needed to tell him. But how?

In the meantime, she had plenty to keep her busy. Mr. Anderson had informed her that the state was coming for an inspection, so all medical files had to be in tip-top shape. Paperwork had to be filled out, medications checked and everything updated. Sabrina patted the stack of files on the desk. This was going to take weeks, not days.

She tuned the small radio on the corner shelf to a country station. The music, combined with the work, soon lulled her into a zone of concentration, and before she realized it, the "done" stack was higher than the "to be done" stack. She carried an armload of files to the cabinet and tapped her toes with the music as she put them away.

She heard a giggle behind her and turned to see Lonnie, a twelve-year-old boy, watching her from the doorway. "Oh, you think my singing is funny?"

A toothy grin lit up his dark face. "No. Your dancing."

"Well come on, hotshot, show me how it's done."

Lonnie didn't need any further invitation. He started jerking and popping in rhythm with the music. Now it was Sabrina's turn to laugh. "You can't dance like that to country music."

He wrinkled his eyebrows. "Whatcha supposed to do?"

"I'll teach you." She took his hands in hers and showed the beginning position for a basic two-step.

"What if I can't do it?" Uncertainty flickered across his face.

"Trust me, if I can teach my son, I can teach anyone. He started out with two left feet." Holding out her hands, she led him through the foundations of the two-step.

Within a few minutes, a small crowd had gathered in the doorway, watching them.

"That's fun." Lonnie's face was red when the song ended.

"My turn, my turn!" One of the girls in the doorway jumped up and down. "Teach me."

A chorus of voices erupted from the hallway and Sabrina laughed. "Y'all really want to learn how to two-step?"

Olivia, one of the few teenage girls at the facility, pushed her glasses up her nose. "The school has dances all the time, but none of us go because we don't know how to dance."

Sabrina's heart ached at the shyness she saw in the girl. "They play all kinds of music at those dances. Not just country."

Olivia shrugged. "I can't dance to any of it."

"I'll teach you."

"Me, too!" Lonnie bounced up and down.

She gave Lonnie a pointed look. "Only if you stop fussing every time you get your insulin shot."

"Yes, ma'am."

"All right," Sabrina said. "I have a lot of paperwork to do today, though. We'll start tomorrow afternoon, okay?"

"Yes, ma'am." Lonnie saluted her before

hopping up on the examine table and holding out his finger so she could check his blood sugar.

She opened the cabinet to get supplies. A reflection in the glass revealed that someone had been watching her with the kids. By the time she closed the door, Tony was gone.

CHAPTER SIX

IT WAS A little after two o'clock in the afternoon when Sabrina got home. She hadn't seen Tony again all day. Had he given up? She wanted him to. Didn't she?

Two boys were playing basketball in front of the garage. She recognized Levi immediately. It took her a moment to realize the other was Bradley. Both of them were soaking wet. Forgoing her usual parking spot, she pulled her rusty Toyota to the side of the building.

"Hi, Mom." Levi tucked the ball under his arm and met her at the car. "Marissa dropped Bradley off this morning. Can he stay the night?"

Her heart jumped. Her son had never invited anyone to spend the night before. "I'll call Marissa and see if it's okay." She frowned. "Isn't it too hot for basketball right now?"

Bradley shook his auburn head. "No. Mr.

Davis set up the sprinkler to spray on us while we were playing."

That explained why they were wet. Her eyes caught the mud puddles around the yard.

Dad opened the screen door to stand on the porch. "I was just trying to call you. The boys helped me move hay this morning, so I promised them fried chicken. I already called the order in. Can you run to The Eagle's Nest and pick it up?"

Levi grinned. "Please, Mom? We're starving."

She rubbed her fingers along her collarbone. "Sure. I guess."

Turning around, she got back into her car. She went to work and came home, and so far she'd managed to avoid spending too much time in town—partly because she wanted to avoid Tony, but mostly because she didn't want to become a topic of local gossip.

In and out. She'd be so fast that no one would even notice her. Oh, who was she kidding? Noticing anyone new or out of the ordinary was a specialty in the small town.

The café's parking lot was surprisingly full—the lunch rush should've died down by now. When she'd worked as a waitress there, the place was dead by two o'clock. But this was good. The more crowded it was, the easier it would be for her to blend in. She tidied her ponytail and headed for the door as fast as she could.

Just before she reached the entrance, the heavy wooden door swung open, catching her toe underneath the corner. "Ow!" She hopped on one foot.

"I'm so sorry. I didn't see you."

Sabrina stopped hopping. No. She had to have the worst luck in history.

"Are you okay?"

"Yes. I'm fine." The sharp pain running up her leg throbbed. She stepped out of his reach.

Tony's eyes narrowed. "I can see blood through your shoe. You're not fine. Wait here."

As soon as he disappeared around the corner, Sabrina hobbled inside.

The café hadn't changed much. Same paint. Same tile. Even the art on the walls were the same. She should know. She'd looked at them almost every weekend for four years. The main dining area was through an archway to her left, with only a few booths against the wall in the small entry. Four barstools sat in front of the counter for those who were waiting for orders to go. She sank onto the closest one, grateful to take the weight off her foot.

"I told you to wait for me." Tony's sharp voice caused her to jump.

She spun on the stool and gave him her best glare. "I told you. I'm fine. I don't need your help."

"Still stubborn as ever," he mumbled as he looked down at her foot. He had a first aid kit tucked under his arm. "The door tore a hole in your shoe."

Her cheeks flamed hot. She wasn't about to admit that the hole was already there. Crossing her leg over her knee, she slid her shoe off. "It's okay. I need new ones, anyway."

She touched the tender area around her big toe. The nail was broken and blood oozed from a cut on the end. "Ow."

Tony opened up a small first aid kit and pulled out a package of antiseptic wipes and a bandage. He ripped open the wipe and cleaned around her toe.

Sabrina gritted her teeth against the sting of the alcohol on her skin. Tony's gentle caress wasn't doing much to help her racing heart.

"Hello, Tony." A sheriff's deputy with bright red hair stood at the entrance to the dining area. His blue eyes darted from Tony to her.

He shook his head slightly and suppressed a smile. "How's it going?"

Tony stood quickly. "Jarrod. I was going to give you a call later this afternoon."

Jarrod? Sabrina glanced at his nametag. Butler. He must be Marissa's husband. How did he know Tony? Did Marissa know they knew each other?

"Catch you later. Keep an eye out for those ghosts." Jarrod walked through the archway and into the dining area.

Ghosts? What was he talking about?

Tony rolled his eyes and turned his attention back to her foot. "I don't think it's broken." He picked up her shoe but didn't hand it back to her.

"Thanks. Can I have my shoe back now?"

"Yes. If you have dinner with me tonight."

She pulled her leg away and turned to the counter. "I'll go barefoot."

"Oh, my goodness! Sabrina Davis!" a shrill voice called from the end of the counter.

"Betty." She tried to stand but was almost knocked over when the large, older woman caught her in a bear hug.

"Gracious, girl. How are you? I was just asking Tony about you a couple of weeks ago."

The ring of the bell over the door signaled Tony's quiet departure. Sabrina glanced at the floor, expecting to see her shoe. He'd taken it. Crud. That was the best pair of sneakers she had. Okay. It was the only pair of sneakers she had.

"Where did you disappear to? How's your daddy?" Betty's chatter pulled her attention back to the counter.

Sabrina answered the questions she could and avoided the ones that were too telling by changing the subject to Betty's grandkids. It took almost ten minutes before Sabrina could ask if her dad's order was ready.

When duty called and Betty went back to the dining area, Sabrina limped to a corner booth in the small front room. She did her best to remain invisible. Too much attention for one day.

The swinging door separating the kitchen from the counter area burst open. "Did I hear right?" a booming voice projected through the area. "Is my saber-toothed tiger back?"

Sabrina covered her face with both hands. She thought she'd gotten rid of that nickname when her braces came off in seventh grade. Straightening up, she waved to the burly man behind the counter. "Hi, Mr. Shannon."

Gary Shannon covered the distance to her booth in three giant strides and pulled her up to give her a hug. "How's my best waitress?"

"I heard that," Betty called from the cash register.

"Don't worry," Gary hollered to her. "You're still the second-best." He set a paper bag on the table and slid onto the bench across from Sabrina. "Are you really back for good?"

"For a while, at least." Sabrina hadn't been hugged this much since she was twelve years old and her mother had died.

After promising to stop by his place for a visit later in the week, she hurried to her car. There, on the front seat, sat her shoe.

TONY POPPED HIS KNUCKLES. If he hadn't been expecting Kyle to show up at the hardware store, he'd march right back into The Eagle's Nest and demand that Sabrina go for a ride with him. There were too many unanswered questions. The biggest one was why she hadn't been back in the last ten years. It was one of the things they'd playfully argued about. She loved Salt Creek, loved being part of a small community, and most all, she loved the farm where she grew up.

Moving away for college had been expected, but she was adamant about coming back. Why hadn't she come back to Salt Creek sooner? This was where she had always wanted her children to grow up. Tony gulped. Their children. The ones he told her he never wanted.

Main Street stretched out in front of him. One red light marked the town's only intersection. A bank, a grocery store, an auto repair shop and an antique store marked each corner. Did teenagers still hang out in the bank's parking lot on Friday and Saturday nights? Aside from being the only place in town with paved parking, it had the added advantage of a view of everyone who drove through town. When he was a teen, it had been the best place around to hang out after all the stores closed.

He turned right and headed a half block toward the train tracks, where Montoya Hardware was located. Papa's truck was in its usual spot, so Tony parked next to it and turned off the engine. He enjoyed helping Papa around the store. It kept him from going stir-crazy when he wasn't at Little Mountain. And the work wasn't challenging. It would give him time to devise a plan to see Sabrina again.

Two hours later, he glanced at the clock.

Again. Where was Kyle? The store closed at five. Would he even show up?

Tony was in the back room when Papa stuck his head through the door. "*Mijo*, there's someone here for you."

"Thanks, Papa. I'll be right there." He rounded the corner to see Kyle standing in the middle of the tool aisle. "Hey, Kyle. Thanks for stopping by."

Kyle shrugged. His shaggy brown hair hung well past his collar in the back and almost covered his eyes in the front. "Mr. Anderson didn't give me much choice."

"I'm sorry to hear that." Tony nodded toward the door. "You're free to go. I don't want to hire someone who doesn't want to be here." He headed back to the storeroom.

"Wait. Hire? You got a job for me?"

Tony wiped the smile off his face before turning around. "Does that mean you're interested?"

"Depends. What is it?"

He motioned for the teen to follow him through to the warehouse portion of the building. He flipped on the fluorescent lights and Kyle let out a loud whistle. Tony walked around the old car. "She's a beauty, ain't she?"

"What year is she?" Kyle's eyes sparkled

as he ran a hand along the faded blue paint of the hood.

"A 1972 AMC Javelin." Teenage boys loved muscle cars. But if he was right about Kyle, it would go much deeper. "I'd let you drive her, but she's not running too good. That's where you come in."

Kyle froze, his brown eyes widening. "Me?"

"Rumor is you're a pretty good mechanic." He leaned his elbows on the roof of the car.

"My old man was a good mechanic, not me."

"You mean you didn't pick anything up from him?"

Kyle's chin lifted in the air. "Yeah. I mean... I helped him sometimes."

"So you think you can get her running again?"

"I don't have no tools."

Tony arched an eyebrow. "*Any*. You don't have any tools. But I do. What I don't have is a mechanic."

Kyle chewed on his thumbnail, his eyes never leaving the car. "I could try, I guess. What do you pay?"

"Fifteen dollars an hour. And you keep the tools you use." With his own tools, Kyle would be able to create his own future. He could almost hear the wheels spinning in Kyle's brain as he thought about it.

"I get to keep the tools?" Kyle looked skeptical.

"Yeah." Tony nodded. "There is one catch, though."

"I knew it." Disappointment filled the boy's face.

"I can't give you a paycheck."

Kyle glared at him. "You said fifteen dollars an hour."

"And that's what I'll pay you." Tony pulled a paper from his wallet and handed it to him. "This is a savings account that I've set up in your name. I'll deposit the money into that account. The money'll draw interest until you turn eighteen and then you're free to do what you want with it."

"Aw, man." Kyle shoved the paper back at him. "I need money now."

"I'll give you twenty percent of your paycheck in cash. But the rest goes in the bank." Where Travis Anderson couldn't touch it. "That's my offer. Take it or leave it."

Kyle's attention drifted back and forth between Tony and the car, clearly weighing his options. "When can I get started?" Kyle's fingers ran over the hood, as if he was itching to lift it up and gaze under it.

"Right now. But first, let me show you something." Kyle followed him through the door to the main part of the building where Tony pointed to a clipboard hanging on the wall.

"What's this?" the kid asked.

"Your inventory sheet." Tony pulled a metal key from his pocket and handed it to him. "This is a key to the back door over there. Feel free to work whenever you want. Just write down whatever tools you take here. If you need something we don't have in stock, mark it here, as well, and I'll get it for you."

Kyle stared at the key. "Are you serious?"

Tony nodded. "Is there a reason I shouldn't be?"

"You're placing a lot of trust in someone you don't know."

"I do have one condition."

"Here it comes," Kyle muttered under his breath.

"If you fail a drug test, the deal is off."

Kyle's eyes widened. "I don't do drugs."

Tony ignored the denial. He'd made his point. Kyle knew that Tony was placing trust in him when no one else would. "I have to get back to help my grandfather. Don't let me down."

In a flash, Kyle was opening the hood and inspecting the belts. Tony paused on his way back into the store. "Can you have it done by the end of the summer?"

"I don't know."

"There's an antique car show at the Harvest Festival in October. You have it ready by then and we'll split any prize money we win." He hadn't attended the town festival in years, but he had the feeling he'd be visiting a lot more often.

"Fifty-fifty?" Kyle looked up from his inspection.

"Yes. Don't forget to log your hours on that clipboard, too."

"Yes, sir." Kyle's voice followed him as he went back into the main store.

"Are you sure you know what you're doing?" Papa's voice was low when Tony resumed his inventory checklist.

"I'm just giving him the same chance you gave me, Papa." Tony reached up to clasp the old man's shoulder. "I'll keep an eye on him, but I have a good feeling about this."

Papa smiled. "I'm proud of you, *mijo*."

"LEVI," SABRINA YELLED, as loud as she could. In the dim light of the setting sun, she couldn't see any movement from the barn. Her toe still hurt from her run in with Tony that afternoon. The thought of putting her shoe back on to look for the boys made her cringe.

"Dad. Levi and Bradley aren't back yet. Can you go check on them? Marissa will be here any minute."

Dad looked up from the news program he was watching. The screen door slammed shut as he stepped outside and off the porch. A loud whistle pierced the air. When he came back inside, he was grinning. "They should be along any second now."

"I forgot about the whistle that can be heard around the world." How many times had that sound beckoned her home when she was roaming the pastures?

The two boys appeared a few minutes later and sat on the front porch, huddled together. Sabrina watched them through the window. "What do you think they're up to?"

"Trying to concoct a plan to get Marissa to let Bradley stay the night, most likely." Dad settled back in his recliner.

"He has a dentist appointment in the morning, so he can't." She hoped Levi wouldn't attempt to change Marissa's mind. It drove her crazy when kids pestered their parents to try to get their way. Although she was hoping to entice Marissa to stay for a while. She needed to find out how Marissa's husband knew Tony.

Headlights flashed through the window, and when she arrived Marissa was greeted by two sad boys with overemphasized puppy-dog faces. She laughed. "Not going to work. The answer is still no."

Sabrina chuckled. "You shot them down before they even got started. They've been scheming for the last fifteen minutes."

"Dang. I should've waited to see what they'd come up with. Bradley's famous for his plotting."

"I was looking forward to watching it. Would you like to come in for some tea?"

"Make it a glass of wine and you've got yourself a deal."

Sabrina shook her head. "Sorry. I don't have any wine. I think Dad may have some beer in the refrigerator, though."

"Tea will be fine." Marissa let out an exaggerated sigh and slumped her shoulders. "You boys play a little longer so I can have some girl time with Sabrina."

In a flash the boys were speeding down the path to the barn.

Sabrina poured two glasses of iced tea and carried them outside. "Let's go to the porch swing on the other side of the house. Dad's watching the news and I don't want to disturb him."

Once they were settled, Marissa said, "It's so quiet out here." She pushed one sandaled foot against the floor, sending the swing into a gentle rhythm.

"Does your husband know about Tony and Levi?" Sabrina got straight to the point.

"No. Why?"

"I ran into Tony at The Eagle's Nest today. Then your husband walked by and stopped to talk to him. I didn't know they knew each other."

"I didn't, either. Jarrod hasn't said anything to me about him." She reached out and squeezed Sabrina's hand. "I haven't told anyone your secret. But do you really think you can hide it forever?"

The lack of judgment in Marissa's voice washed over Sabrina. She took a deep breath. "I wasn't trying to be vindictive, you know. He left me. One day things were fine and the next day he said he was leaving and there was nothing I could do to keep him here. Then I found out I was pregnant. Was I supposed to use a baby to make him love me?"

Marissa shrugged. "Of course not. But he didn't read your letters. His grandparents could've found him for you."

Her stomach tightened. "I did go to his grandparents. They were so busy telling me how good he was doing and how proud they were that he got out of Salt Creek and was trying to make something of his life, I couldn't tell them."

Marissa ran a hand through her short blond hair and fluffed it. "Do you think Mr. Montoya would've forced him to come back?"

Sabrina pushed the swing a little harder. "He wouldn't have had to. Tony would've dropped everything, rushed back here and insisted on getting married."

"And that would have been a bad thing?" Marissa cocked her head.

The worst. "He didn't love me and I wasn't willing to settle for anything less."

"Marriage is hard, even under the best circumstances. But raising a child on your own is harder. At least he could've helped financially."

"Tony wouldn't have settled for being an

absentee dad. And getting married would've doomed us both to a life of misery." Him for being stuck in Salt Creek and her for loving someone who didn't love her back. She toyed with the diamond on her left hand.

Unable to meet Marissa's gaze, she stared at the pasture beyond the yard. "After a few years, I told myself it didn't matter anymore. I was fine on my own."

"Levi thinks his father is dead." Marissa arched one eyebrow. "Are you going to tell him now that Tony's back?"

"I don't know. I know I should, but the other part of me says it's too late. Levi and I don't need him."

"Speaking from experience, I can tell you it's not too late."

Sabrina heard pain in Marissa's voice. "What do you mean?"

"I have a stepson." Marissa shrugged. "Jarrod had a child with his high school girlfriend."

"And she didn't tell Jarrod?"

Marissa took a long sip of her sweet tea. "She did. They got married, but they were too young and it ended within a couple of years. Jarrod wasn't much of a dad in the beginning. He rarely saw Scott. He thought the child support check he sent every month was enough."

"A lot of men feel like that." But not Tony. Not after being abandoned by his own father. It was the reason he'd never wanted kids. *Don't bring them into the world if you're not going to take care of them*, he'd said. And he didn't want to take care of anyone but himself.

"When Bradley came along, Jarrod realized how important it was to really be a dad. By then, Scott was almost twelve years old and he wanted nothing to do with Jarrod."

Twelve. Three years older than Levi was now. How would her son react if Tony suddenly appeared in his life? Would he be angry at Tony? Or her? "How long ago was that? How's their relationship now?"

"Almost five years ago. Things are still touch and go. Amanda really ran Jarrod down to Scott, and since Jarrod had never been around to defend himself, Scott believed her." Marissa tucked a strand of gold hair behind her ear.

"So you think I should tell Tony." It wasn't a question.

Marissa smiled. "You should do what feels right. I'm not here to judge. I pushed Jarrod to build a relationship with his son, but I have to admit, there were times the drama became too much. There were days I just wanted Scott to go away."

Sabrina's mouth dropped open. "You don't mean that."

Marissa pressed her lips together and nodded. "I'm ashamed to admit it, but it's true. The kid was so angry at everyone that he made life miserable for all of us. Don't let that happen to Levi. Either tell them both the truth soon, or don't tell them at all. If they accidentally find out, you'll all get hurt."

TONY AND KYLE were busy under the hood of the car when Papa popped into the workshop. Without a word, he jerked his head, signaling for Tony to follow him.

He wiped his hands off on a rag. "Be right back," he said to Kyle.

Why was his dad on edge? As he rounded the corner he realized why Papa's eyes had been conveying a silent warning.

The sight of the man at the end of the aisle caused the hair on the back of his neck to stand up.

"I heard you were back in town."

"Hi, Kurt." Tony placed one elbow on the shelf and assumed a casual position. "Can I help you?"

"I didn't think you'd have the guts to show your face around here again." Eyes so dark the pupils were hidden glared at Tony.

"Is there something you need?" Tony took a deep, cleansing breath. What a way to have his good mood shattered.

"I read about a hotshot cop in the paper a few weeks ago." Kurt glanced around the room. "I came by to see for myself if it was really you. You sure managed to pull the wool over a lot of people's eyes."

Tony silently counted to ten. "I'm sorry you feel that way."

"My wife told me you were volunteering at Little Mountain."

"I am."

Kurt looked around the room again. "Anderson thought he was being sneaky, putting a cop in the home to spy on the kids. I told him there wasn't nothing going on, but he fired me, anyway."

Something about his movements didn't sit right with Tony. "I'm not here to spy on anyone. Why'd you get fired?"

Kurt ignored his question. "Maybe you just get your kicks being around a bunch of little boys. Don't get too comfortable. As soon as I talk to my brother, you'll be out on your ear."

Tony refused to let Kurt bait him. It was obvious the man was there to start something. "I'm not on staff. I'm a volunteer. And I'm only in town for a few more weeks."

The man's glazed eyes narrowed. "Well, that's rich. You helping out with juvies. Do you tell them about your own life of crime?"

"I don't hide anything from them." Tony popped his knuckles. What he really wanted to do was to knock the man on the floor and search him for drugs.

"How many times were you arrested?" Kurt clearly enjoyed needling him. "Was it six or seven? I forget."

"Actually it was four." Tony had had enough. He stepped closer. The intimidation factor worked. Kurt moved away. "All but one of them were before I moved here and charges were dismissed the last time. It seems someone tried to set me up. You don't know anything about that, do you?"

Kurt shifted uncomfortably. "You were caught red-handed but somehow convinced your little girlfriend to lie for you. That's the way I remember it."

"I remember it differently." That evening would forever be etched into his memory. "I remember seeing a blue truck speeding away from the parking lot behind the school where I was parked. When I got to my truck, I found stolen tools in it. Didn't you used to drive a blue truck?"

Kurt refused to look him in the eye. "It's a good thing your girlfriend was able to vouch for you."

His patience reached its limit. "What do you want, Kurt?"

"To warn you. Stay away from Little Mountain."

Tony struggled to keep his voice calm and not betray his temper. "And let me warn you, if I find out that someone is using those kids for their own personal gain, I will use every available resource I have to lock that person behind bars."

Kurt grinned. "You won't find much help around here. You're nothing but a punk with a shiny badge."

Tony stood rigid, waiting for the chimes over the entrance to signal Kurt's departure.

Jarrod walked through the entrance as Kurt stormed out the door. "What was that about?"

"Just an old friend welcoming me home."

"Could've fooled me."

Tony beckoned Jarrod over to him. He looked around to make sure Kyle wasn't in the main part of the store. "He accused of me spying on the kids and warned me to stay away from Little Mountain. Now, why do you think he'd do that?"

Jarrod raised his red eyebrows. "Huh. Maybe we've been focusing too much energy on Travis. I'm going to see what kind of dirt I can dig up on Kurt and his wife."

"His brother Allen is the regional manager. He has the power to sweep any problem under the rug before it attracts attention. You think he's behind it?"

"I don't know. I've met with Allen a few times. He seems to be on the up and up. Kurt, on the other hand..."

"*Mijo*," Papa called from behind the counter. "Kyle is going to lunch with me. You coming?"

"Jarrod and I have some things to discuss and I'm helping out at Little Mountain this afternoon. Do you want me to lock up or wait until you get back?"

His dad flipped the lights off. "I'll lock up. Most people know I close at lunch, so I doubt anyone will come in."

Kyle and Papa went out through the back and Tony pulled the rolling warehouse door closed after they exited.

"He's a good kid." Jarrod picked up a wrench off the counter and tapped it against his hand. "You don't think he's involved in drug smuggling, do you?"

"No way. Not Kyle." Tony remembered the way Kyle spoke about drugs that night in the alley. "His mom walked out on him because of drugs. I can't see him selling them."

Then Tony remembered something else Kyle had said. "But I do think he knows more than he's saying."

"No wonder the kid won't come forward. Not after what happened to his dad."

"What?" In all the time they'd spent together, Kyle refused to talk about his father. Tony sensed they'd been close.

"His dad helped the police out a few times. One day he ratted out the wrong guy. There wasn't much left of him, from what I understand." Jarrod's face was somber.

Tony shuddered. The extent dealers went to to protect their supply never failed to amaze him. The amount of pain one human being could inflict on another in the name of drugs. "He once said he knew what happened to narcs. Poor kid."

Jarrod shook his head. "His dad was a good

guy. It's a shame that Kyle ended up in a children's home."

Was there something he could do about that? The kid deserved to spend his last year of high school in a real home, with people who cared about him. Tony couldn't help him with that from San Antonio.

He scratched his chin. "What are the chances I could transfer to the sheriff's department here?"

CHAPTER SEVEN

THURSDAY. THE DAY both Sabrina and Levi had been dreading. Sabrina locked the door to the medical office and looped her purse over her shoulder. She stopped at the open door to Karen's office. "I'm taking my lunch break."

Karen looked up from her computer. "Going to pick up Levi?"

"Yes. Dr. Moore has agreed to a one-on-one with him after his group counseling session." Hopefully he'd be willing to fill out the paperwork she needed to enroll Levi in Salt Creek Elementary in the fall.

"There's no shame in sending Levi to a therapist. Everyone needs help sometimes." Karen gave Sabrina a pointed look.

"I know that." The words came out sharper than she'd intended. Sabrina took a deep breath. "Can I get you anything in town? A Coke?"

Karen took her glasses off and rubbed her temples. "A Dr Pepper would be great. Thanks."

Sabrina opened the front door to leave and plowed into Tony. She jumped back. What was he doing here? He always volunteered in the mornings and helped his grandfather at the hardware store in the afternoons. And this was Thursday. He didn't come in on Thursday.

"Where are you rushing off to?" The dimple on his left cheek deepened when he smiled at her.

It was on the tip of her tongue to tell him that it was none of his business. She had to stop being so defensive when he was around. "I'm running out to the farm for lunch."

Tony smiled gently. "This is the first time you haven't gotten a panicked look on your face when you saw me. I'd call that progress."

"What are you doing here? Are you volunteering this afternoon?" *Please say no.* She needed to keep Tony and Levi apart for as long as she could. At least until she could figure out what to do.

"I'm doing a presentation for Dr. Moore's teen session on gangs."

Her shoulders relaxed. The younger kids met while the teenagers did a group activity. With any luck, he'd be busy with them and she and Levi wouldn't even see him. "I have to go. Have fun."

She strode away from him as fast as she could. For ten years, she'd hated the man. Or, at least, she'd thought she had. How was she supposed to feel now? Every time she saw him, conflict raged. With the children at the home he was patient, kind. All the things she'd wanted him to be for their own child.

And he would've been. For a while. His sense of responsibility wouldn't have allowed him to walk away if she'd told him she was pregnant. But how long would it have lasted? Until Levi was a few months old? A toddler? Her biggest fear was that she'd wake up one morning and he'd be gone. And that would be worse than never knowing his father at all.

What kind of person was she? Still trying to justify keeping her secret. Her cheeks burned with shame. Had he changed? If only she knew. Marissa's words echoed in mind. *Either tell them both the truth soon, or don't tell them at all.* She wasn't ready to make a decision yet. Not until she knew he wouldn't break her son's heart.

A movement by the barn caught her eye and she saw Levi disappear through the breezeway as she parked in front of the house. Her dad leaned against the gate, his face somber.

"Where's Levi going?"

"I'm not sure. As soon as he heard your car he hightailed it to the barn."

She groaned. Not today. Squaring her shoulders, she headed down the path. The sweet aroma of cut hay was mixed with manure and mud. Her gaze darted around the breezeway. "Levi Michael Davis, get out of that loft right now."

His head appeared over the rail. "How did you know I was up here?"

The wooden ladder nailed to the barn wall creaked under her feet as she climbed up into the loft. She scooted on her bottom across the wood floor until she was next to him. "Are you kidding? This was my hideout long before it was yours."

His anxiety was palpable. Sabrina couldn't blame him. The last, and only, time he'd seen a therapist, the good doctor declared him to be suffering from oppositional defiant disorder. The school wanted to place him on a modified behavior plan and pull him out of regular classes. Sabrina, desperate to get her son help, signed the permission forms and saw her bright, happy son turn into the angry eight-year-old the school claimed him to be.

"Why do I have to go? I'm tired of everyone thinking I'm some kind of freak." Levi sat on the edge of the door that swung open to overlook the pasture.

"You're not a freak. But you have to go the counseling session to get that five-oh-four removed from your file before you start school."

He looked at her, his hazel eyes wide. "Does that mean I don't have to be in special classes anymore?"

She shuddered at the memory. It was a self-fulfilling prophecy. Because of his new label, the school had expected bad behavior from him. Other students had teased him for being in a special education class and the fights only increased. A fight that broke out the last week of school was the final straw. He'd been expelled and wouldn't be able to return after the summer.

Levi confided in her, weeks later, that a group of boys had been bullying Evan, a boy who lived in the same apartment complex. The boy's thick glasses and cleft lip made him an easy target.

The initial fights happened because Levi was defending Evan on the bus. The older boys retaliated by turning their attention to her son. Unlike Evan, Levi defended himself and wouldn't back down. Unfortunately, the other students were much better at convincing the teachers that Levi was the instigator.

In her mind, the therapist had made the situation worse. And now her son would forever be labeled as a problem student. She'd hoped teachers at Salt Creek Elementary would allow him to start off with a clean slate. But first, she had to prove to the principal that her son wouldn't be a trouble maker. And Levi needed to learn to control his anger better if that was going to happen.

"They don't have special classes at the elementary school. They have a separate school for kids who need help. Which one do you want to go to?"

Levi lifted his chin, the muscles in his jaw twitching as he gritted his teeth. A habit he inherited from Tony. "I want to go to the same school as Bradley."

"I want that, too." She pulled him closer and hugged him. If the doctor decided Levi's anger was too much for public school, at least he'd be at the school where she worked. She only hoped it didn't come to that. "I'm starving. Let's grab a bite before we leave."

After eating sandwiches, Sabrina and Levi got in the car to go into town. The ride was quiet. She reached over to stroke his head. "Don't worry about this. Just be yourself."

Levi shrugged. "This is stupid. I don't know why I have to do this again."

"Because the last time you saw a counselor, you threw a book at him and ran away."

Sabrina kept her hand on his shoulder as she walked with him to the recreational room where the residents of Little Mountain were waiting for the counselor to join them.

The buzz in the room quieted. Levi stopped, his shoulders tense. There were six other children sitting in the chairs that had been placed in a circle in the middle of the room. With her hand, she urged him to take another step, but he refused to budge.

Behind her, a door closed. "Hi, guys. Dr. Moore is going to be a little late, so I get to entertain you for a while."

The sound of Tony's voice shot her heart into overdrive. She gripped Levi's shoulder tighter.

"Hi. You must be Levi." Tony appeared in front of them. "I'm Tony. It's nice to meet you."

TONY HELD HIS hand out to the boy Sabrina was clinging to. He had to admit, he was surprised when he found out that the new addition to the group counseling session was Sabrina's son. Dr. Moore had asked him to keep the group occupied until he got there. He couldn't divulge any information to Tony about why the kids were in his therapy session, but he did tell Tony that Levi had been in some trouble at his old school.

Levi threw his shoulders back and shook Tony's hand.

"Firm grip," Tony said. "I like that. It says a lot about a man."

The small chest puffed out more. "Yes, sir. That's what my mom says, too."

"Your mom's a pretty smart woman." His gaze drifted to Sabrina.

Her face had gone pale and she moved behind Levi to place both hands on his shoulders. "Maybe we should come back another time."

"Dr. Moore will be here in a few minutes. I'm just here to get the games started." He motioned for Levi to join the others at the center of the room.

His step forward was stopped by Sabrina, who pulled him back. "Mom," he whispered, "let go. You're embarrassing me."

Her face flushed and she shot a panicked

look at Tony. "Let's just go, okay? We can do this later."

Tony's eyes narrowed. Why'd she bring her son if she had a problem with him being included in this group? Talk about overprotective. If she'd smothered him like this his whole life, it was a wonder he was able to get into any trouble. "I've known Dr. Moore for five years. Levi'll be fine."

Levi jerked his arm from Sabrina's grasp. "Bye, Mom." He slid into the first empty chair. He crossed his arms and turned his back on her.

Her chest heaved and Tony was afraid she was about to cry. He ran one hand up her arm. "We'll take good care of him. I promise."

"I'll be in my office." Whirling around, she fled from the room.

Tony watched her leave. What was she so worried about? A clatter behind him caused him to jump. He turned just in time to see Levi standing toe to toe with one of the boys from the home. The other boy towered over him, but Levi wasn't shrinking back. When Tony saw Levi's hand curl into a fist, he stepped between them.

"Settle down. What's going on?" Dr. Moore

had left him in charge for ten minutes and a fight was already on the verge of breaking out.

The larger boy, Andrew, gave Tony a smug smile. "Nothing."

Tony looked at Levi. "You got something to say?"

"No." His eyes never left Andrew, but his body seemed relaxed.

Tony recognized the stance. The kid had street smarts. He stood his ground and appeared calm. Only his clenched fists gave away the anger below the surface. *Never show emotion.* It was the unspoken rule. The question was, where had Levi learned it?

Lonnie stepped forward. "Andrew called him a mama's boy. Told him to go crawling back for a bottle."

Tony took both boys by the shoulder and led them back to their chairs. "Andrew, go get the cards from the game shelf."

Andrew rolled his eyes. "Why should I?"

"Humor me." Tony met Andrew's glare without batting an eye.

After a long, exaggerated sigh, Andrew went across the room and got the cards.

All the children settled into their chairs, comfortable now that their routine had resumed. He didn't need access to their records to know that Andrew's dad was in prison. Deja's mom had died from a drug overdose. Over the last two weeks, he'd learned their stories. Most of them were there because drugs had ruined their families. Tony's chest was heavy. This was why he did what he did. Children shouldn't have to bear the burden of their parents' choices. Parents were supposed to take care of their children. Love them. Not abandon them to the streets.

Lonnie poked him. "It's your turn, Mr. Tony."

Before he could play his card, Dr. Moore, a tall balding man, came through the door.

"I'm sorry I'm late," his voice seemed to echo in the large room. "I see Mr. Tony has kept you busy."

Tony gathered the cards up from the kids. "We had fun. I'll let y'all get started."

"Before you go," Dr. Moore said, "I wondered if you would be willing to tell your story."

Seven pairs of curious eyes stared at him. He swallowed. Dr. Moore hadn't said anything about him having to speak. Would his story help these kids? He rubbed the back of his neck.

"My name is Tony. My mom died from a drug overdose when I was eleven. For the next few months, I lived by myself on the streets. I got caught robbing a store, and social services put me in a foster home. For the next three years, I was in and out of over ten foster homes. When I was fifteen, social services located my grandparents and they took me in. It was the first time I'd ever had a real home."

"And tell the kids what you do for a living now." Dr. Moore took his place in the circle.

"I'm a police officer in San Antonio. I try to keep kids out of gangs and away from drugs like the ones that killed my mother."

A slew of questions erupted around him. It seemed everyone wanted to know more. Dr. Moore raised his hands. "Tony will have plenty of time to talk with you later. Right now, I'd like to welcome Levi to the group. Levi, you don't have to tell us about yourself today. Unless you'd like to."

Levi shook his head, his hazel eyes wide as he stared at the kids around him. There was something about him that struck a chord with Tony. He waited for Dr. Moore to involve the kids in another activity before he got up and slipped out of the room.

A flash of blond hair disappeared around the corner. Had Sabrina been eavesdropping?

He hurried to the medical office and rapped lightly on the open door.

Sabrina glanced up from a chart she was holding. Oh, yeah. She'd been standing outside the doors. "Are they finished already?"

"No. They're just getting started." He stepped in and sat down across from the desk. "Why did you bring your son to counseling sessions?" He seemed like a good kid, even if he did have a chip on his shoulder. "Are you trying to scare him?"

"No." She pressed her lips together and stared at him. "Will it?"

"It might. The kids in that room have had a lot rougher life than your son ever thought about."

"What do you know about my son's life?" Her eyes sparkled with anger.

Tony suppressed a grin. She was cute when she was mad. How many times had he purposely angered her? Making up had been so much fun. His gaze dropped to her lips. Could he still defuse her with just a kiss? God, how he wished he could find out. But he didn't dare.

"Nothing. Maybe you're just being overprotective to make up for his dad not being around. What's the worst thing he's ever done? Stolen a candy bar from the grocery store?"

"Get out." She stood and pointed at the door.

SABRINA POINTED AGAIN. "I'm not kidding. Get out." Did he really think she'd send her son to counseling because she was overprotective?

He stood and stepped in front of her. "Calm down. I didn't mean to offend you. I just meant—"

"I know what you meant," she snapped. "Try telling his last school district he doesn't fit the profile of a juvenile delinquent."

Tony's brow wrinkled. "I never called him that."

"You didn't have to. Plenty of other people have. This is his chance for a fresh start. I won't let you ruin it for him." She clasped her hands together to stop the shaking.

"Hang on. We're on the same side here." Tony took her hand in one of his. Heat shot through her body. His fingers brushed her ear as he tucked a strand of hair behind it. "I want what's best for Levi, too."

Her heart rate escalated. He was still holding her hand and his face was inches from hers. And he was staring at her lips. She swallowed. Jerking her hand away, she stepped back. What would he say if she told him what was best for Levi was to have a father around? To have him around? The problem was, she wasn't convinced yet.

Tony's eyes dropped and he stepped away from her. "Is Levi here voluntarily, or was it court ordered?"

Sabrina bit her bottom lip. How much could she reveal to him? "Neither, actually. Levi got into some fights at school. After his second suspension, he had to see the school therapist, who decided he was angry at the world because his father wasn't around and that he was emotionally disturbed. They recommended he be placed into a special class where he wouldn't be able to harm other students."

Tony let out a whistle. "I've seen some kids who are in those classes. Levi doesn't strike me as that type."

She blinked back the tears welling up in her eyes. Levi counted on her and she'd let him down. A ragged breath tore through her. "I thought I was doing what was best for Levi. So I signed the papers."

"Let me guess." Tony sat on the edge of the desk. "Things got worse."

"Much worse. He started skipping school. I had to take him to the bus stop just to make sure he went. Then he started running away from school."

"But not home?"

Sabrina shook her head. "No. He always came home."

He reached out to squeeze her hand again. "Did you ever find out what was really bothering him?"

"Yes. I should've seen it sooner. I should've had more faith in my son." Emotion bubbled in her chest until it threatened to strangle her.

Tony pulled her close and hugged her. "Levi doesn't blame you."

How did Tony pinpoint her deepest fear? She allowed herself to relax on his shoulder, inhaling the scent of him. Was this what it felt like to have support? She could get used to this. "How do you know?"

"Because he came home." Tony held her face in his hands and wiped the dampness from the corners of her eyes with his thumbs. "And now you need a second opinion to get him back into a regular classroom."

She nodded. "Levi has a temper. If one of the boys in there baits him, he's liable to get into another fight. What will happen then?"

"Dr. Moore is one of the best I've ever seen. I even worked with him a few times in

San Antonio. He can tell the difference between a kid with an emotional disability and one that's just trying to survive a bad situation. Don't worry."

Never had words comforted her so much. Throwing her arms around Tony's neck, she kissed his cheek. His arms tightened around her and pressed her body to his. She could feel his heart beating against her chest and she jumped back in alarm. What was she doing? "I'm sorry. I didn't mean to do that."

He held her gaze for several seconds. "Did you love him?"

She frowned. "Of course I love my son."

"Levi's father. Did you love him?"

Her heart stuttered. At least she could answer this question honestly. "With all my heart."

Pain flashed in his eyes and he stood suddenly. "So you didn't run off with him in an attempt to forget about me?"

He was jealous. She twisted her engagement ring. Getting over him had been an impossible task. "What do you care? I was just another notch in your belt. I'm sure it didn't take you long to get over me."

Tony's jaw clinched. "Yeah. It was so easy to get over you that I've never had more than one date with another woman. I'm too busy comparing them to you."

What was he saying? That he still loved her? She sucked her breath in. "You were the one that left. Not me."

"You're never going to forgive me for that, are you?" His voice was low. "That's okay. I've never forgiven myself, either."

The silence in the room pressed on her. She needed to change the subject before she blurted out the truth. "You've done okay. I mean, you're a police officer now. An upstanding member of your community. You should be proud of how far you've come."

Her words broke the mood. He nodded. "I love my job. I may not prevent drugs from getting on the streets, but I'll never stop trying."

Sabrina read between the lines. Every drug dealer he put away was one step closer to avenging his mother's death. Did he still blame himself?

"I almost forgot. I got something for you."

She frowned. "What?"

"I didn't know if I'd see you today, so I left it in my truck. Be right back."

Tony opened the door and returned a few minutes later, putting a shoebox on her desk. "I felt really bad about ruining your shoes."

She blushed. "You didn't have to do that."

He shrugged. "Don't even think about telling me to return them, because I can't. They were on clearance and I already lost the receipt. If you don't want them, give them to someone who needs them."

She tapped her fingers on the top of the box before letting her curiosity get the best of her. Inside was a pair of slip-on sneakers. They were a style and brand that many of the nurses she'd worked with over the years wore, ones she'd never been able to afford. If she hadn't really needed them, she'd probably have thrown them at him.

"Are they okay? I did an internet search to find out the best shoes for nurses."

"I'm not a nurse." She put the lid on and slid the box toward him.

Tony smiled slightly. Just enough to deepen that dimple. "You will be."

The confidence in his words shook her. Her coworkers in Houston had warned her that nursing school would be too hard, too long, and too expensive, and the chances of her making it through the program were slim. Her father thought she should be happy as a medical assistant and spend more time on the farm. It seemed no one really thought she could do it. Except Tony.

CHAPTER EIGHT

SABRINA MANAGED TO avoid Tony for the rest of the day. She breathed a sigh of relief when Karen told her he wouldn't be in on Friday. Being around him was too unsettling. Every time she saw him, she came closer to telling him about Levi.

She and Levi were both looking forward to the weekend. Weekends off were a luxury she'd never had before. Since Levi was three years old, she'd juggled two jobs, and tried to fit in all the prerequisite college courses for the nursing program while taking care of him. The few days she had off, she was too exhausted to do anything.

Levi was looking forward to Bradley's birthday party. It was all he'd talked about for the past week. After work on Friday, they'd driven to Lampasas and he'd spent an hour walking through Walmart trying to find the perfect gift. He'd wrapped and rewrapped the present at least five times.

Saturday morning, Levi bounced up and down in the seat next to Sabrina. "How many kids do you think will be there?"

"I don't know. Ten? And put your seat belt on." Levi had never been to a birthday party before. He'd been invited to some in Houston, but her budget had been stretched so tight she couldn't afford a gift. And her son wasn't going to a party without being able to take a gift.

Their destination was on the outskirts of town. It was still hard to believe the town had a regional park, complete with picnic tables, barbecue grills and a playground. The only playground in town when she was growing up had been the one at the school.

Levi barely waited for her to stop the car before opening the door and jumping out. "Bye, Mom!"

She waited until she saw Marissa greet Levi and wave to her before heading home. As she exited the park, she glanced into the back seat and moaned. Circling back, she pulled into a parking space next to the playground and reached into the backseat for the neatly wrapped present.

Marissa met her halfway across the park

and gave her a hug. "Sabrina! I'm glad you changed your mind and decided to stay!"

She glanced down at her cutoff shorts and wrinkled T-shirt. "I'm not staying. Levi forgot Bradley's present in the car. I'm helping Dad fix some fences this afternoon."

"You can spare a few minutes to meet some of my friends." Marissa pulled Sabrina toward the picnic table.

"Ladies, I want y'all to meet one of my oldest and dearest friends. Actually, I guess I should say reintroduce, since most of y'all probably know her already." Marissa pointed out the women. "Adalie Conradt, Carol Martin, do y'all remember Sabrina from high school?"

Her Texas drawl dripped with feigned innocence. Marissa knew very well that Adalie had been in Sabrina's class and they'd once been good friends. The other woman, Carol, was a classmate of Marissa's.

"And this is Mary Kay Blodgett. She moved here about three years ago. She teaches fifth grade now that Mrs. Graham is retired."

"Nice to meet you." Sabrina nodded at the pudgy brunette. "How do you like teaching in Salt Creek?"

"It took some getting used to. In Austin,

there were four classes for each level and I had to coordinate everything with the other teachers in my grade. But I love being the only fifth grade teacher."

Sabrina nodded. Levi's old school had been like that. "How many kids are in a class here?"

"Last year I had fifteen kids." Mary Kay smiled.

Out of the corner of her eye, Sabrina noticed Carol and Adalie whispering. She shifted her weight. She could imagine what they were talking about.

When Tony was accused of a string of robberies, his refusal to give an alibi all but guaranteed a conviction. So she'd come forward and admitted they'd been together the entire night.

In some places, people might not have batted an eye. But in Salt Creek, when the valedictorian and president of the National Honor Society confessed to being involved in a tryst with a rebellious boy who'd already caused a heap of trouble, well…people talked about it for weeks. She suddenly found herself the topic of town.

Adalie had been one of the first ones to jump on the "How could you ruin your life over a boy like that?" bandwagon. She leaned over and whispered, "I'm so sorry. I've felt horrible all these years for the way I acted in high school. Can you forgive me?"

Sabrina couldn't tell if Adalie was sincere or not. No matter. If she was restarting her life, might as well give everyone a fresh slate. Even friends who had turned their backs on her. "It's okay. It's water under the bridge now."

Mary Kay waved at Adalie to get her attention. She pointed across the park to a group of about ten teenage boys. They sat still, listening intently to a dark-haired man. Mary Kay was almost drooling. "Who is that man? Is he new in town?"

Sabrina followed her gaze to the other side of the park. He was turned away from her, but she knew who it was. His denim jeans hugged his thighs and there was no mistaking his curly black hair or the way his shirt stretched across his broad back, hinting at supple muscles underneath.

Adalie gave Sabrina a sideways glance. "Yes, that's Tony Montoya. Sabrina used to date him."

"You did?" The chunky brunette sauntered

closer. "Are you friends? Could you introduce me?"

Sabrina pressed her lips together. "It was a long time ago. I wouldn't feel comfortable saying anything to him."

Adalie waited for Mary Kay to drift away. She leaned close to Sabrina. "Did you read the article about him in the paper? He really turned his life around."

Yes, he did. But why did he have to leave her behind to do it?

Sabrina sank onto the picnic table. The chances of Tony noticing Levi on a crowded playground were slim, but she was going to stick around just to make sure. The more he saw Levi, the more likely he'd recognize the similarities between them. It wouldn't be hard to put two and two together. Unable to concentrate on the conversation around her, she moved to the edge of the table.

A few minutes later, Tony waved goodbye to the boys and walked down the sidewalk. He was going to pass right by them. Her heart pounded and she held her breath. He was almost past their table when Mary Kay got his attention.

"You're Tony Montoya, aren't you? I read about you in the newspaper." She rushed over to him and touched his arm. "Your grandparents must be so proud."

Sabrina bit her tongue. There was no reason for her urge to knock Mary Kay's hand away. She wasn't jealous. Just disgusted over the way Mary Kay was gushing over him.

Tony shifted uncomfortably. "Thank you. Just doing my job."

His eyes fell on Sabrina and he made a beeline for her. "Hi."

She swallowed. "Hi."

"I was just heading to your house." His voice slid over her like silk.

"Why?" Out of the corner of her eye, she saw Levi running toward her from across the playground. Her stomach clinched.

Levi's face was red from playing when he ran up to them. A grin spread across his face. "Tony. What are you doing here?"

"I was just about to ask your mom if you could come with us to Spring Ho next weekend. I'm going to help chaperone some of the boys at the fishing tournament. Do you like to fish?"

"I sure do. I fish at the pond almost every day."

"The stock pond in the back pasture?"

Tony leaned over and whispered, "Don't eat any of the catfish. They taste like mud."

Levi laughed. "How do you know?"

Tony gave Sabrina a warm look. "I used to fish there with your mom when we were kids."

"I didn't know you knew my mom. What else did y'all do?"

Sabrina's throat went dry. "Levi, your friends are waiting. You better go play."

"I forgot my present in the car."

"I already put it on the table."

"Thanks." Levi grinned and ran back to the playground.

Tony watched him run off, a thoughtful look on his face. "He really is a good kid."

"So can I con you into chaperoning the girls so Levi can go fishing with us?"

"Do you think that's a good idea? I mean, what if Andrew tries to pick a fight with him again?" *What if you spend too much time with Levi and realize he's your son?*

"Andrew won't do anything as long as I'm around. I'll take good care of Levi. I promise."

"You better be careful." Sabrina eyed him. "The last promise you made to me was broken two weeks later."

DIGGING HOLES FOR FENCE posts the old-fashioned way did wonders to work out Sabrina's frustration. She slammed the post-hole digger into the ground. Her shoulders protested as she yanked the handles apart to scoop the dark earth from the hole. She tried to wipe sweat from her eyes with the back of her arm, but all she accomplished was wiping dirt across her face. Her arm was as wet with sweat as her head.

Farther down the fence line, Dad pounded a metal pole deeper into the ground with a sledgehammer. His shirt was soaked with sweat, too. With one final swing, he nodded at her. "That one 'bout done?"

She checked the depth. "Yes, sir."

Digging holes and stretching barbed wire in the middle of the afternoon was not for the timid. The high heat and humidity could dehydrate a person quickly. But fences had to be fixed, especially when the fence was next to a major roadway.

When she was a little girl, one of their cows got out onto the highway in the middle of the night. It was too dark for the semi-truck driver to see it until it was too late. It had left the driver shaken, but thankfully, the cow was the only casualty. Had it been a smaller vehicle, the results could've been deadly.

Dad stopped long enough to take a drink from his Thermos. Then he carried a new post to the hole she'd just finished digging. "Dip your handkerchief in the ice chest again. Don't let it dry out."

How could it dry out when she was sweating so much? Sabrina opened her mouth to protest but paused. Dad was just trying to take care of her. She untied the handkerchief from around her neck and opened the ice chest sitting on the tailgate of the truck. She dipped the material in the icy water and squeezed it out. Her body temperature seemed to drop five degrees as soon as she placed the cold fabric on her neck, and she splashed some water on her face.

"Good job." Dad's breath came in gasps by the time they'd placed the last post. He wiped his face with his own handkerchief. "Now let's go home and cool off."

Sabrina tossed the tools in the bed of the truck and they climbed in. As the truck bounced down the rutted road, she pulled the heavy gloves off her hands to examine her blisters.

Dad reached over and ran his thumb over her palms. "You lost your calluses, girl. They'll be back soon enough."

"Just what every woman wants. Ripped, calloused hands." The wound stung and she blew on it. She'd be so sore tomorrow she probably wouldn't be able to get out of bed, but she wouldn't trade this day for anything. Just her and her father, working under the hot Texas sun.

Her cell phone rang and she pulled it out of the glove box. Marissa's number showed on the caller ID. "Hello?"

"Hi, Mom." Levi shouted over the noise in the background. "Bradley wants to know if I can stay the night with him."

A few minutes later, she hung up the phone. "Looks like it's just us tonight, Dad. Levi's staying over at Bradley's."

"Actually, it'll just be you. Soon as I get showered, I'm heading to San Saba. I'm helping Ray haul some cattle to the Waco auction in the morning."

"Oh. Okay." What would she do with herself for an entire night? She hadn't been alone since Levi was born. Maybe she'd drive to Killeen and catch a movie. A real, grown-up movie. A chick flick, even. She settled back in the truck seat. Yes, a night alone might be just what she needed.

But by the time they got to the house and

she'd showered, the soreness had set in and she didn't want to do anything but lie on the couch.

Picking up the television remote, she flipped through the three channels. The rumble of an engine caused her to hit the mute button. Had her dad forgotten something? She walked out to the porch.

It wasn't a Ford truck, but a gray Dodge Durango. Sabrina swallowed. It pulled to a stop by the gate and Tony got out.

He leaned against his vehicle. "Any chance I could convince you to have dinner with me tonight?"

She crossed her arms over her chest. "Sorry. I'm exhausted. No way am I getting dressed and going anywhere."

Reaching into the open window of his SUV, he held up a white paper sack. "Too exhausted for the best hamburger in the world?"

"You brought me Storm's?" It was embarrassing how excited she was over a burger from the Lampasas drive-in. She met him at the gate and he followed her into the house.

Neither of them spoke as they spread the meal out on the table.

"Where is everyone?" Tony dumped the fries on the paper plate she handed him.

"Dad is helping a friend haul cattle and Levi is staying the night at Bradley's." She shoved a handful of fries into her mouth. "I can't believe I've been back in Salt Creek for a month and this is the first time I've had a Storms burger."

Laughing, he pulled a drink from a second bag. "I even brought you a frosted Coke."

Unwrapping her burger, she lifted the top bun. Her hand paused and she gave him a puzzled look.

"No tomatoes." Tony handed her a ketchup packet.

"You remembered?"

"I remember lots of things."

She ignored the implications and devoured her burger, pausing just long enough to take a sip of her drink. "No place makes burgers like Storms."

"And I didn't even know it existed until I was sixteen. How sad is that?"

Sabrina cocked her head. "I was the first one to bring you there." That had been the first night he had kissed her. Did he remember that, too?

His golden gaze dropped to her mouth. Oh, yes. He most certainly remembered. She licked her lips.

He reached across the table to pluck one of her fries off the napkin. "I like this. Sitting and talking like friends. Does this mean you don't hate me anymore?"

"I'm tired of hating you."

"I'm glad." He swallowed the last bite of his burger.

Tell him. The annoying voice in the back of her mind was determined not to let her have any peace. "The newspaper article said you got shot. What happened?"

He rolled his eyes. "That stupid article is a pain in the neck."

"Was it true?"

"Parts of it." He shrugged.

Her knee bounced under the table. *Just spit it out.*

Tony didn't seem to notice her nervousness. "I could use a female chaperone for the girls. Interested?"

It seemed like yesterday when they'd lain on the banks of the Sulphur Creek and enjoyed their own fireworks. She shook her head. "Thanks, but I've already got plans."

HER WORDS SURPRISED HIM. Plans? With who? None of his business. Still, it didn't stop the bile from burning his throat. "I see."

She studied him for a moment. "Why do you spend so much time with the kids at the home? Most of the people in town want to shut the home down."

"That's why I do it."

"Where will it leave them when you go back to San Antonio?" Her brown eyes bored right through him.

Guilt hit him like a ton of bricks. "I'm going to do everything in my power to make sure they'll be okay before I leave." *And you.*

Her eyes widened. "And when will that be?"

"Right after Spring Ho." Why did he feel like he was about to walk away from her again? "If I can get my doctor to give me the all clear, that is."

"I'm curious." Sabrina sat back down in her chair. "Where have you been the last ten years? How did you end up becoming a policeman?"

She was trying to have a conversation with him. This was new. He didn't question why. "I've been everywhere, really. The construction job in Lousiana only lasted about six months, so I traveled a lot. After about a year, I ended up in Dallas." He leaned his elbows on the edge of the table. "While I was there, my boss offered extra incentives for volunteer work, so I started helping with the

Boys and Girls Club and found out I was really good at relating to teenage boys."

"When did you decide to become a cop?"

"While I was in Dallas." The memory of that day was forever etched into his memory. "I'd got real close to some of the kids. They were growing up on the streets, just like I did. I felt a kinship with them. Then cops came to the construction site one day. They needed someone to identify a kid's body and they'd heard I was friends with him."

A strange look crossed her face. "Tony. I'm so sorry."

He rubbed the back of his neck. "Retaliation for refusing to sell drugs for the local dealer. I signed up for the police academy the same day."

"You love your job."

It wasn't a question. He nodded. "I do. And I'm good at it."

Sadness flickered in her eyes. "You could get killed."

"I could get killed walking across the street. If I get killed taking down a drug dealer or as retaliation for arresting a gang member, at least I will have died for something. I'm okay with that."

"But what about the people who care about you?"

Tony's heart sang. She was worried about him. After all this time, she still cared about him. Now, if he could just get her to admit it. "My grandparents will be taken care of if I die. I don't have anyone else."

He held his breath, waiting for her to deny it. For her to say that she still cared about him, despite having loving someone else. The thought sobered him. Not only had she loved someone else, she'd had a child with him. He'd let her down and she'd moved on.

He stood up. "I better go. I promised some of the kids I'd stop by for a basketball game."

She wrinkled her brow. "I thought you were injured?"

"I can handle it."

TONY WAS STILL on a high from his dinner with Sabrina when he pulled into the parking lot next to the basketball courts and got out.

Kyle waved him over. "Glad you made it." He turned to the players. "Tony's going to join us."

A collective laugh came from the group. "You think you can keep up, old man?" one of them asked, grinning.

Tony snatched the ball from his arms and launched it across the court to the hoop. When it effortlessly swished through the net he shrugged his shoulders at the boys, who gaped at him. "I'll try."

"He's on my team," a tall, lanky redheaded boy called out. "I'm Scott," he held his hand out to him.

"Tony." He shook the outstretched hand. "Let's play."

An hour later, sweat dripped down Tony's forehead. His lungs burned, but he'd been able to keep up with the teenagers. Had it really been two months ago since he'd been lying in a hospital bed? If Mr. Chan had used a higher-caliber gun, the bullet would've penetrated his lungs instead of deflecting off a rib. Still, breathing wasn't as easy as it should be, even if he was out of shape.

"Where're you from, man?" one of the boys, Jacob, asked during a break.

Tony shrugged. "Everywhere. I moved a lot."

"Ah." Jacob nodded knowingly. "Military brat like me?"

"Foster home brat," Tony corrected.

Kyle asked, "How many?"

Tony tossed Jacob the ball. "About ten. Come on, kid, you're down by four." He sensed that the boys had a lot more to say, especially Jacob and Scott, the ones who weren't from the home. But if he wanted to gain the boys trust, he needed to approach it the right way. Slow and steady.

At the end of the game, Tony's team lost by six points, but he gained some measure of respect from the teens. It felt good to be around boys that age again, helping them out. It felt right.

They'd played for almost an hour and not once had Tony seen anyone checking on the kids. The basketball courts were just two blocks from the home, but they still should've had an adult with them. Where was the evening supervisor?

A shiny black truck pulled into the parking lot and its engine stopped. Tony waited for someone to get out but no one emerged from it.

"Good game." Kyle slapped Tony on the back and kept his hand on his shoulder.

Tony watched him glance at the truck several times. Was the truck waiting on Kyle? A few seconds later, the loud engine roared to life and the truck squealed out of the parking lot, disappearing on the dirt road going to the top of Little Mountain.

He was pretty sure the truck didn't continue around to the road going down the other side. With mufflers like that, it could be heard for miles.

Kyle bent down to tie his shoes. "I'll see you later, Tony."

Tony nodded and turned back to the rest of the boys while keeping Kyle in his sights. As he expected, Kyle headed up the mountain road instead of walking toward the home.

Kyle's departure seemed to be a signal to the rest of the boys. Within a few moments, Tony was alone on the court with Scott and Jacob. "Does Kyle take off like that a lot?"

"Yeah," Jacob said. "Nick shows up and Kyle disappears."

"What do you think they're up to?"

Scott shrugged. "Not sure. But whatever it is, it ain't good."

Jacob nodded. "There'll be trouble in town tomorrow, for sure."

The leading comment sent Tony's cop senses into full alert. "What do you mean?"

"When Nick and Kyle get together, something always gets broken, stolen or disappears." Scott twirled the basketball on one finger. "My dad'll tell you all about it tomorrow."

"Your dad?"

Scott pointed at his red hair. "Can't you tell? Jarrod Butler's my dad. You're coming to my house for dinner."

Tony laughed. "I should've recognized you. Your dad talks about you a lot."

"Don't believe anything he says. See ya."

He'd missed bantering with the boys he worked with in San Antonio. Until tonight, he hadn't thought he would find that feeling anywhere else.

CHAPTER NINE

"WOULD YOU LIKE anything else?" A feminine voice pulled Tony from his fog.

He gave Marissa a slight smile. "No, thank you. Everything was really good."

"Really?" She arched one eyebrow at him. "You hardly touched anything."

Tony frowned. He'd hoped that she wouldn't notice. His stomach rolled at the sight of the table. He hadn't had an appetite all day. "Sorry. I'm just not very hungry right now. I think I may be coming down with a stomach bug."

Scott leaned over and plucked another taco from the platter. "Does this mean I can have the rest?"

Jarrod rolled his eyes. "How can you still be hungry?"

The teenager grinned. "I'm a growing boy."

Jarrod laughed. "After you finish, you and Bradley can do the dishes."

Tony watched the interaction between father and son. He'd never known his father and he envied their relationship. "Y'all are great together."

"It wasn't always like that." Jarrod opened the French doors leading to the patio. "When he first came to live with me, we couldn't see eye to eye on anything. It was rough."

The room spun a little when Tony stood up to follow him. He gripped the edge of the table for a minute. The room settled and he went out to the patio with Jarrod. "What do you mean? When he first came to live with you?"

Jarrod cocked his head toward Tony. "I thought you knew. Scott is from my first marriage."

"You were married before?"

"Yeah." Jarrod nodded. "Right after high school. We thought we were grown-up enough to understand what marriage was. All we really did was play house for a little while. It wasn't as much fun when you don't have enough money to pay the bills or put food on the table."

"How old was Scott when you divorced?"

"Two." Jarrod rested one hand on his knee. "When I couldn't handle it anymore, I took off. I'm not proud of it, but that's what I did. I left a note." He shook his head. "He was twelve when his mom was killed in a car accident and social services brought him to me."

Tony understood the turmoil that Scott had gone through. To lose his mother and be sent to live with someone he barely knew. Someone who was supposed to be his father. "It must've been tough on him."

"You don't know the half of it." Jarrod sighed. "I'd been a failure as a husband and an even bigger failure as a father. So I pretended that part of my life never happened. Other than the child support check I sent every month, I didn't have a kid. You can imagine Marissa's surprise when my twelve-year-old son showed up at the door."

"Marissa didn't know?" Tony found that hard to believe. The couple shared everything.

"I had been too ashamed to tell her about my past before then. I spent so much time hiding from it, it almost cost me my son and my second marriage."

Tony shook his head. "So what happened?"

"You could say Marissa and I had a come-to-Jesus meeting." Jarrod chuckled. "It took a while, but we were finally able to heal and become a family."

"I had no idea."

Jarrod opened an ice chest and pulled out

a couple of beers. He settled into the lawn chair next to Tony. "Scott said you played basketball with them last night. Did you get any impressions of the kids?"

Tony opened his bottle and took a swig. "I'm still watching Kyle. He's pretty much a loner from what I can see at the home. What do you know about Nick Johnson?"

"Didn't take you long to figure out that one." Jarrod shook his head. "The kid is nothing but trouble. He gives Scott a clear berth, probably because I'm a cop, but he's been known to rough kids up. You think he's involved in something besides being meaner than a possum trapped in a wood shed?"

"I'm not sure. What about the people who work at the home? Anyone there who could use the kids to move merchandise?"

Jarrod nodded knowingly. "You and I think a lot alike." He disappeared into the house and returned with a clipboard.

Tony looked over the papers. Time sheets for all the employees at Little Mountain for the past six months. "What are the highlighted dates for?"

"Yellow for nights that vandalism or thefts were reported in town. Pink for reports of drugs in town."

"Rachel Johnson is the campus monitor every time a yellow highlight appears. Have you checked her out?"

"So far, she's clean."

"Any relationship to the rest of the Johnsons?"

"Nick's stepmother."

Tony shook his head. "A lot of coincidences. I'm only here one more week. What do you want me to do?"

"Just what you're doing. Observe what you see on the inside. The relationship between some of these boys and Rachel."

"You think Travis is involved?"

Jarrod shook his head. "My bet is on someone inside the home using the boys for runners. But not Travis. He's stupid, but he's no criminal."

The bottle slipped out of Tony's hand and shattered on the concrete. He wiggled his fingers but he couldn't feel them. His entire arm had gone numb. Man. He'd really overdone it tonight. He slid off the chair and scooped up pieces of glass. "I'm sorry."

"Happens all the time. You okay? You're looking a little pale."

Tony rubbed his shoulder. He didn't feel

okay. "I think I may have overdone it playing basketball last night. I should go."

"Need me to drive you home?"

Tony waved him off. "No. I didn't have but a few sips. I'm good."

"Maybe so, but if you're getting sick, I can give you a hand."

Once again, Tony waved him off. He'd be fine with some rest. He was sure. Mostly.

THE TEMPTING AROMA of bacon made Tony's stomach growl. Last night, the pain in his chest had caused the nausea that had kept him from enjoying his evening with the Butlers. He hoped he hadn't insulted Marissa by not eating much.

There was a lot he admired about Jarrod. The man had everything Tony had once wanted. A wife who adored him, two great kids, respect in the community and a job he loved. Family. Respect. Job. The trifecta of happiness. Tony sighed. He'd given up his chance for a family when he walked away from Sabrina. As a police officer, he'd earned respect among his coworkers and the community he served. But being around Sabrina reminded him that there was more to life than just his job. No matter how much he loved it.

He rolled out of bed, ignoring the sharp stabbing sensation in his chest. He shuffled down the hall and sank onto a dining room chair. "Morning."

Papa's eyes narrowed at him over his newspaper. "Good morning. How are you feeling?"

Tony took a bite of the warm tortilla his grandmother slid onto his plate. "Fine."

"You groaned a lot last night." Abuela placed a glass of orange juice in front of him. "Are you sure you're feeling all right?"

"I must have had a bad dream." Determined not to let Abuela see his pain, he avoided looking her in the eye. Instead he turned to Papa. "I'm going to Little Mountain for a while this morning, but I'll meet you at the store when I'm done."

Papa glanced at the watch on his wrist. "Sounds good. It's Monday, so I expect Kyle will show up sometime, too."

Kyle. What was he involved in? True to Scott's prediction, someone had plowed through a whole section of fence near the Johnson ranch, leaving deep ruts from oversized tires. Little Mountain Children's Home was less than two miles from the damaged property. He didn't want to believe Kyle was involved, but it looked like he was.

"Great. I can check his progress." And get some answers. Pressing a kiss to Abuela's cheek, he twirled his key ring around his finger and headed outside.

"You been spending a lot of time with Sabrina?" Papa followed him outside, on his way to work.

"I had dinner with her Saturday."

"Be careful." Papa opened his truck door. "That girl's been through a lot. There were some who weren't very nice to her after you left. If you ain't planning on sticking around this time, it's best she knows that up front."

"She knows my leave is up at the end of the week." Tony should be excited about going back to work, but he wasn't. She'd asked him if he'd ever give up his job and he'd answered truthfully. Being a cop was who he was. But he could be a cop somewhere else. Like here. If she'd give him a reason to stay.

"What if I did want to stick around?" Tony asked. "If I don't get the promotion in San Antonio, there's nothing holding me there. What if I wanted to transfer and be closer to home?"

"Don't give up anything for us," Papa said. He paused before sliding into the cab of his truck. "Or her. You've come too far to try to make up for past mistakes. Moving forward together is one thing, but don't feel like you have to give up something to makes amends to anyone."

Tony shifted his SUV into gear and followed Papa into town, contemplating the words he'd said. Tony wasn't giving anything up. He'd never thought he'd like living in the small town. In his memories, the community had been too judgmental. Too hard to please. Time had matured him enough to see that the chip on his shoulder had caused him to think everyone was against him.

What about Sabrina? Would she give him a second chance if he could prove he was here to stay?

Speak of the devil. Parked in front of Little Mountain was Sabrina's car. What was she doing here so early? She didn't normally show up until nine. Was something wrong?

He signed in at the front office and then headed to the medical room. The door creaked as he pushed it open and his stomach did a flip. Curled up in an overstuffed chair, Sabrina was sound asleep, one arm tucked underneath her chin, her long blond hair hanging over the edge of the chair. How could she sleep like that? Her neck appeared to twist at an awkward angle. She shifted in an attempt to get more comfortable.

Blinking at the bright light coming through the window, her eyes focused on him.

His heart skipped a beat. "Morning."

She stood up and stretched, rolling her neck to loosen it up. "Hi." She yawned.

Tony smiled. "You look awful."

Shooting him an irritated glare, she rubbed her neck. "Thanks. I didn't intend to fall asleep in that chair."

"Here." In two steps he was next to her. Turning her around, he began to massage the knots in her neck.

Tony's pulse quickened when she relaxed against him. The fire started slowly, burning its way from his hands and flooding all the way to his toes. Every nerve screamed with awareness of her. The clean scent of her shampoo tickled his nose.

Her chest was heaving when she stepped away from him. She'd felt it, too. "What're you doing here?"

"I could ask you the same question. You're never here this early."

Her brows creased. "Apparently, one of the boys got cut trying to sneak back in a few weeks ago. He didn't tell anyone about it and it got infected. He started running a fever in the middle of the night and they called me in to check him."

"Who was it? Why didn't they take him to the emergency room?" Which boy had it been? Hadn't Carter been limping the other day?

"They didn't know the fever was from an infection. He only fessed up when I saw the cut. Mr. Anderson took him to the doctor this morning. Just as I was about to leave, one of the girls had an asthma attack." She gestured to a girl sleeping on a nearby cot. "I must have fallen asleep after that. Your turn. What're you doing here?"

"It's eight o'clock."

"So?" She leaned down to check the girl.

"I come by every morning at eight. Jake insists on working on the playhouse before it gets too hot."

The door burst open and a large man came into the room. "Here you are, Tony. I've been looking forward to meeting you. The boys speak very highly of you. I'm Travis Anderson."

The elusive director. Finally. "Nice to meet you in person. Can we talk in your office? I have some questions for you."

"Sure. Sure." Travis checked his watch.

"But it'll have to wait for about an hour. I have a meeting with the school board over at the district office."

"All right. I'll be in the backyard with the kids. Let me know when you get back." At least this gave him a few more minutes with Sabrina.

"Mr. Tony!" A small voice squeaked from outside the door. The little girl shouted down the hallway. "Jake. Mr. Tony's here."

So much for spending more time with Sabrina. He shrugged one shoulder. "Guess I'll see you later."

ALL MORNING, SABRINA jumped at the slightest sound. Was Tony going to come back to her office? She sat at her desk with the files Karen had sent her. A throat cleared and she looked up. Tony leaned against the frame, his hazel eyes on her. "Good morning. Again."

Her pulse went into overdrive. She took a deep breath, willing her heart to slow down. "Hi."

"I forgot to tell you. I met a friend of yours last night."

"Who's that?" She walked over to the file cabinet and slid the file into its place.

"Marissa Butler. She said she was a couple of years ahead of you in school."

"I'm surprised you don't remember her from high school. There was only one Marissa." She smiled. "I don't think the town could've handled more than one."

Tony let out a hearty laugh. "She is a little… enthusiastic."

Enthusiastic. That was a good way to put it. Thinking of Marissa made her chuckle. "I think the word our teachers used was *loud*."

"She told me to stop by and tell you she said hello."

Why would Marissa do that? They talked to each other on the phone every few days. If it wasn't about work, it was to make plans for the boys to play together. Sabrina chewed on her bottom lip. She hoped Marissa wasn't thinking about playing matchmaker.

"Thanks. If you see her, tell her I said hi, too." She held up the stack of files on the desk. "I need to get to work, so I'll talk to you later."

The edge of his mouth turned down, but he pushed away from the door. "Travis is expecting me, anyway."

Karen appeared at noon, carrying a tray of food for each of them. Sabrina made room on the desk. She looked forward to eating lunch with the assistant director. Karen didn't pull any punches. Sabrina admired people who were straightforward.

"What did you do to Lonnie? He be-bopped in here this morning to get his insulin checked without me having to chase him down."

Sabrina chuckled. "I've been teaching some of the kids how to dance. But he has to get his blood sugar checked first."

"That explains it." Karen picked up both of their trays. "I think your dance party is here."

Her eyes followed Karen to the door where four boys and three girls waited.

She busied herself going over the paperwork, pretending not to notice the impatient children at the door.

"Ms. Sabrina," Lonnie groaned. "Hurry up."

She pasted a look of surprise on her face. "Oh. I didn't see you there. What can I do for you?"

Olivia tapped Lonnie on the shoulder. "She's busy, Lonnie. Let's go. We'll come back later."

Guilt pressed on Sabrina's chest. These kids were used to adults letting them down. "Stop, Olivia. I was just teasing you. Let me check Lonnie's blood sugar and we'll meet you in the big room."

"Really?"

"Really." She patted the exam table. "Hop up here, Lonnie. Let's poke that finger."

"Come on," Olivia hollered to some other children waiting in the hallway.

Ten minutes later, Sabrina joined the kids in the recreation room. They were already practicing the steps she'd taught them the week before. She paired them up and turned music on to lead them through a practice dance. Lonnie grabbed her hand and did his best to duplicate the steps she'd shown them.

When the song ended, applause erupted from the hallway. Tony and three teenage boys whistled. Sabrina and Lonnie bowed. Another song began and Lonnie, enjoying the attention, held up his hands for another dance.

After a few bars of the song, Tony tapped him on the shoulder. "May I cut in?"

Lonnie grinned and stepped back. Sabrina's heart caught in her throat as Tony pulled her into his arms. If there hadn't been a roomful of children watching, she'd have turned the music off. Instead, their movements blended together as the tempo increased.

Extending his arms, he twirled her around and pulled her back, never missing a beat. The kids oohed and awed. By the time the song was over, she was almost out of breath. A slower song began and he pulled her closer. His hand on the small of her back sent goose bumps up her spine, his eyes focused on her lips.

"That was awesome." Lonnie danced in a circle around them. "Did you teach Mr. Tony?"

The spell that had been weaving its magic around them was broken. She glanced down at the little boy. "Actually, Mr. Tony taught me."

"Wow, Tony." Matthew, the oldest of the boys, stepped forward and gave him a playful punch to his shoulder. "I had no idea you had moves like that."

Tony's shoulder dropped and he grimaced. But the pain on his face was masked by a smile when he turned to Matthew. "That's nothing. You should see me when I get my groove on."

Sabrina recognized the signs of pain. She also knew when Tony was covering something up. The kids headed for the door, Tony at the rear of the line. She stepped in front of him. "Boys, Tony will catch up with you. I need to talk to him for a sec."

Tony's face was blank as he followed her to the exam room. His shoulders were stiff and he barely looked at her. Was it because he was in pain, or something else?

"Sit down." She nodded to the examining table and shut the door.

Tony's face was a little paler than before, confirming her guess. He clenched his jaw. "Why?"

His voice lacked the warmth of earlier. Was he angry about the pain, or at her for noticing? "Take your shirt off."

"Why, Sabrina, I'm not that kind of boy." All the emotion was missing from his voice.

"Shut up and take your shirt off." She rubbed hand sanitizer on as she approached the table.

In one quick motion, Tony pulled the T-shirt over his head, exposing fine curling hairs on a massive chest wrapped by an ACE bandage. Gently she began unrolling the bandage. "How long has this been hurting?"

"It's just normal aches and pains from healing. Nothing to worry about." Tony winced when she touched the area around his scar.

A mass of black and blue bruises greeted her. There was no way he was able to function normally. She was tempted to press her fingers into his ribs to get his attention. "These bruises are new, Tony. Don't tell me you're healing. What did you do?"

"Nothing." He shrugged.

She wanted to strangle him. Why had he downplayed his injury?

"Who shot you?" Her voice was almost as shaky as her hands.

"Mr. Chan, a convenience store clerk."

"Why?" She moved around to his back to look for more signs of trauma.

"I was trying to talk a kid out of robbing him. Mr. Chan's gun went off accidentally."

"Flesh wound, huh? Does this happen often?" Knowing he'd been shot and seeing the wound were two different things.

"Getting shot? First time." Tony flinched when she lifted his arm.

Was it possible for her heart to get broken again? That was how it felt. The ache in her chest grew and she blinked back a tear. What if she told him about Levi, and then he got killed in the line of duty? Would it be fair to Levi to risk putting him through that?

CHAPTER TEN

THE EXERTION OF dancing with her had caused his lungs to burn again and he'd been fighting dizziness for the last few minutes. He thought he'd done a good job covering it up. How had she noticed?

Tony closed his eyes, ignoring the sensation of her hands on his skin. *Ow.* The tender spots she hit sent a fresh wave of nausea and he prayed he didn't pass out on her table.

She moved around in front of him. "You've obviously fractured a rib. What else was damaged? Did the bullet puncture your lung?"

He couldn't concentrate on all the questions she asked. All he could think about was how much he wanted to kiss her. He reached up to touch her face, but she batted his hand away.

"Are you having trouble breathing? Shortness of breath?" The cold metal of the stethoscope touched his bare chest and he shivered.

"No. I'm fine."

Anger flashed in her eyes. "It's me, remember? I can tell when you're lying."

No, she couldn't. She'd believed him when he told her didn't love her anymore and didn't want her around. "You should be a nurse. You're very good. Tell me again, why haven't you finished nursing school?"

"I can't afford it." She held up her finger to silence him as she listened to his heart and lungs.

"What about your inheritance? I know you got one when your mother died." Focusing on her face kept his mind off the waves of pain threatening to black him out.

"It costs a lot of money to raise a baby." She picked up his hand, two fingers wrapped around his wrist.

Suddenly it all made sense. Why she looked so tired. Why her shoes were worn out and why she'd suddenly moved back home after being gone for ten years. "Didn't you get any money when Levi's father was killed?"

She heaved a sigh of frustration and snapped her fingers in front of him. "Tony. Focus. Have you done anything lately to damage your ribs? Stretch too high? Move too fast?"

The panic lacing her voice pulled him out of the fog he was in. "I played basketball with the boys on Saturday. After our dinner. I've been pretty sore ever since."

"You idiot," she murmured. She picked up the phone.

"Hi, Mr. Montoya. This is Sabrina Davis. Listen, I've got Tony over here in the medical office of the children's home. I think you need to take him to the emergency room. Right. Now."

"What did you do that for?" He slid off the table. As soon as the room stopped spinning, he'd call his grandfather back. He leaned back against the table.

She hung up the phone and gave him a smug look. "Because you're too stubborn to do what I tell you. I may not be a nurse, but I've been around medical facilities enough to know you're in danger. Your fractured rib may have punctured a lung, or you may be getting pneumonia. I'm not sure, but something is going on in your lungs and you need to be seen."

The seriousness of her tone caught him off guard. "But I'm supposed to go back to work soon."

She shook her head. "I'm sorry. That's not going to happen. Now sit back down and let me wrap you up again."

Those words should've devastated him. So why did he feel relief? He wanted more time in Salt Creek. More time with his grandparents. More time with the boys. More time with her.

Sabrina pulled a chair away from her desk. "Sit down and wait for your grandfather. Now."

She was cute when she was bossy, too. The room stopped spinning when he sank into the chair. He needed to keep his mind occupied or he'd pass out. "Tell me about Levi's father."

Her body stiffened. "Why?"

"I want to know about the guy that stole you from me."

"He didn't steal me. You left. Remember?" She changed the paper on the exam table without looking at him.

Tony caught her hand as she walked by. "I went looking for you. But I couldn't find you."

Sabrina took a sharp breath. "When?"

"Just before I entered the police academy. I wanted to be someone you could be proud of." His words tumbled out and he couldn't seem to stop. "But you weren't where you were supposed to be. You weren't at school. I told you to move on, but I didn't really want you to. I wanted to come back and tell you, but you changed the plan and fell in love with someone else. How could you do that?"

His eyes locked onto hers and silence blanketed the room. Sabrina's hand came to her chest and she rubbed her collarbone. Tony remembered that quirk. She did it when she wanted to avoid answering a question.

A bell chimed in the hallway but Sabrina stood frozen.

"Hey, Mom." Levi called from the doorway. "Jake asked me to help paint the playhouse today, so Grandpa dropped me off."

Tony tore his gaze from Sabrina to her son.

Levi stepped across the room to stand in front of Tony. "Dude. You don't look so good. Are you sick?"

Sabrina took Levi by the shoulders and turned him to the door. "Yes, he's sick. Go on and find Jake."

Tony's eyes narrowed. Why the sudden panic in her voice?

Levi shrugged away from her and came back to face Tony, his hazel eyes wide with concern. "What's wrong?"

Funny. He'd noticed Levi's hazel eyes before, but now it struck him why. Green, with flecks of gold that lightened them. It was an unusual color. At least, that was what everyone said about *his* eyes. His breath hitched in his chest and his pulse raced. Could it be? Had Sabrina lied to him?

He stared at the boy. "I'm fine. Your mom is just a worrywart."

"Welcome to my world." Levi rolled his eyes and grinned, causing a dimple to deepen on his cheek. One dimple. On his left cheek. Exactly like Tony's.

His heart went from racing to pounding. "Levi, how old are you?"

Tony's grandparents burst into the room before Levi could answer. Abuela rushed over to him to place her hand on his cheek while Papa asked Sabrina question after question. Tony searched the room for Levi, but he had slipped out in all the chaos.

Sabrina averted her gaze and didn't look at him. Her hands were shaking as she scribbled on a clipboard. She handed the notes to Abuela. "I wrote down all his vital signs for you. It might encourage them to take him straight back and not make you wait. I'll call and let the ER know he's coming."

At last, her gaze flickered over to him. And he knew.

THE FAMILIAR SMELL of antiseptics and cleaning supplies enveloped Sabrina as she hurried down the hospital hallway. She'd been working with patients for ten years, but adrenaline shot through her system every time she stepped through the sliding doors of a hospital.

The closer she got to Tony's room, the more her heart pounded. She had seen the moment it dawned on him that Levi was his son. His accusing glare said more than words ever could.

When Tony left ten years ago, he'd made it clear he never wanted to be burdened with the responsibilities of a family. But if she'd told him, would he have still walked away? No. He didn't want responsibility, but he would've accepted it. Especially since he knew firsthand how it felt to be abandoned by a father.

If she had a lick of sense, she'd turn around and go home. And stay there. But she couldn't run from this. Tony wanted her to believe that he'd left to make things easier on her. What were the chances he'd believe that she'd done the same thing? Her hand shook as she knocked.

Elaina, Tony's grandmother, opened the door. When she saw Sabrina, a smile lit her face and she hugged her. "Sabrina."

She hugged the tiny Hispanic woman back.

"How is he? They wouldn't tell me anything at the front desk."

Antonio stood up from his post by the hospital bed and strode across the room to give her a hug, as well. "He's going to be okay, thanks to you."

Elaina settled Sabrina in the chair next to hers, still holding her hands. "The doctor said he rebroke his rib and the end of it almost punctured his lung." She wiped a tear away from the corner of her eye.

"There, there, Mama." Antonio patted her on the back. "His lungs weren't punctured. Just bruised. Our Sabrina saved him."

Sabrina stood next to Tony's bed. He looked so pale. She resisted the urge to stroke his hair. "What does the doctor say about his recovery? How long will he be in the hospital?"

Antonio was the one to answer. "At least a week. I talked to his captain and they are extending his leave another six weeks."

Elaina sniffed. "He's not going back to San Antonio. He needs to stay here."

"Mama." Antonio shook his head. "You can't do that to him. They are promoting him to detective. It's his calling. There's nothing for him in Salt Creek. You have to let him go."

The words may have been meant for his wife, but they cut Sabrina to the core. She bit into her bottom lip. A promotion to detective. What did that mean? Would it put him in more danger?

"Maybe you can talk some sense into him, *mija*." Elaina patted Sabrina's cheek.

The warmth of her hand reminded Sabrina of the times her mother would cup her face. She fought to swallow the lump building in her throat. "I'll try. But it never worked before."

Elaina pressed a kiss to her forehead. "God didn't bless us with lots of children, and when we lost Teresa we thought there was nothing left for us. Then Tony found us. I don't know what we'd do if we lost him."

Sabrina averted her gaze, her cheeks flaming red hot. By keeping Levi from Tony, she'd kept him from his great-grandparents as well. Her anger with Tony had prevented her from seeing the bigger picture. By disappearing from Salt Creek, she'd protected her pride and her heart, but she'd robbed her son of a loving set of grandparents.

She squeezed Elaina's hand. "Tony's lucky to have you."

Light hazel eyes, so much like Tony's,

gazed right through her soul. "And Tony is lucky to have you. I'm glad you two found your way back to each other."

Sabrina sucked in her breath. She'd be willing to bet that Tony didn't feel that way.

"Bree?" A weak voice whispered from the hospital bed. Tony's eyes were half open, his expression unreadable. "You're here."

Antonio took Elaina by the elbow. "Mama, let's give them some time together."

Elaina nodded and stood next to her husband. "We'll be down in the cafeteria if you need us."

She pressed a kiss on Tony's forehead and the two of them shuffled out the door, leaving Sabrina alone with Tony.

Her chest constricted. She shouldn't have come. He was still in a lot of pain and needed to rest. Could she make him understand why she did what she did? Should she bring it up? No. She'd wait for him to broach the subject. Until then, she'd play it cool.

She sat in the chair next to his bed, placing her elbows on the rail. "You look awful."

"I feel like someone parked a truck on my chest." Tony frowned. "Where's Levi? Where's my son?"

So much for playing it cool. She shifted

away from the bed. "He's at home with my dad."

"So you admit it. He's mine." Tony shifted in the bed, adjusting so he could sit up. Each time he moved, his face twisted in pain.

"Be still," she said. "You don't need to move so much."

"Now you want to act like you care?" Sarcasm dripped from his words.

She clenched her fist. "Since you were the one who walked away from me, that's a little like the pot calling the kettle black."

He gritted his teeth. "Why didn't you tell me?"

"I tried. You sent my letters back without opening them and I didn't even know where you were." Yes, it'd been wrong not to give him a say in Levi's future, but at the time, she didn't feel like she had much choice. She wasn't about to let him forget it. "And weren't you the one who told me I'd have to play house by myself?"

Tony's mouth dropped open. "That's when I thought you were giving up college for me. I was trying to make you go to school."

"And what if you'd known, Tony? Would it have made a difference?"

"We'll never know, will we? You didn't trust me enough to give me a choice."

A wave of nausea hit her. Confrontations always made her sick. The urge to flee was overwhelming. "Only because you didn't love me enough to stay."

"I told you why I left," Tony snapped.

"So it's okay for you to make a decision for both of us when you think it's for my own good, but I can't?" She stood up. "Believe whatever you want, but I wasn't going to use a baby to blackmail you into staying. Especially after I found out how you really felt."

"Where are you going? We're not done talking."

A weight dropped onto her shoulders. She swallowed the lump in her throat. "You believe I did this to get back at you. You don't want to talk, you want to be angry at me and you have every right to be. I've been mad at you for ten years, so go ahead. But right now is not the time to talk about it."

He snorted. "When is the best time? When he graduates high school?"

"Goodnight, Tony. We'll talk when you're out of the hospital." Steeling herself, she turned and walked out the door. And she didn't look back.

THE TICKING OF the clock on her nightstand mocked Sabrina's inability to sleep. It had been over a week since her conversation with Tony at the hospital and she still wasn't any closer to deciding how to handle it. Time was up. He'd gotten out of the hospital two days ago and she wouldn't be able to avoid him much longer. With a groan, she tossed the blanket off and crept through the dark house. The screen door creaked as she stepped onto the porch. The cold stone sent shivers up her legs, but she made her way to the swing and stretched out on it to stare up at the stars.

The constant humming of the cicadas during the day had been replaced by crickets. Somewhere in the distance, frogs joined in the chorus.

Sabrina closed her eyes. There wasn't an orchestra on Earth that could've played any sweeter sound. It was like they were welcoming her home.

"Bree." Someone shook her.

Her eyelids wouldn't open. The swing tipped and fell on the ground with a thud.

Dad grinned down at her. "Good morning, sleepyhead."

She stood. "What time is it?"

"Almost five." He picked up the blanket

crumpled in a mess at her feet. "Good thing I covered you up around two this morning or the mosquitoes would've eaten you alive."

Her heart stuttered. He'd brought her a blanket? The simple action spoke volumes to her. "Why didn't you wake me up?"

"I figured you had some pretty serious thinking to do or you wouldn't have been up half the night. You worried about that boy?"

She stiffened. It was the same tone he'd used when she and Tony were dating in high school. "That *boy* isn't a boy anymore, Daddy. He's grown. Just like me."

"You gonna tell him 'bout Levi?"

Her heart caught in her throat. "How did you know?"

He sat next to her on the porch swing. "It wasn't hard to figure out."

She rubbed her arms, chasing away the chill of the early morning air. "Yeah. Tony figured it out, too."

"That explains why he's been calling non-stop since he got out of the hospital. When are you going to tell Levi?"

"I don't know. I'm hoping I can talk Tony into not telling him at all." Her cheeks burned. It was one thing to think it. Saying it out loud made her feel like a heel.

"Why? Levi has a right to know." Dad's brow wrinkled.

"He's a cop, Dad. He works with kids from gangs. He's already been shot once. Do you know what it would do to Levi if something happened to Tony?" Not to mention what it would do to her.

"So you're basing your decisions on what-ifs?" Dad lifted his chin.

"I have to protect my son."

He raised his eyebrows. "That's a pretty big what-if."

Sabrina stared at the horizon. The rising sun painted the sky with pink and purple and already the hum of bees in the rose bushes by the fence could be heard. "So you think I should tell Levi?"

Dad stood, straightening the baseball cap on his head. "There's an auction in Dublin tomorrow. I want to get down there this afternoon so I can inspect some of the farm equipment before the auction. I think I'll see if Levi wants to go with me. It'll do you good to have a night to think."

Code for "go talk to Tony." She stood, too. "Thanks, Dad."

Without Tony popping into her office, the morning seemed to drag. Even the kids seemed quieter. By lunch time, Sabrina felt like screaming.

"Karen, I'm taking a longer lunch today. Dad and Levi are going out of town and I need to get Levi's things ready."

Karen waved at her as she headed out the door.

The branches on the rose bushes bent under the weight of the blossoms and the buzz of bees in the mimosa tree echoed in the little house. The thickness of the stone walls kept the oppressive heat at bay, but the humidity was impossible to escape. It was no wonder she'd resorted to wearing a ponytail just to keep the hair from sticking to her neck and back.

Time was running out. Soon Dad and Levi would go to Dublin. Then she'd go talk to Tony. Her insides quivered at the thought. She put a paper towel over the sandwiches she'd made for her boys and went to let them know lunch was ready.

Sidestepping cow patties, she picked her way along the path to the barn. The smells overpowered her. Fresh-cut hay, dirt, cows. Nothing smelled better. She found Levi pounding nails into a board at the back of the building.

"Where's Grandpa?"

Levi pointed to the hayloft and went back to driving nails into the wood.

"You run inside and get cleaned up. Lunch is ready and you smell like manure."

He hung his hammer up on the wall and dashed to the house.

"Dad," she called up to the loft. "Lunch is ready."

Levi was finished with his sandwich by the time she made her way back to the house. "I need to pack some clothes to go with Grandpa. What should I use?"

"I have an old duffel bag in my closet. I'll get it for you in a second. Did you have fun riding around on the tractor with Grandpa this morning?" She turned on the faucet to wash dishes.

"Yeah. Grandpa said there used to be a lot more cattle here, but he sold most of them. How come?"

"Raising livestock is a big job," Sabrina told him. "After I moved away, it probably got too hard for him to do it all by himself."

"This place is great." Levi poured himself a glass of water. "There's so much neat stuff. Chickens, cows, fish. Why did you leave?"

"My Uncle Troy had a stroke and Aunt

Patty needed someone to help her take care of him."

Levi chugged the water and placed the glass in the sink. "I'm going to jump in the shower."

She couldn't resist reaching out to touch the soft curls that hung at the back of his neck. After tonight, would she have to share him with Tony? How would Levi react to the news that his father wasn't an army staff sergeant killed in action, but Tony?

A few minutes later, the water in the shower started and Sabrina went to get the duffel bag from her closet. She opened the door and reached up to take the bag from the top shelf. She heard a thud as something fell when she closed the door. Whatever it was, she'd pick it up later.

By the time Levi got out of the shower, Sabrina already had his bag packed for him. She placed the bag on top of his bed and looked around the room, taking in the signs that he was growing up. The cartoon characters that used to decorate his wall had been exchanged for posters of muscle cars and bands. The action figures he used to play with sat untouched on the dresser, while an intricate design of building blocks sat on the floor at the foot of his bed. He was growing up too fast.

She went back to the kitchen to start washing dishes. What was taking Levi so long to get out of the bathroom? She glanced down the hall. The bathroom door was open. A noise from her bedroom alerted her to where he was. He was probably looking for her duffel bag.

At the door to her bedroom, she stopped short. Levi stood outside her closet, holding the photos, her treasure box at his feet.

Levi turned his gaze to her. "Tony's my dad, isn't he?"

Gripping the edge of the door, she tried to calm her skyrocketing pulse. "What?"

"You have a picture of him in your treasure box. It was dated the year I was born." Levi held the picture out. "And he looks like me."

Her heart raced. She entered the room and sat on the edge of her bed. Would her son ever be able to forgive her? "Yes. Tony's your father."

Levi's brow furrowed. "Is that why we never came to visit? Because you didn't want to see him? Or he didn't want to see us?"

Sabrina sucked in a breath. "We were young and Tony hated living in Salt Creek. He got offered a job in Louisiana and left. By the time I realized I was pregnant with you, he was already gone."

The muscles in Levi's jaw twitched and Sabrina knew he was trying to mask his emotions. Tony used to do the same thing. "So he didn't know about me?"

"No, he didn't." Her hands shook. "I never told him."

Levi lifted his chin. "You lied to me. You made up a story about my dad being a war hero and the whole time he was alive?"

The pain in Levi's eyes ripped her heart out. She blinked back tears. "It's a little more complicated than that, but I was trying to protect you."

She reached out to touch his shoulder, but he pushed her away. "I hate you." He ran outside.

"What's going on?" Dad met her in the hallway.

"Levi knows." Tears streamed down her face. "He hates me."

Dad shook his head. "He doesn't hate you. He's mad, but he'll get over it."

"I have to go talk to him." She started for the door, but her dad pulled her back.

"Give him some time. He's got a lot to think about."

She pressed her lips together. "What am I going to do?"

"I'm going to shower, and then Levi and I are going to Dublin. You're going to go talk to Tony, and tomorrow evening y'all are going to sit down together and work this out."

"No way. He can't go with you now." She rubbed her temples.

"Yes. He can. He needs time alone just as much as you do." Dad put his thumb under her chin and raised her face to look at him. "It'll be all right."

A half hour later, Sabrina stood on the front porch and watched the big Ford bounce down the dusty road. Levi refused to come back into the house and tell her goodbye. The afternoon stretched before her and she'd never felt so alone.

Then the phone rang.

CHAPTER ELEVEN

TONY HELD HIS breath waiting for Sabrina to answer the phone. What would her excuse be today? Did she really think she could avoid him by not answering her phone?

"Hello." Sabrina's voice came over the line. She sounded...upset.

"What's wrong?"

The phone was silent for a moment. "I'll be there in twenty minutes."

His heart leaped. He hadn't even had to beg. "See you then."

Abuela set a glass of iced tea on the coffee table in front of him. "Who will you see?"

"Sabrina's on her way over." Tony wrinkled his brow. His grandmother hovered over him like he was going to collapse any minute. How was he going to have any privacy here? "Abuela, when she gets here, do you and Papa mind giving us some time alone?"

Papa looked up from his reclining chair. "Why do you need to be alone?"

What was he going to tell his grandparents? Would they be angry with Sabrina? Abuela's Latin temper would surely flare, but it would ebb quickly. The joy of having another child to fuss over would outweigh any hard feelings she harbored toward Sabrina.

And what about *his* anger? Would any excuse she gave him make up for losing out on ten years with his son? Keeping the truth from him hadn't made things any easier on her. How had she survived in Houston? How did she support herself with no education and a small child to raise? What factors had led to Levi's counseling? Most of the troubled kids he came across had one thing in common: no father. It made his blood boil to know that his own son was one of those statistics when he didn't have to be.

Rubbing his hands on his jeans, he sat next to Abuela on the sofa. "Sabrina and I have a lot to discuss. Last week, just before I went to the hospital, I found out that Levi is my son."

Papa turned the television off and Abuela set her needlepoint down. She moved to sit closer to him. "What are you talking about, *mijo*?"

Where to begin? *Just tell them.* "Levi isn't

the son of a GI killed in Afghanistan. It was just a story she made up. I'm Levi's father."

Abuela's mouth fell open. Her fiery temper was on the verge of exploding. "Ten years. She is just telling you now?"

A stream of rapid Spanish escaped from her lips. Tony tried to calm her down. "Abuela. Stop. She didn't know she was pregnant until after I left town."

Papa nodded. "That explains why she left."

"It doesn't explain why she didn't tell him," Abuela snapped. She turned to Tony. "She could've come to us. We would've helped her."

How could Tony explain something he didn't understand himself? He wanted to defend Sabrina, but the same questions had crossed his mind. "I don't want to waste time being angry with Sabrina. I've lost nine years already. I don't want to lose more because we can't get along."

Was it too late for him to build a relationship with his son? Levi wasn't much older than Tony had been the first time he met his dad. He'd been thirteen when he finally found out where his father lived. The first time he'd run away from foster care it was to take a six-hour bus trip from Dallas to Houston. The tall blond-haired blue-eyed army sergeant had been less than thrilled to meet the son he'd never wanted. He'd greeted Tony with a bus pass home and a warning to never return. Tony had never forgotten that he wasn't good enough for Steven Elliot. Levi would never feel that type of disappointment.

"Oh, *mijo*! You'll make a good father." Within seconds she had her arms around him and was peppering his face with kisses.

"Mama, you'll hurt him." Papa pulled her away from Tony. "He's still very sore."

"Of course." She dabbed tears from her eyes. "*Lo siento*. I'm just so happy. We have a great-grandson, Antonio. I never thought I'd see this day."

Tony pulled her close and hugged her again. "Don't apologize, Abuela. And you didn't hurt me."

Papa folded his newspaper and stood. "Elaina, it's still early. Let's go into town and eat dinner at The Eagle's Nest. We can bring something back for Tony."

Tony could almost see the wheels spinning in Abuela's head. The last thing she wanted to do was leave. He wasn't sure if it was because she wanted to confront Sabrina or just eavesdrop on their conversation.

Papa recognized her hesitation, as well. He took his wife's arm. "Let's go, Mama. Tony and Sabrina need some time alone. I'm sure he'll tell you all about it when we get home."

She let out a sigh. "Fine. I'll get my purse."

Their truck had just disappeared down the road when Sabrina's car pulled into the driveway. His pulse pounded. From the moment he first saw her at the grocery store, he knew her life hadn't been easy. Faded clothes, worn-out shoes. Until now, it hadn't dawned on him that Levi's clothes and shoes were new, even if they weren't name brand. How many things did she go without so she could provide for her son? He bit his lip. Their son.

"Hi," she said through the screen door. Her voice was shaky.

He pushed the door open. "Where's Levi?"

The smell of honeysuckle and vanilla drifted in the air as she brushed past him. "My dad took him to an auction in Dublin."

Tony's throat tightened. Robert had never liked him. How many of Sabrina's lies had been concocted by Robert in an effort to keep Levi away from him? "I'm sure he's upset that I discovered his little ruse."

Dang. He didn't want to start off their conversation with sarcasm.

Her face fell, but she threw her shoulders back and lifted her chin. "He had nothing to do with it. The fault is mine. No one else's."

"He didn't try to stop you, though, did he?" There he went again. He needed to get a grip.

Sabrina crossed her arms in front of her. "Maybe I should leave and come back when you actually want to have a conversation."

Sabrina was one of those rare people who never seemed to get mad—unless she was pushed too far. Then it was best to stay out of her way. She was almost to that point. He held up his hands in surrender. "Let's sit down. I'll be good."

Her shoulders relaxed and she strolled over to the couch, avoiding his gaze. Finally, she stared up at him. Her dark brown eyes masked any emotion she was feeling. "Where do we go from here?"

"How about backward?" Tony sat in Papa's chair, across from Sabrina. For the last week he'd thought of dozens of questions. But he wasn't sure where to start. So why not at the beginning? "Start from the day I left. I won't interrupt. I just want to understand."

SABRINA RUBBED THE back of her neck. The speech she'd practiced was forgotten. Did he really want to hear the whole story? She doubted she'd make it halfway, but at least he wasn't barking at her.

The harshness in his eyes softened and he leaned back in the chair.

Sabrina took a cleansing breath. "I don't remember a lot about the first week after you left. I didn't do much. I didn't even go to work at The Eagle's Nest. One morning Dad dragged me out of bed and told me to quit wasting my time waiting for you to come back."

Amazing how the pain was just as sharp as it had been ten years ago. She twisted the ring on her finger. "All my friends were going to the river to celebrate graduation. I decided to go to work, instead. The gossip mill was still having a field day with our relationship. One of the ladies from my church asked for a different waitress because she didn't want to associate with a harlot."

Tony leaned forward, the muscles in his jaw tense. Whatever he wanted to say, he kept quiet.

"All I wanted was to get through the summer and go to Texas State University. I already had my dorm room assignment and everything was ready to go." She rolled her shoulders, trying to relieve the tension.

"Three weeks after you left, I realized I was pregnant. I didn't know what to do. Dad was already so embarrassed by what we'd done that he barely spoke to me. I knew when he found out, he'd storm to the hardware store demanding to know where you were.

"You'd made it clear that you hated Salt Creek and wanted out. The last thing I wanted was for your grandparents to force you to come back."

Tony shook his head. "I wish you had. By that time, I was already regretting leaving. I was just too ashamed to come back on my own."

"Call it pride, but I didn't want to use a baby to make you want me. I wanted… No. I *needed* you to *want* to be with me because you loved me. Not because you wanted to do the right thing."

Tony moved from the chair to sit next to her. The heat from his leg pressed into hers and she closed her eyes.

"I drove to San Marcos to find out what my options were. I still wanted to go to school and use my scholarship. I told them I would only be attending part time. The admissions office informed me that one of the conditions of my scholarship was to be a full-time student. Since I was pregnant, I couldn't do that." She took a breath. "So they revoked my scholarship. I didn't know what to do, so I called my Aunt Patty."

"Her husband had a stroke right after you graduated from high school, right?"

Sabrina nodded. "I told my dad that I was going to put off school for a while and go help Aunt Patty. He was furious. He thought I was throwing school away because I was waiting for you."

She paused to stop her shaking hands. "I never told him I was pregnant. Uncle Troy was retired from Fort Sam Houston, and they had a lot of friends from the base. Michael used to come by the house every weekend to see if Patty needed anything. He felt sorry for me. He even told me that if you hadn't gotten your head on straight by the time he got back from Afghanistan, he'd marry me himself."

Tony's head jerked toward her. "You mean there really was a GI you were involved with?"

"*Involved* isn't the right word. We weren't even friends, really. He was so much older than me, but I admired him. His wife had died from cancer and they'd never had children. I think he was lonely and he thought I needed rescuing.

"It felt nice to have someone want to be with me. You can't imagine how scared I was. Wondering how I was going to take care of a tiny baby all on my own. I felt like a bum who was sponging off Aunt Patty."

"Sounds involved to me. Were you going to marry him?"

No more lies. Sabrina shrugged. "I told him I'd think about it. He wanted to get married before he went overseas. That way, if something happened to him, the baby would be taken care of."

She tried to decipher the look on Tony's face, but it was unreadable. "But I couldn't. I didn't want my baby to have another man's name. Maybe a part of my heart kept thinking you'd come back to me. Whatever it was, I couldn't.

"He wrote me every day. Then the letters stopped coming. I thought he'd finally come to his senses and it wasn't until his unit returned stateside that I found out. One of his buddies came to find me and bring me his last letter."

Tears filled her eyes. What a fool she was.

Crying over one man while begging for forgiveness from another. "I never loved him, but he was important to me. He gave me hope that someday I'd find my happy ending."

"He sounds like he was a great guy."

She nodded. "After Levi was born, Patty told my dad that I'd been seeing a soldier before he got deployed and that Levi was his son. She knew I didn't want to risk letting anyone find out you were his father."

Tony stood and paced the living room. "That's where you lose me. Was I such a horrible person that you didn't want me around my own son?"

"No." How was she supposed to make him understand? This was ridiculous. "I was eighteen years old. I was alone, scared and you'd broken my heart. I knew you'd come running if you found out about the baby. But if you didn't want me, then I didn't want you. I went with Patty's story because it saved me from admitting to people that I wasn't good enough for you."

He jerked as if she'd burned him. His mouth dropped open. "Okay. I get why you didn't tell me then. But what about now? What stopped you from telling me when you found out I was back in town?"

"You're not back in town." She avoided looking at him. "You're on medical leave from a job that almost got you killed. Could still get you killed."

"That's why? Because you don't like my job?" He stopped pacing to stand in front of her. His hazel eyes sparked with new anger.

She stood up, forcing him to take a couple of steps backward. "Yes. I didn't want Levi to get attached to you and then lose you."

"You're lying." His voice was low but strong.

"About what? About wanting to protect my son from having his heart broken?" Her voice cracked and tears welled up in her eyes again. Stupid tears. A side effect of getting angry.

"Tell me what you're really afraid of." He stepped closer, just inches separating their bodies.

The scent of his shampoo mixed with his aftershave and did weird things to her senses. She looked him straight in the eye. "I told you."

"Tell me the truth."

She couldn't think with him so close. His golden eyes bored into hers. The truth? She wasn't ready to admit it to herself yet, much less him.

He cupped her face in his hands. "What are you the most scared of?"

She wanted to turn her head away but couldn't. "Falling in love with you again. Losing you again. Coming in second to my own son." She closed her eyes when she said the last sentence, her cheeks burned hot.

Her eyes were still closed, so she didn't see what was coming. Warm lips covered hers and he gathered her close to him. Her senses were assaulted by the taste of him.

TONY HADN'T MEANT to kiss her. But when he felt her pulse beneath his hand and saw the pain in her eyes, he couldn't resist. The anger he'd felt all week began to ebb against her soft lips. For a split second she stiffened under his touch. Then she kissed him back and he sank his hands into her hair and deepened the kiss.

Fireworks exploded and the world spun out of control. By the time he pulled away, neither one of them could breathe. He pressed his forehead against hers. "You've never been second to anyone. Ever."

For what seemed like an eternity, they stood staring at each other. Finally, Sabrina pulled back. "Does this mean you forgive me?"

Did he? He'd meant what he said to his

grandparents. Nine years was a long time to lose with his son. He wasn't about to risk more because he and Sabrina couldn't get along. Judging by the way his lips still tingled, getting along wasn't going to be a problem.

Taking her hand, he sat them both on the sofa. "We can't change the past. Let's figure out how to move forward."

She tucked a strand of hair behind her ear. "First, I just want you to know that I'm not expecting anything from you."

"Well, that's good, because I'm expecting a lot from you."

Panic filled her eyes. Her muscles tensed and she pulled her hands from his. "Like what? Please, don't try to take my son from me."

His brows creased. "I don't want to make trouble for you, Bree." He leaned closer to her. "And I would never try to take *our* son away from you. But I do want time to get to know him."

"I understand that, but I don't know if that's what's best for Levi."

"Having a father in his life is what's best for Levi."

Her eyes widened. "Not one that won't be

there all the time. Have you been shot at before?"

"Excuse me?" He wasn't expecting that.

"How many times?" Panic laced her voice.

The muscles in his jaw twitched. What was she getting at?

She stepped back from him. "You were lucky this time. What if it happens again?"

"I don't take unnecessary risks."

"But you have been shot at before."

He let out a slow sigh. "Only a couple of times."

She gasped. "And it may happen again. If something happens to you, I'm the one who'll have to pick up the pieces."

Tony ran a hand through his curly hair. "Nothing is going to happen."

"Sabrina, I know I hurt you. Not one day has gone by that I haven't regretted walking away from you. I can't change what I did. But don't punish me by keeping me away from my son."

Her hands reached up to grip his forearms. "I'm not trying to punish you. I just want to protect Levi."

Even in the fading light, Tony could see the tears in her eyes. "I would never hurt him."

She pushed his hands away. "Not intentionally. But your job puts you at a risk I'm not willing to take. It'll break his heart."

Tony's eyes narrowed. "If you think I'm going to walk away from him because you're scared, you don't know me at all."

"For the first time in his life, he feels like he belongs somewhere. Now his whole world is upside down. He needs some time to adjust."

He took her by her shoulders. "Are you telling me he already knows?" When had she told him? Did he think Tony had abandoned him all those years ago?

She sniffed. "Today. He found a picture of us together and he figured it out."

"You kept a picture of us?" That had to mean something. "How'd he take it?"

"Not well. He wouldn't even speak to me before he left with my dad."

"He's probably mad at me, too." Tony sank back onto the sofa.

"No. He knows I kept the truth from you." She fought back a sob. "He said he hates me."

Her tears were too much for him and he wrapped his arms around her. "You must be doing something right, then. Don't all kids hate their parents at least once a week?"

A small laugh escaped between the tears.

"I guess. My dad said he'll get over it. But it hurts so much."

He stroked her head, the blond tresses like silk under his fingers. She was the one who'd lied to him and kept him from his son for almost ten years, but here he was, comforting her. How'd that happen?

"Can't you understand what I'm scared of? Even a little bit? You're here now. But what will happen when you're not?"

"I'm not going anywhere. I want to be a part of his life. Whatever your terms are. Whatever you want."

Sabrina leaned her head back to look up at him, her hand resting on his chest. "Fine. On two conditions. One, you never lie to him. And two...don't make promises you can't keep."

"Done."

CHAPTER TWELVE

IT WAS ALMOST three o'clock in the afternoon when her dad's dusty Ford bounced down the road to the farm. The flatbed trailer behind it carried his finds from the auction. Sabrina waited on the porch, unsure if she should greet Levi, or let him say something first.

The heat was unbearable and sweat dripped down her neck. She wasn't sure if she'd make an entire summer with no air-conditioning. Levi slammed the door to the truck and stopped at the gate. She held her breath. He walked by her without a word. A few seconds later, the door to the bathroom slammed shut.

Dad strolled up the walk and stopped in front of him. "Things are going to be okay. Did you talk to Tony?"

"Yes. He's coming to dinner tonight to meet Levi officially."

"I think I'll go to Arnold's and have dinner with him and his wife. I haven't seen them in a while." He took his cap off and dusted it off against his pants. "I'll get all the feeding done early, but make sure Levi still does his chores. I'll unload the trailer tomorrow."

Sabrina heard the toilet flush, followed by the sound of running water.

"Be careful going to San Saba."

Levi perked his head up. "You're going to San Saba? Can I go?"

"No, Levi," Dad told him. "You need to stay here and do what I said."

Levi's gaze darted back and forth between his grandfather and his mother. "Hi, Mom." His welcome lacked warmth, but at least it wasn't dripping with anger.

"Did you have a good trip?"

He shrugged, looking down at the ground.

She stepped toward him and placed her hands on his shoulder. He didn't push her away or take off, so maybe there was hope. "I'm sorry I lied to you. I want to say I was trying to protect you, but I think that would be another lie. I was trying to protect myself. And that was wrong. I'm sorry."

Levi lifted his chin. "Protect yourself from what? Is Tony a bad guy?"

"Not at all." She tried to think of an easy way to explain love and fear to a child. "You know the way you felt yesterday? When you found out I lied to you? Well, that's how Tony made me feel once. But instead of talking about it with him, I ran away. And I was so scared of feeling that way again, I lied to everyone."

"Does he still make you feel like that?"

A flashback of yesterday's kiss went through her mind and her heart did a little stutter. "No. And if I had talked to him about how I felt before, things wouldn't have gotten so messed up."

"Grandpa said you were going to talk to him while we were gone."

"I did."

Levi looked over her shoulder toward the house and back to the driveway. "You told him and he doesn't want me." His chest heaved.

"No. Why would you think that?"

"Then how come he isn't here?"

She clasped her hands together. "He's coming over tonight to talk to you. That's why Grandpa wouldn't let you go to San Saba with him."

Levi's lip stopped quivering. "Really?"

Sabrina stared at her son. Anticipation replaced anger in the blink of an eye. If he could get excited that quickly, how much faster could he be crushed? She was trying to do the right thing but looking at her son's hopeful expression reminded her how fragile his ego was.

She waved her hand at the door. "He's coming for supper. Now go do your chores and I'll start cooking."

He paused in the doorway to look back at her. "Do you think he'll like me?"

Sabrina took a deep breath. "He already does."

With that, Levi sprinted to the barn to gather the eggs and lock up the chicken coop.

As she started cooking, she tried to keep her panic under control. Levi paced around the house like a caged lion, asking question after question about Tony. Finally, she couldn't stand it anymore.

"Go get in the shower so you don't have to do it after he gets here. That way, you can stay up as late as you want."

Levi froze. "You're gonna let me stay up past my bedtime?"

"Yes. Only if you go take a shower right now."

A couple of minutes later, gravel crunched in the driveway signaling Tony's arrival. After checking her hair, she met him on the porch. He smiled as he rubbed the back of his neck. "Hi."

Goodness, he looked nice. A light blue shirt tucked into black slacks, emphasizing the muscular figure beneath the clothes. He'd even gotten a haircut. She bit back a smile as he rocked back and forth on his feet. She'd never seen him so nervous. "Levi's in the bath right now."

Tony shifted from foot to foot. "Does he think I abandoned him?"

She shook her head. "No. He's very excited about meeting you." *Too excited.*

HE WAS AT a loss for words as he looked at the woman in front of him. Her long hair was piled on top of her head in a messy semblance of a bun. An apron was tied around her waist and the smell of fried chicken followed her through the air. With her hands on her hips, she blocked his entrance into the house.

Before she could voice whatever was on her mind, a slamming door made them both jump. Levi came out to stand between them, his dark hair still wet. "Oh. Hey. I didn't know you were here." He eyed Tony for a moment. "Mom, I think the chicken is burning."

"Oh, marmalade!" Turning, she ran into the kitchen, leaving Tony and Levi alone.

Levi rocked back and forth on his bare feet. "So you're my dad. What am I supposed to call you?"

Tony swallowed. He'd approach him like he did the teens he worked with. Trust had to be earned. "How about what you called me before? Tony. I'd really like the chance to get to know you. To be your dad. But you don't have to call me anything you don't want to."

The boy studied him through narrowed hazel eyes. The same color he shared with Abuela. Tony stood up tall, waiting for Levi to finish his inspection. What did Levi think of him?

"We better go inside. Mom thinks she makes good fried chicken, but she really doesn't." The last part came out in a whisper.

Tony chuckled and followed Levi through the living room into the kitchen. The house had changed since the last time he'd been there. An alcove had been added onto the end of the large country kitchen to hold the dining room table. The door to an additional room was open. Must be Levi's room. Unless Sabrina had taken a liking to race cars.

Sabrina eyed them suspiciously. "Go ahead and sit down. It's almost ready."

Sitting in the chair next to him, Levi propped his head up his hands, his elbows resting on the table. "Do you have any brothers or sisters?"

"No. I'm an only child." At least as far as he knew. His father had married shortly after abandoning him and his mother. No telling if they had children or not. Tony didn't want to know.

Levi spooned some mashed potatoes on his plate. "Did you want kids?"

Tony gave Sabrina a wary look. "I always wanted kids, but I told everyone I didn't. I think that's why your mom was afraid to tell me about you. She was afraid I'd be mad and not want you."

"So you lied about wanting kids, and mom lied about the one she had." Levi wrinkled his nose. "It looks like my entire family is a bunch of liars."

"Levi Michael Davis," Sabrina snapped. "That was rude. Apologize now."

Tony lifted his hand. "It's okay, Sabrina. He's right. Maybe it'll teach him to always be honest about his feelings. No matter what."

"Why did you lie about wanting kids?" Levi wasn't ready to let the subject go.

"My mom died when I was young and I never really knew my dad. He left when I was very young." Tony buttered a piece of bread and took his time answering the question. "I was afraid that I wouldn't be a very good dad. I was so scared of it that I tried to convince myself I didn't want kids."

Levi asked questions between bites of food. Sabrina sat across the table from Levi and shook her head slightly as if to apologize. Tony gave her a slight smile.

At the end of the meal, Sabrina began clearing the dishes away and Tony turned to Levi. "My grandparents are dying to meet you. Do you think that'd be okay?"

"Can I, Mom?" His face was hopeful as he turned toward Sabrina.

She nodded. "Yes, of course."

Tony relaxed. He'd worried she might be difficult about letting his grandparents know. "I'd like to pick him up for breakfast in the morning, if I could. I'll have him back whenever you say."

Sabrina shifted in her chair. "I have to work until two. I guess I could pick him up when I get off work."

What? She was letting him take Levi without an argument. This was going far better than he'd hoped.

"I better clean up. Dad will be home soon. Why don't you two go into the living room? Levi, you can teach him that new card game."

Levi hurried to the living room to set up the game on the coffee table. Tony pushed his chair in and carried his plate to the sink. "Thank you. You could've turned him against me, but you didn't."

Sabrina toyed with the ring on her finger. "I didn't do it for you. I did it for Levi. If he thought his father was a bad person, he might think that made him bad, too."

"Whatever your reasons, thank you."

"I'm ready," Levi called. "Mom, you play, too. It's more fun with three people. I'll help with dishes later, I promise."

Sabrina shot Tony a look of defeat. "Okay, Levi. I'll be right there."

Two rounds later, Tony had figured out the strategy of the game. He was just about to play his final card when Sabrina's cell phone rang.

She stepped out of the room, but not before Tony heard her say, "Hi, Craig."

Levi won the next three games, as well. Tony couldn't pay attention. He was too busy trying to eavesdrop on Sabrina's conversation. Jealousy was not something he'd ever been prone to, even in high school, but then again, he'd never been fighting to win Sabrina's affections back.

The rumble of a truck engine got closer. Robert must be coming home. Funny, he'd been so worried about meeting Levi, he'd forgotten about Robert.

"I better get home. What time do you get up? I'll pick you up in the morning."

"I get up with the chickens." Levi grinned.

"That early?" Tony laughed. "What time would you like me to pick you up for breakfast?"

"He usually eats around seven thirty." Robert stood at the doorway. For once, he wasn't glaring at Tony. "How are you?"

Tony jumped to his feet. "Fine, sir." He stepped around the coffee table to shake Robert's hand. "Thanks for letting me come over this evening."

Robert hung his hat up on the antlers on the wall. "You lock up the chickens?"

"Yes, sir." Levi imitated Tony's stiff stance. "Fed them, too, and made sure there was water in all the troughs."

"Good man." Robert ruffled the boy's hair.

"Almost bedtime. You better go brush your teeth."

A burning sensation traveled from Tony's stomach to his chest. Pure jealousy. He should be the one getting Levi ready for bed. The one tucking him in. "I'll see you in the morning."

"Okay." Levi took a step toward him and then paused. "Good night." Turning, he headed back through the kitchen. He disappeared into the bedroom that'd been added onto the house.

"Good night." Tony nodded to Robert. "Tell Sabrina she can pick him up at my grandparents' house when she gets off work."

Sabrina was still on the phone when Tony left.

As soon as she heard Tony drive away, Sabrina came back into the living room. Her call had ended fifteen minutes before, but she wasn't ready to face Tony yet. Her heart had jumped in her chest when he looked at her across the coffee table during their card game… She shivered. What was he trying to do to her?

Levi emerged from the bathroom. "I forgot, I promised to help you with the dishes."

"It's okay. I'll do them. I'm going to be up awhile, anyway." Like she could sleep now.

He threw his arms around her waist and hugged her. "Thanks, Mom."

At nine years old, his hugs were getting scarce so she pulled him tight. "You're welcome. I love you."

"Love you, too."

He waited for Levi's door to close. "I hope you know what you're doing."

"Me, too." If only she had a crystal ball and could look into the future.

"I picked up the mail earlier." He tossed some envelopes on the kitchen table. "There's some for you."

She sank into a kitchen chair and flipped through the mail. Her fingers stopped on a cream-colored envelope from the closest junior college. What if her credits didn't transfer? Could she retake the courses and apply again?

She slid the envelope open. Yes! Everything had transferred and her application for admission to the college had been approved. Now she could submit her packet to the nursing program. By the time she got finished with the application process, her six-month probation period with Little Mountain would be complete and the bonus they promised her would cover the first semester of the two year program.

Dad had already turned off the living room lights and gone to bed, and the house was quiet. Trudging down the hall, she pulled a ledger from her nightstand. The original balance had been just large enough to disqualify her from financial aid and grants for school, but not large enough to pay for tuition and living expenses.

While she lived in Houston, she'd taken only one or two classes a semester. She worked enough hours to pay for her rent and living expenses and she'd only used her savings to pay tuition. She'd been able to stretch the money to complete her prerequisite classes. Of course, the process had taken her six years instead of two.

Once she got into the nursing program, she wouldn't be able to work full-time. The program was too demanding. She'd planned to use what was left of her money for tuition and living expenses. The balance jumped off the page at her. She was going to have to come up with another plan. And fast.

The shrill ring of the phone made her jump. She hurried to answer before it woke Levi or her father. It had to be a wrong number. No one called this late.

"Hello?" she whispered.

"Oh, good, you're off the phone." Tony's rich timbre came across the line.

Was he calling to cancel the breakfast plans? "Yes. What do you need?"

"I thought I'd give you my cell phone number, in case you wanted to call and check in with Levi tomorrow."

Oh. That was thoughtful. "Sure, okay. What is it?" She jotted down the number he gave her on a pad hanging on the wall.

"Could I get your cell number?"

She bit her bottom lip. Why did it seem like a big deal to give him her number? Her insides quivered like a schoolgirl with her first crush. She rattled off the number. "I won't be able to answer my personal phone at work. But you know the number of Little Mountain if you need it."

"Thanks."

Sabrina waited but he didn't say anything else. "Anything else?"

Tony sighed. "Who's Craig?"

Was he jealous? "A friend I worked with in Houston."

"A good friend?"

Yes. He was definitely jealous. "One of my best friends. I forgot to ask, how are your ribs? You're not playing basketball anymore, are you?"

He chuckled. "A few aches and pains, but I think as long as I stay off the court, I should be recovered in no time."

She bit her lip. "When are you supposed to go back to work?" What she really wanted to know was what his plans were when that day arrived.

"I go for a reevaluation at the end of August. Then they'll decide when I can go back to work."

"Are you taking any pain medication?"

Very few people knew the truth about Tony's past. But Sabrina did. His entire childhood had been spent taking care of his drug-addicted mother. He avoided any type of drug at all, even for pain.

"I don't take pills."

She nodded. "They're not all bad. Sometimes they help, you know."

"Children of addicts are more likely to become addicts themselves."

"But not all. If you were predisposed to be an addict, I think it would've shown up by now."

"Still not a chance I'm willing to take." Tony's voice was quiet. "I have someone counting on me now."

The intensity in his voice touched her. Sabrina yawned. "I have to get up early for work. I'll see you tomorrow."

"Okay. Good night."

Somehow, she didn't think it'd be a good night. She'd be awake for hours, tossing and turning and wondering how she was going to keep from falling in love with him again.

CHAPTER THIRTEEN

IT WAS A quarter after seven when Tony parked in front of the farmhouse. Sabrina met him on the porch.

"Levi just got up." She looked down at her feet. "He was up half the night going through old pictures."

"Going through your treasure box again?" He already knew his picture was in there. Did the box still hold the things he'd given her? "I hope he's hungry. Abuela's been cooking all morning."

She blushed. "Do they hate me?"

The worry in her eyes pulled at his heart. "No. They don't understand why you didn't come to them for help, but they don't hate you."

"What about the children's home? Don't you go there every morning?"

"Usually, but I haven't been back since I got home from the hospital." His life used to revolve around spending extra hours at St.

Paul's with kids. Funny. He hadn't thought of it once in the last week.

"I better get going. I have a lot to do today, so I'll see you after two."

Levi joined them on the porch.

"Bye, Levi. I'll pick you up this afternoon. Be good." She threw him a sharp glance.

He rolled his eyes. "Mom."

His insides twitched as Sabrina drove away. He was alone with his son. He walked to his SUV and waited for Levi.

Levi opened the passenger door and climbed in. "I still can't believe I have great-grandparents."

The boy was desperate for a family. Just like he'd been at that age. "Yes. And they're dying to meet you. Ready?"

He slammed the door shut. "Let's go. What's for breakfast?"

"I'm not sure. Did you think of any more questions for me? I know I have a lot for you."

Levi shrugged. "I don't want to make you mad."

Tony's heart wrenched. When he was a child, his mother had paraded dozens of men in and out of their lives. Occasionally, she'd bring home one that seemed smarter, nicer, better than the rest. If he was good enough, maybe the guy would stay and his mother wouldn't be so unhappy all the time. It never happened. Sooner or later they all left. His mother blamed it on him. No one wanted to be saddled with a rotten kid like him.

He started the engine and turned to Levi. "Don't ever be afraid of that. You can tell me anything. You can ask me anything. I'm not going to be mad at you. As a matter of fact, I couldn't sleep last night worrying that you're mad at me."

Levi wrinkled his nose. "That's funny. Why would I be mad at you?"

He headed down the bumpy dirt road. "Because I haven't been there for you and your mom. It's okay to be a little mad at me."

"I guess I was a little mad at you."

Tony shot him a sideways glance. "Just a little?"

The boy shrugged. "Maybe a lot. But Grandpa told me it wasn't your fault."

Robert had defended him? Miracles did happen. "If I'd known, I would've been there. I hope you know that."

"My mom really messed things up, didn't she?" A trace of anger laced his words.

"Don't be too upset with her. She only did

it because she loves you so much. She's a really great woman."

"Do you still love my mom?" Behind Levi's question, Tony saw a glimmer of hope in his eyes.

"She is the first and only woman I've ever loved." He couldn't deny it. He didn't want to. "I think the question is, do you think she could ever love me again?"

"She's pretty stubborn." Levi scrunched his face.

"That she is." Tony parked the SUV. Abuela waved from the porch. He glanced at Levi, who was fiddling with his seat belt, his eyes darting all around. "Don't be nervous."

"I'm not."

"You look nervous." Who could blame him? So was he. "Whenever I get nervous, I just say a prayer."

Levi gave him a sheepish grin. "I already did."

Tony's chest swelled. Leaning over to him, he whispered, "I said about fifty of them last night before dinner and fifty more this morning."

"You were nervous about seeing me?" Levi laughed, his body relaxing a little.

"Are you kidding? I've never been a dad before. This is the scariest thing I've ever done."

More giggles.

He opened the door. "Let's go eat."

Throughout breakfast, Tony tried not to stare. He couldn't believe that Levi was his. Did they share anything besides looks? Would he have anything in common with his son?

Between Abuela hovering over him and Papa asking questions, Tony was afraid Levi would be overwhelmed. But Levi laughed and talked with them like he'd known them his entire life. He giggled when Abuela spoke to him in Spanish and she taught him some phrases he picked up right away.

The conversation continued nonstop and Tony found it hard to get a word in. When Abuela got up to refill their juice glasses, he seized his opportunity. "Did you get to go to Spring Ho?"

"Yeah." Levi's face lit up. "We went to the parade on Saturday and Grandpa took me to the carnival for a little while afterward."

"Didn't your mom go with you?"

Levi shook his head. "No. She met some friends from Houston for dinner, so Grandpa took me."

Friends from Houston? Was one of them Craig? Jealousy wasn't something he'd ever been prone to. He didn't like it.

Later that afternoon, he watched Papa teaching Levi to whittle and his heart swelled. He felt…content. The reasons to stay in Salt Creek kept racking up.

It was getting close to time for Sabrina to pick Levi up and Tony dreaded it already. He hadn't had enough time. What was he going to do when his medical leave was over?

His cell phone rang. "Hello?"

"Hey," Sabrina said. "I'm going to be stuck at Little Mountain for a few minutes and Levi has chores to do. Would you mind taking him home and I'll be there as soon as I can?"

Tony grinned. More time. "What's going on? I can swing by there if you need me to."

"That's okay. I forgot where I left the key to the filing cabinet and Karen can't find it. I'll probably remember as soon as I retrace my steps, though."

"All right. Levi and I will see you at home."

"Thanks." The line went dead.

Just the sound of her voice made him buzz with electricity. The reasons for staying were definitely adding up.

ALL THE WAY HOME, Sabrina worried. Was she doing the right thing? Maybe she shouldn't have let Levi spend the day with Tony so soon. He needed more time to adjust. Twice last night she'd picked up the phone to call him and tell him not to come. But Levi was so excited she didn't have the heart to.

A tiny part of her felt betrayed. Levi shouldn't be so eager to accept Tony. Wasn't he angry that he'd been absent for his entire life? No. He was just thrilled that he had a dad. Parking her car, she hung her head. Shame on her. She'd raised a good, fair child who was willing to give Tony the benefit of the doubt. Willing to give him a chance. It was more than she could say for herself.

Tony's SUV was parked next to the shed. She took a deep breath. Time to see how their day had been. Laughter greeted her as she strolled to the door.

"Uno," Levi told Tony, and the two of them laughed.

With her hip leaning against the front door, she watched them interact. Levi seemed more relaxed than he had during dinner last night, but there was still a part of him that he held back.

Levi laid down his last card and erupted in a fit of giggles. Tony tossed his cards on the table and grinned at her. "You should've warned me he cheats."

Don't smile back. Don't do it. The corners of her mouth betrayed her. Giving in, she shrugged. "I wouldn't play checkers with him, either, if I were you."

Tony stood up and pushed his chair in. "Thanks for the tip. I guess I better go."

"See ya later." Levi dismissed him with a wave of his hand, swept the cards up into a pile and carried them to his room.

Disappointment flickered across Tony's face as he watched Levi go.

"He's not really the huggy type, if that's what you were expecting." She folded her arms.

His eyes tightened. "I'm not really sure what I was expecting." He rubbed his palms together. "Uh…thanks for letting us hang out. Can we do it again tomorrow? You work every morning, don't you?"

"Not tomorrow morning. I have a meeting in Lampasas at nine, so I have the day off. You can pick him up on Wednesday, though."

"Oh, okay." Tony didn't try to hide his disappointment. "I guess I'll see you then."

She followed him outside to his SUV. "How did it go this morning with your grandparents?"

"That could be a problem."

She whipped her head around to face him. "Why?"

He made a show of glancing at the door to see if Levi was listening. Leaning close to her, he whispered, "He's still young enough to spoil. They're going a little nuts."

"When you say 'going nuts,' what does that mean, exactly?"

The dimple deepened as he gave her a mischievous grin. "I hope you have room for a lot of boxes."

"Boxes?"

"Birthday presents. Christmas presents." He held up his hands. "I want it on the record that it wasn't me."

She pulled her long hair over one shoulder and combed her fingers through it. "It's not Christmas. Or his birthday."

"No. But they want to make up for the nine they've missed."

"What?" She lifted her eyebrows. "You can't be serious."

He took a step closer, his hand stroking the hair she was playing with. "You've always had the softest hair."

Shivers danced down her spine. "Stop changing the subject. You can't let them buy him nine, no, eighteen gifts. Where would we put it all?"

His deep laugh resounded through the night air. "I'll try to rein them in. But I can't make any promises."

"I'm used to that." She clamped her hand over her mouth. "I'm sorry. Knee-jerk reaction."

The flicker of pain in his eyes was like a kick to her gut. She reached out with one hand and squeezed his biceps. "I didn't mean it. I don't why it came out like that."

"Yes, you did." He covered her hand with his and gave it a gentle squeeze. "It's okay. You're right. I always avoided making promises. But I'll make you one now."

He lifted the hair from her neck and leaned close. His warm breath tickled her neck, his mouth inches from her ear. "I'm not leaving Levi. Or you. I promise."

She shuddered. He pulled away, his hand still buried in her hair, cupping the back of her head. The air froze in her lungs. The gold flecks in his hazel eyes seemed to glitter as he stared into hers. "I promise," he repeated and climbed into his vehicle.

It took several minutes for her to get her heart rate back under control. Why did she let him affect her like that? She sat down on the leather couch. What was she going to do? It would've been so much easier on her heart if he could just be angry with her. She kept his son from him for ten years. Be mad. Be unapologetic. Not understanding. And sweet. She let out a puff of air. She was in big trouble.

His grandparents weren't really going to bring boxes of stuff over. Were they? She groaned. Boxes. Years ago, she'd boxed up all her mother's things and stacked them in her room. Now they were piled against the wall. Before going to bed each night, she'd promised herself that she would go through at least one box.

Levi ran to the barn to do his evening chores and she settled herself on the floor of her room, determined to put away the contents of at least one box.

"Mom, I'm hungry." Levi appeared a while later at her door. "When will Grandpa be home?"

Her stomach growled in response and she glanced at the window. It was dark outside. She'd been so engrossed in her task, she hadn't noticed how late it was. Boxes and their contents were scattered over the floor like the lily pads in Dad's stock pond. Stepping over the piles she followed Levi to the kitchen.

"He went fishing with Ray. He won't be back until tomorrow night." She scanned the contents of the refrigerator. "Did you feed the chickens and the goat?"

Thank goodness she didn't have to worry about the cattle. Mr. Morgan ran some stock in the pastures with Dad's. In return for the use of the land, he fed the cattle and checked the water in the troughs and ponds when Dad was gone.

After dinner, Levi disappeared into his room without offering to help her with the dishes. She'd just put the dishes away when the ringing of the telephone startled her.

"Hi. Sorry to call so late." Tony's smooth baritone voice flowed across the line.

"It's okay." Why was he calling?

He cleared his throat. "I wondered if I could take you both to breakfast tomorrow morning."

"I don't think that's such a good idea." She wasn't ready to spend time alone with him. Especially in Salt Creek. The gossip mill would have a field day with it.

Almost as if he read her mind, he said,

"Since you're going to Lampasas, anyway, I thought we might go Gene's."

Her grip on the phone tightened. He remembered. How was she supposed to keep him at arm's length when he kept doing things to tug at her heart? She chewed on her bottom lip.

"We can ride together, and Levi and I can go to the river walk or something while you're at your meeting."

Warning bells went off in her head. *No. Just say no.* "What time?"

"Pick you up around seven thirty?"

"Okay. See you in the morning." She hung up and tried to settle the butterflies in her stomach. There were good reasons to say yes. Monitoring the conversation between Tony and Levi. Saving gas money. Sure. That was why she said yes.

She flipped the lights off and headed for her bedroom. Pausing at her bookshelf, she looked for something to read. Once again, she had a feeling that sleep wouldn't come for a long time.

TONY ARRIVED A little after seven. Before he could knock, the door swung open and Levi came barreling out. "Ooph," he huffed as the boy ran into him.

"Oh. Sorry." Levi gave Tony a sheepish grin. "I didn't see you. I gotta go feed the chickens."

Levi tore past the gate and ran toward the barn. Tony turned his attention back to the house. Should he go in? Wait on the porch? He hesitated for a split second before knocking. No answer. No sound came from inside, so he turned and followed Levi's path to the barn.

Levi was scooping corn from a barrel with a can. Tony leaned on the fence. "Can I help?"

"No, thanks." Levi headed for the chicken coop on the other side of the barnyard. "I already fed the pigs and the goat. Mom usually feeds the chickens, but she's still trying to decide what to wear."

Tony didn't miss the boy's tone of dismay. "Does she do that a lot?"

"Never." Levi opened the gate to the yard for the chickens, leaving it propped open with a rock. Chickens mobbed him, pecking at the corn as fast as he could scatter it. Dropping the can back into the feed barrel, he let the lid slam shut. Levi's eyes narrowed as he looked Tony up and down. "She's been acting weird all morning."

Tony's heart jumped. Could she be as nervous about spending the day together, too? Women didn't spend inordinate amounts of time getting ready for someone they hated. "Should we go find her?"

Levi shrugged and walked ahead of him. "What're we gonna do while Mom is talking to the college lady?"

College lady? Tony hadn't asked her about her meeting. Was she trying to finish school? He turned his attention back to Levi. "I know you like to fish. We could go to the river."

"Sure. I hope it's better than Grandpa's tank." He nodded at the stock pond toward the back of the property. "I haven't caught anything yet."

They were loading Levi's pole in the trunk of his Durango when Sabrina came out of the house. "What are y'all doing?"

Tony almost slammed his hand in the trunk. He couldn't help but stare. Her yellow sundress rippled around her slender legs as she headed for them. The light summer breeze blew a strand of her long blond hair across her face. She tossed it back with a flick of her wrist.

"Loading my fishing pole." Levi walked

around to the passenger side of the car. He paused as he opened the door. "We going?"

Tony exchanged looks with Sabrina. "Ready?"

"Sure."

The sweet scent of honeysuckle filled the air as she brushed past him. Every nerve in his body sprang to life and he fought the urge to pull her into his arms. He reached out to touch her hand. The way Sabrina stiffened doused him like a bucket of cold water.

She stepped back, breaking the contact and replacing the impenetrable wall around her. Dropping his hand, he gave her the space she needed. "We better get going."

Sabrina didn't speak much on the ride to Lampasas, letting Levi fill the silence with chatter. By the time they arrived at the small café in the town square, Tony had fallen into an easy rhythm with the boy. He was surprised at how many things they had in common. Music. Sports. They even liked the same colors.

An elderly couple stood just inside the doorway to the small restaurant, and Tony lingered with the door open to allow the pair to go out. By the time he was able to close the door, Sabrina and Levi were already seated. In a booth. On the same side. He sighed.

Levi picked the conversation back up. "Bradley said Salt Creek has its own festival that's even better than Spring Ho."

Sabrina played with her napkin. "The Harvest Festival takes place at the end of September. It may have changed, but when I was a kid, it didn't have a carnival. It was mostly vegetables and animals."

"Animals? Like dogs and cats?" He perked up.

"No. Farm animals. Sheep, steer and lots of pigs. It's where a lot of kids get their animals for the livestock show."

"What's a livestock show?"

Tony bit his lip to suppress his smile. Levi had been raised in the city, just like he'd been. "Kids across the county spend months raising farm animals. The stock show is like a contest to see who's done the best job."

"They judge you for feeding a farm animal?" Levi's voice raised an octave. "Maybe I should be in it. I feed Grandpa's pigs and goat every day."

This time, Tony couldn't hold in his chuckle. "It's a little more complicated than that. Not only do they feed the animal, but they work with it every day to get it to do what they want. Some of the animals, like steers and sheep, have to hold still a long time so the judges can check them. It takes a lot of practice to teach the animals to do that."

Sabrina glanced up from the menu. "You also have to keep a log every day on how much you feed them and how much they weigh. Sometimes you even have to take their temperature."

Her eyes caught Tony's and they both stifled a grin. He gave Levi a pat on the arm. "Whatever you do, don't ever let your mom talk you into helping her with *that*."

She leaned over to her son and whispered, "Don't listen to him, Levi. It's not my fault Tony didn't know how to check Daisy's temperature."

"Daisy?" Tony snorted. "You mean Killer."

Levi gave Tony a confused look. Four coffee cups sat upside down on their saucers on the back edge of the table. He slid one of the cups toward Sabrina and then one toward himself, flipping them right side up so the waitress could fill them.

Sabrina laughed again. "Levi, in case you didn't know, in order to take an animal's temperature, you have to insert the thermometer in their rear end."

"And, by the way, sheep don't much like

getting their temperature taken." Tony gave Sabrina a mock glare. "I had hoof prints on my chest for two weeks."

"It kicked you?" Levi was fascinated.

Sabrina broke into another fit of giggles. "Kicked him. Butted him. Ran over him a few times. Sheep, one. Tony, zero."

Tony was struck with an overwhelming desire to run his fingers through her silky hair. His gaze lingered on her lips. "I almost forgot what a cute giggle you have. It's nice to hear it again. Even if it was at my own expense."

Levi made a face. "You showed animals, Mom?"

"Sheep and pigs. Dad wouldn't let me have a steer. He thought they were too much work."

He leaned back in the seat and tapped one finger on his chin. "Do you think I could try?"

"What kind of animal would you want to show?" Tony ignored the glare from Sabrina. "It's a big commitment. You'd have to take care of it every day."

Levi lifted his chin. "I can do it."

"Maybe you should check with your mother before you decide anything." Sarcasm laced Sabrina's words. Her eyes never left Tony as she spoke. "I don't think Tony is the best one to talk to about commitment, anyway. He never raised show animals."

Tony winced at the subtle dig. "No. I didn't raise animals when I was a kid." He returned Sabrina's stare. "I didn't really understand how commitment worked then. Now I do."

She shifted in her seat, but continued to hold his gaze. He held it as long as he could before turning his attention back to the window. Out of the corner of his eye, he could see her staring at him.

CHAPTER FOURTEEN

GENE'S RESTAURANT SAT on the town square in Lampasas. Like so many other places in Texas, the town square had once been the hub of activity. Now most of the stores were situated along the highway that cut through town. She picked up a menu and scanned it quickly before setting it down. "The choices haven't changed much." With her elbows on the table, she rested her chin on one hand, her eyes unreadable as she stared at him. "I haven't been here since high school."

"Me, either." Tony turned his attention to Levi. "This was your grandpa's favorite place to eat. Once he woke your mom up at one o'clock in the morning so she could drive him down here for breakfast."

Levi raised his eyebrows. "Really, Mom? One o'clock in the morning?"

Sabrina nodded, biting her lip. "More than once, actually. He'd get a craving for biscuits and gravy, and off we'd go."

Only Sabrina usually wasn't asleep. Or alone. Tony had made a habit of crawling through her bedroom window after her curfew so they could spend more time together. No one would've believed that two teenagers would sit up all night, just talking. They'd hear Dad stomping down the hall just in time for Tony to hide in the closet. The memory made her smile and the pensive look on Tony's face said he was thinking about it, too.

"You seem to be enjoying your time in town. Did you change your mind about living in the middle of nowhere?"

He shrugged. "It's growing on me. You lived in Houston a while. Did you like the city?"

"Not at all." She let out a wistful sigh. Closing the menu, she turned her attention to Levi. "Did you decide what you wanted to eat?"

"Can I order whatever I want?" Levi asked.

"Anything."

"Okay." Grinning, he set his menu down.

The waitress appeared. "What can I get y'all?"

Levi spoke up. "I'd like a grilled bacon and cheese sandwich, please. With hash browns."

Tony handed the waitress his menu. "I'll have the same thing."

Sipping her coffee, Sabrina avoided his

gaze. Tony was probably wondering why Levi had just ordered Tony's favorite sandwich.

"Levi, you said you like baseball. What other sports do you play?"

Levi shrugged. "I don't know. I only played at the Y. I've never been on a real team."

Tony cleared his throat. "What about soccer? That starts soon."

Sabrina had already looked into it but the registration fees for new players were too high. There was no way she could afford it. "I think it's too late to register."

"Jarrod's the coach and he said he needs a few more players." Tony leaned forward. "Let me talk to him and see what I can do."

"Bradley's dad?" Levi asked.

"Yes." Tony looked at Sabrina. "Is that all right with you?"

Sabrina tucked a strand of hair behind her ear. Giving Levi a sorrowful glance, she lifted her chin. "Thank you, but that won't be possible."

"Why?" Both Tony and Levi spoke in unison.

Gritting her teeth, she glared at Tony. Didn't he think she'd already looked into it? "What do you think I'm in Lampasas for? I'm applying for the nursing program. I'll have classes every day after work. How am I supposed to get him to practice when I'm going to be at class?"

"That's not a problem." Tony met her stubborn gaze with one of his own. "I can take him to practice."

But he wasn't going to be here. By that time, he'd be back at work in San Antonio. Levi didn't know that yet and she wasn't about to be the one to tell him. She took a deep breath. "It's not possible right now."

Levi watched the exchange. "Why not, Mom?" His eyes opened wide as a thought occurred to him. "It's because of the money, isn't it?"

"We'll discuss this later. At home. Alone."

Tony ignored her. Leaning forward, he asked Levi, "Do you have a soccer ball or any equipment?"

"No."

"I guess fishing can wait until after we go shopping."

Sabrina stood up. "I want to speak to you. Outside. Now."

Levi whistled. "I think you're in trouble."

"I'll deal with you later, young man." She walked out and paced back and forth along the side of the building until Tony joined her.

He was confused. "Exactly what did I do wrong?"

Was he just teasing her or did he honestly not know? Her nostrils flared. "You are deliberately trying to undermine me in front of my son."

"That's not what I meant to do."

"Don't you think I want to let him play? I looked into that team when Marissa told me about it, and there's no way I can afford it."

"And if I pay for it?" He arched one dark eyebrow.

Sabrina shook her head. "I've raised him for almost ten years without accepting charity from anyone. I'm not going to start now."

Now it was Tony's turn to be angry. "It's not charity. He's my son. Stop being so stubborn and let me do something for him."

"Fine. You can pay for it. But that doesn't solve the problem of him getting to practices."

Tony's mouth gaped open. "I just told you I'd take him to practice."

"How're you going to take him to practice in September when you go back to San Antonio? I had two conditions, Tony. Don't make promises you can't keep."

He stepped back like he'd been burned. "You're so sure that I'm going to flake out on you. September is less than two months away and you've already pushed me out of the picture."

The only way to protect her heart was to remind herself that he was leaving. "What do you want from me?"

Tony took her by the shoulders. "I want you to give me the benefit of the doubt. I want you to trust me."

"I'll give in, for now. But I don't trust you." She couldn't.

Levi was already eating when the two of them sat back down at the table. He exchanged a worried glance with Tony. "Look, Mom. Tony ordered the same sandwich as me."

"Really? What a coincidence." Except it wasn't. She hadn't realized how much of Tony she'd impressed upon her son.

"Since your mom agreed to let you play soccer, what's your favorite position?"

The conversation between the two of them continued as Sabrina played with her food.

Levi was enjoying the attention, but she sensed something was wrong. He'd always been a *what you see is what you get* kind of kid. He didn't pull punches with anyone. One more personality trait he seemed to have inherited from Tony.

When Tony left the table to pay, Levi turned to her. "Do you still love him?"

She almost choked on her coffee. "I haven't

seen the man since high school. Why would you even ask me that?"

"You look at him funny."

She brought her hand to her mouth. Levi was more intuitive than she'd given him credit for. "He's changed a lot since we were kids. I guess I'm just trying to figure him out."

"Ready?" Tony reappeared at the table.

"Sure." Levi took one last sip of his drink before standing up.

Tony's hand at the small of her back burned a hole through her thin cotton dress as she followed Levi to the door. He kept his hand on her waist all the way to the car, only moving it to open the door for her.

The ride to the college admissions office was quiet. When Tony pulled into the parking lot, he turned to her. "We can wait here if you'd like. How long will it take you?"

Sabrina shook her head. "You promised Levi a new soccer ball and that's exactly what you're going to do." She opened her car door. "Take your time. I'll text you when I'm ready."

THE FOLLOWING WEEK the soreness in his chest and shoulder had eased enough to allow him to go back to Little Mountain. He wanted to spend as much time with his son as possible, but he couldn't back out on his commitment to the kids at the home. Especially when Jarrod informed him that he'd received a tip that a major drug deal was running through the home. So Tony spent every morning with Levi and dropped him back home on his way to Little Mountain.

By the end of the week, Tony's cop senses were on full alert. He didn't miss the glances exchanged between a few of the older boys when he walked into the room. Only Martin went out of his way to be friendly to Tony and stuck to him whenever he was there. Tony wasn't fooled. It was the age-old mantra. *Keep your enemies closer.*

Martin, the oldest, thought himself to be the leader of the boys. He'd been raised by an elderly grandmother who let him run wild on the streets, and he had a rap sheet longer than any other boy there. The two things missing from his impressive résumé of crimes were drugs and weapons. If Martin was involved in either, he was smart enough not to get caught. From the judge's perspective, Martin was a troubled kid who needed a second chance. Little Mountain was a way to keep out of juvie.

At the home, Kyle rarely spoke to Tony. He kept to himself for the most part, but some type of animosity had developed between Kyle and Martin. More than once Martin stepped into Kyle's path to bump shoulders with him. Not once did Kyle rise to the bait.

Whatever Martin was up to, Kyle wasn't going along with it. Now, if he could just get Kyle to tell him what that was.

In the back of the hardware store, working on Tony's old car, Kyle was in his element, a totally different kid. He chatted and joked with Tony and Papa. Blasting the radio on an old country station, he knew the words to songs that were even before Papa's time. Red Sovine. Hank Snow. Kyle knew them all by heart.

Since Kyle had begun to let himself in and out of the building, Papa had started taking inventory twice a week. Tony busied himself by straightening the shelves. He didn't relax until Papa tapped his pencil on the clipboard and nodded. Then he would hang the clipboard on the back wall, whistling happily.

Was that how everyone had felt about him at one time? Saying that they trusted him but going behind him and double-checking his work?

"Tony?" Kyle called to him from the door to the back room.

Tony looked up from the shelf he was stocking. "How's the work going?"

Kyle pulled himself up straight. "I'm finished."

In less than three weeks? "Really?"

"Yes, sir. Would you like to check it out?"

Tony patted the young man on the back. "Can't wait. Let's go." He followed the lanky teen to the back room.

Even though the roll-up door to the warehouse was open, the smell of grease and oil hung thick in the air. A fan in the corner of the room worked overtime, trying to blow the fumes outside. The old car sat in the middle of the room with its hood up. Not a speck of dirt marred the floor, and the tools lay on the counter in an orderly line. Tony's chest swelled with pride.

Kyle bounced with impatience as Tony climbed into the muscle car and turned the key in the ignition. The car roared to life. Pressing his foot on the gas pedal, he felt the hum of the engine vibrate through him.

"Well?" Kyle's brown eyes searched Tony's. He tapped a wrench against his leg as he waited for Tony's approval.

Tony turned the ignition off and pulled

himself out of the car. "You think you did a good job on the car?"

Kyle stepped back. "No one could get that car running better. No one."

"Good." Tony pulled a card from his wallet and handed it to him. "A friend of mine in Lampasas could use some help in his garage. Interested?"

"You mean, like a job? A real job?" Kyle looked at the business card. His shoulders slumped. "Mr. Anderson will never let me do it."

Tony grinned. "Chris will, if you've got a sponsor who is willing to accept responsibility for you while you're out of his supervision."

"I don't have a sponsor."

"You do now." Tony patted Kyle on the arm. "Chris Mortenson offered you a job, and I'll be your sponsor. And you can use the car whenever you want."

"You mean to go to work."

"No. I mean whenever you want." Tony tossed him the keys. "Keep it parked here when you're not using it."

Kyle's eyes narrowed. He fingered the keys in his hand. "Why? What's in it for you?"

Redemption. Peace. Could a seventeen-year-old identify with any of those? Probably not. "Revenge," he said. Kyle could relate to that.

"On who?"

"Everyone who told me I'd never be worth anything. Everyone who's still waiting for me to fail." Tony didn't want to get too serious with him, but now Kyle needed to know. "If you fail, I fail. I trust you. Don't let me down."

Looking Tony in the eye, Kyle nodded. "I won't. See you at the counseling group tonight." Walking over to the pegboard on the wall, he carefully hung the keys up and headed out.

The heavy metal door rolled shut with a thud, leaving Tony alone in the room. Most boys would've taken the keys, jumped in the car and been gone. Leaving them behind was a promise he wasn't going to take advantage of Tony's trust.

Mimicking his grandfather's happy whistle from earlier, he sauntered back into the main building and almost ran into Sabrina.

"You busy?"

"No. What's up?" Her long hair, usually pulled into messy bun, hung long and loose around her shoulders. Tony's fingers itched to touch it.

"Dr. Moore wrote a letter to the school board for Levi. The principal agreed to let him start school. Dad's grilling steaks to celebrate. Levi wanted to invite you over."

Sabrina had avoided him for the last week, so Tony never stuck around her place after dropping Levi off. No way would he miss out on a chance to spend the evening with her and Levi. Even if it was under the watchful eyes of her father. "What time can I be there?"

SABRINA'S HANDS SHOOK when she got back in her car. Levi's explosions had become a thing of the past. Until this afternoon. He accused her of making Tony feel unwelcome because Tony left as soon as he saw Sabrina. She'd promised Levi she would invite Tony to dinner again.

To outsiders, Levi seemed to be content and happy. When Tony or her father was around, he was on his best behavior. But when they were alone, his anger seeped through and showed itself not through outbursts, but disrespect.

Whenever she told him to do something, he ignored her. A couple of days before, he'd told her he'd done something when she knew he hadn't. When she'd confronted him, he shrugged and said, "I lied. I thought that's how we did things now." Trying to discipline him had turned into a battle of wills. She was now the bad guy and Levi picked Tony at every turn. And she hated it.

Her dad told her not to take it too personally. Levi was going through a lot of changes and needed time to adjust. Of course, Levi was on his best behavior in front of her father. Every night she'd go in to her son's room to say good-night and he'd roll over to face the wall and pretend to be asleep. It was tearing her up inside. She was trying to be patient, but she wasn't sure how much more she could take.

Tony still hadn't told Levi that their daily visits were only temporary. It was the end of July. At the end of August, Tony would go back to San Antonio. If he thought he was going to leave it to her to tell Levi, he had another think coming.

Tonight she was going to get some answers from him. Mainly, when was he going to tell Levi he was going back to San Antonio? And what would happen when he did go back? Did he want to see Levi every other weekend? Or just when he had time? Would Levi be okay with seeing him only on the occasional weekend? Every time she broached the subject, Tony would shrug and tell her not to worry. He couldn't wait until the last minute to tell Levi.

Sabrina turned off the farm-to-market road and followed the dirt road leading to the farm. She topped the last hill before home and stopped. Acres of waving prairie grass stretched as far as the eye could see. Cattle dotted the landscape and fields of alfalfa, and corn rose up at the edge of the rolling hills. She got out of the car and leaned against the hood.

One hundred and fifty years ago, a broken wagon wheel had interrupted her great-grandfather's journey to California. By the time he got the wheel fixed, his wife had fallen in love with the area and refused to leave. What else could he do but build her a house?

In the distance, the same house stood on the skyline. Only now, an addition with wood siding nestled up against the flagstone structure. It was Sabrina's sign that she was where she was supposed to be. Why couldn't Tony feel the same way about this place? If only he loved Salt Creek like she did.

After their first kiss he'd told her, "I don't stay in one place very long." The last words he'd said to her before he left were "I told you I don't stay in one place very long." She was under no illusions that he was here to stay in Salt Creek. She wouldn't even ask him to. Especially not with a promotion waiting for him in San Antonio. She knew he would always be there for Levi. If only she knew how he planned to juggle his job and Levi. And could she handle the dangers his job put him through?

She'd never quit loving him. Even when she hated him, she loved him. How did he feel about her? Before he left the first time, she'd been sure of his love. After he left, she'd convinced herself that his love had been a lie. But lately she caught him looking at her in a way that made goose bumps dance across her skin. The one kiss they'd shared replayed itself in her dreams every night.

Often, while lying in her bed listening to the crickets chirp outside her window, she wondered if they could ever be a family. But even when she finished the nursing program, she had no desire to return to Houston, or any other city. So what if she couldn't make as much money here as she could in a larger town? Life was about more than money.

Tony might agree with her about money,

but he had a mission. While she was happy to stay in Salt Creek forever, his quest to put drug dealers behind bars wouldn't allow him to be content here. His ambitions were driven by his mother's death. Would he ever feel that he'd been redeemed? Probably never. If they got together, he would want her to move to San Antonio with him, where the dangers of his job would be front and center every day. At least in Salt Creek, she wasn't inundated with reminders.

The smell of burning charcoal filled the air with a tantalizing aroma when Sabrina pulled into the driveway, but the yard was quiet. She picked up the paper bag full of groceries she'd bought in town and went inside. Levi sat on the floor in the living room. Her dad sat in his chair. Both of them leaned over the coffee table, studying the checkerboard between them.

"Hi, Mom." Levi nodded to her before he turned his gaze back to the checkerboard. A smile tickled his lips as he made his move. The same move Sabrina had made a million times. She held her breath. Levi was competitive. When he first learned to play, she'd let him win the first few times. He was a sore loser, so now she beat him occasionally to try to teach him sportsmanship. Her father had never let her win when she was a child. He didn't believe in it. How would Levi react to getting beaten by Dad?

Dad glanced at the checkerboard and back at Levi. Then he did something that surprised her. The easy move. The one that would leave his final two checkers vulnerable to Levi.

Grinning, Levi took advantage of the perceived weakness and eagerly jumped his checkers. "Yes! I win!" He reached over to give his grandpa a high five.

"Good job." Robert nodded. "Winner gets to clean it up."

Levi dumped the checkers into the box and tucked the board beneath his arm.

When he was out of the room, Sabrina walked over to her dad. "I never thought I'd live to see the day that someone beat you at checkers."

He shrugged. "Levi's good."

With one arm wrapped around his neck in a quick hug, she whispered in his ear, "Don't make a habit of letting him win."

"I'm going to check on the charcoal."

"Thanks. I'll have the macaroni salad ready soon. It can chill while you grill the steaks."

"Knock, knock," an all-too-familiar voice called from the doorway. "Am I too early?"

CHAPTER FIFTEEN

THROUGH THE SCREEN DOOR, Tony saw Sabrina and Robert exchanges glances. He braced himself as Robert opened the door.

"No, you're not too early. I was just about to check the grill." Robert extended his hand to him.

Tony stared at it for a moment before gripping it in a handshake. "Is there something I can do to help?"

"Sure. The steaks are on a cutting board in the kitchen. When I whistle, bring 'em out to me."

"Yes, sir." He smiled at Sabrina as Robert walked past him outside. "How about you? Is there something I can do?"

She started to say something, then stopped and smiled. "Actually, you can wash some potatoes for me and wrap them in foil while I start on the macaroni salad."

"Aye-aye." He gave her a mini salute and followed her to the kitchen.

"Tony!" Levi bounded out of his bedroom. "You're early. I'll go get my checkerboard. I bet you can't beat me."

The sparkle in Levi's eyes warmed him. His son seemed to be accepting him. He still wasn't ready to call him dad, but he wasn't avoiding him, either.

"Sure. Right after I help your mom. Sabrina, is there anything Levi can do?"

Sabrina stiffened and gave her son a guarded smile. "Levi, why don't you wash the asparagus?"

Levi gave her a defiant stare. "Because I don't want to."

She blushed and turned back to what she was doing. Did Sabrina always let him speak like that to her? Or was this a new development?

"Levi, your mother asked you to do something."

The boy huffed and jerked the door to the refrigerator open. He splashed a couple of drops of water on the asparagus. "Here."

Before Tony could say anything, Levi ran out the door. Sabrina's back was to him, but her posture told him everything. Touching her shoulder, he turned her to face him. "Is this new? Is he always that disrespectful?"

Sabrina sniffed and wiped a tear from the corner of her eye. "It started last week. I thought he was adjusting fine and then he was angry at me all over again. He'll never be able to forgive me for lying to him. And you."

Tony pulled her close. She relaxed against him for a moment. Nothing he'd done since leaving Salt Creek felt as right as holding her in his arms.

"I'm sorry. I'll go talk to him."

"No." Sabrina shook her head. "It'll just make it worse. He'll have to get over it on his own."

Tony shook his head. "No matter how angry he is with you, it doesn't excuse him behaving toward you that way. You are his mother. Put your foot down and demand his respect. It's the only way you'll get it."

She glanced down. "That's what my dad says, too."

A shrill whistle pierced the air. Tony picked up the cutting board with steaks on it. "I'm being summoned."

Robert's whistle had Levi running toward the house. He vaulted over the low rock wall at the back of the yard. When he saw Tony he stopped, as if unsure what to do.

Tony grinned at him. "I'll be ready for that

checker challenge as soon as you go in and wash that asparagus correctly."

Levi shifted back and forth for a moment. "Okay."

Robert waited for Levi to disappear in the house. "Well done."

"Thanks," Tony said.

"You and Sabrina may not be a couple, but you have to be united in your expectations of Levi. I appreciate you backing her up."

"I never wanted to make things hard for her." Tony handed Robert the spatula from the end of the grill. "Even ten years ago. I swear, I thought she'd be better off without me. Otherwise, I'd never have left. I loved her."

Loved. Past tense. Or was it? When he strolled back into the house, Levi had just finished washing the asparagus. He opened the checkerboard and set it up. They were almost finished with their second game when Robert whistled for a plate to put the steaks on.

During dinner, an easy silence stretched between Tony and Robert. Tony's chest tightened. Why hadn't they been able to do this ten years ago? He'd been too busy trying to prove to the world that nothing bothered him. Sabrina had seen right through him when no one else could. Everyone else found him cocky and belligerent. No wonder Robert had threatened to run him off his property with a shotgun on more than one occasion.

After dinner, Sabrina began to clear the dishes away. Tony stood to help.

"Want to play cards?" Levi got up without cleaning his place.

Tony shot Sabrina a look. She took a deep breath. "Levi, put your plate in the sink."

"I have Go-Fish or Uno." Levi didn't even acknowledge her. He ran into his room and came out with several decks of cards.

Sabrina snatched the cards from his hand. "No dishes, no cards."

Levi made a face, but he did as he was told. When he was done, she handed the cards back to him. "What game do you want to play?"

Tony took a deep breath. "Actually, Levi, I want you to finish the dishes so your mother and I can talk."

Despite the open windows and the screen door, the air was thick with humidity. He opened the door and quietly walked out onto the porch. "Is there someplace we can talk alone?"

Sabrina's lip quivered and she nodded. She opened the door and hollered inside. "Daddy,

Tony and I are going for a walk out to the barn."

The full moon cast an eerie light over the Texas landscape as they walked to the barn's breezeway.

He stopped a few feet from her. The wind rustled in the pecan trees and somewhere in the depths of the barn, an owl hooted in the rafters.

As soon as Sabrina stopped walking, he pulled her into his arms. He rubbed his hands along her back. "I've been wanting to do this all day."

Sabrina hugged him for a moment. "We need to talk, Tony."

"I know. We have a lot to discuss." He pulled her hands to his chest and pressed a kiss against her knuckles. "Give me the chance to make up for the mistakes I made. For our son. For us."

She took a few steps away from him. "I accept that you want to spend time with Levi. But there is no us. Not anymore."

"Why? Why won't you give us a chance?"

She took a deep breath before looking him straight in the eye. "That's the same question I asked you ten years ago."

Tony's nostrils flared. "So that's it. That's all I get?"

"That's all I can give you."

She was lying. He could feel it in the way her pulse raced beneath his hand. He stopped inches from her. "No. I need a reason."

"We have different lives now." She played with the ring on her finger. "Your future is in San Antonio and mine is here."

"What do you have here that you can't have in San Antonio? School? A job? If it's your dad you're worried about, we can visit every weekend. Don't we owe it to Levi to try to be a real family?"

Sabrina took a deep breath. "I can't walk on eggshells every day wondering if today is the day that your luck ran out and you won't come home to me."

"So that's it? My job? I would never put my job over you and Levi."

The phone is his pocket chirped. He opened it up to read the text message from Kyle. Trouble at the hardware store. Hurry.

Crap. "I'm sorry, Sabrina, but I have to go. We'll talk about this later."

THE KEYS WERE still in his pocket, so he didn't need to go back to the house. No sense in bothering his grandparents. In a flash he sped into town and turned down a small back alley to cut across to the main street. Out of the corner of his eye, he saw a light flash and disappear. A flashlight? Two streets over, he shut off his engine and crept toward where he'd seen the light.

A noise ahead stopped him in his tracks. He dropped to the ground, blending into the shadows of the alleyway. The back entrances to all the businesses on Main Street sat along the alley. Crawling, he managed to get close enough to the corner to hear the sound of someone trying to pry a door open, but couldn't see which business they were trying to break into.

"Hurry up," a whispered voice demanded.

"I'm trying. I'm not as good at this as the kid." Scuffling noises drifted to Tony.

At the end of the alley, a third, louder voice joined the group. "What are you doing?"

"What's it to you? You didn't want a piece of the action."

"I won't let you do it."

The first voice laughed. "You think you can stop me?"

Muffled curses followed some more scuffling. Tony eased his head around the corner to see what was happening.

One figure lay in a heap on the ground. Kyle had a larger boy pinned against the outside wall of the hardware store. "You're not breaking into this store," he said through gritted teeth and let the boy go.

"You'll be sorry." The other boy picked his companion up off the ground and they scurried away from Kyle to the road, right past Tony.

Kyle hollered at the retreating figures. "I'll be here all night to make sure you don't come back."

Tony didn't recognize the smaller boy, but when they ran by he'd gotten a good look at the bigger kid's face. Nick Johnson. When they were gone, he stepped out of the shadows. "Looks like you didn't need me, after all."

"Why didn't you text me back?" Kyle threw up his hands. "I thought I was on my own."

"I'm sorry. I should have. Pretty brave for someone who thought they were working alone." Tony patted him on the back. "Thanks for watching out for Papa's store."

"You're not gonna try to make me talk to

the police, are you?" Kyle followed him down the alley to his truck. "I won't do it."

"No." Tony nodded to the truck. "Get in and I'll give you a ride home. How did you get out of your cabin?"

"Martin put a sleeping pill in Mr. and Mrs. Cordova's drinks after supper. When he left, I followed. They're probably still out of it."

Tony's eyes narrowed. "Where did he get the pills?"

"I don't know. He has lots of pills." Kyle climbed in the SUV. "And don't ask me anything about it. I don't know, and even if I did, I'm not a rat."

"You realize how dangerous it is to deal drugs."

"My mom got hooked on drugs and took off with her dealer when I was little. I won't have anything to do with them."

Tony started the truck. "One more thing we have in common. But covering for a drug dealer is as bad as pushing them yourself. I hope you realize that."

"Yeah, well, I also know what happens to narcs." Kyle stared out the window, confirming Tony's suspicions.

Someone was using the group home to run

drugs. Nick? Martin? Mr. Anderson? It was only a matter of time until he found out.

SABRINA PULLED INTO the Montoya's driveway when she got off work. Mr. Montoya and Levi sat on the porch, their legs hanging over the edge. Tony was on the porch swing, watching them. He stood up and met her at her car.

She almost lost her nerve, but she deserved to know why he'd skipped out on her so fast. "What happened last night? Why did you have to leave?"

"Jarrod asked me to keep an eye on some of the boys at the home. One of them texted me about some trouble that was going down."

This was why she couldn't let herself fall in love with him again. It was just like Tony to go rushing off to help other people, even when he wasn't on the job. Wasn't he helping out a kid when he got shot?

Tony's phone rang and he glanced at the caller ID. Whoever it was, Tony didn't look excited about talking to them. "I really have to take this. It's my captain."

Why was his work calling him if he wasn't due back for three more weeks? She stepped far enough away to give him some measure of privacy, but still hear the gist of the conversation.

"Hello, Captain Rodriguez," Tony answered quickly. A smile broke out a few moments later. "That's fantastic. Thank you."

A short silence followed and Sabrina felt his eyes on her. "I appreciate the opportunity, sir. Can I think about it and get back to you?"

He ended the call and leaned against her car.

"Good news?"

"Yes. The mayor was pushing for an investigation and threatening to file charges against me. He's dropped them."

"Why would he want to do that? What did he accuse you of doing?"

Tony ran a hand through his hair. "He's been pushing an anti-gang coalition. I talked Mr. Chan out of pressing charges against the teen who tried to rob his store. The mayor thought I was too close to some of the gang members and accused me of hampering the investigation."

"Is that true?" Her pulse roared. How close was too close to gang members?

"Adolfo wasn't a gang member yet. I was trying to get to him before the leader of one of the gangs did. Adolfo volunteered to wear a wire and help bring him down."

Sabrina swallowed. How much more dangerous could his work be? "The mayor dropped his charges. That means your job isn't in any danger, right?"

Tony smiled, excitement hummed in the air. "Better than that. Adolfo and several others came forward because of the relationship I'd developed with them. The captain had no idea how much influence I had over some of the kids. Not only does he want to give me a promotion, he wants me to lead my own undercover task force."

Sabrina's heart went from racing to stopping. Undercover? That was the most dangerous thing there was. She pasted a smile on her face. "Congratulations."

He nudged her. "How about going out with me on Friday night? There's supposed to be a great band playing in Llano this weekend. We can celebrate."

"I can't. I'm working all weekend." Dancing together at Little Mountain had unnerved her and that had just been one dance. An entire night of dancing with him? Nope. She couldn't do it. Especially when she felt like he'd just signed his own death warrant.

Tony's face fell. "Okay."

Levi looked up, a chunk of wood in one hand and a pocketknife in the other. Piles of wood shavings littered the ground.

"*Hola*, Mom." Levi hopped up. "That's Spanish for *hello*. Abuela is teaching me."

"*Muy bien*," Sabrina said. "That's Spanish for *very good*. Are you ready to go?"

"I gotta get my stuff." He ran into the house.

She let out a sigh of relief. Although things weren't completely back to normal, they were better. Tony had been right. Once she put her foot down, Levi's bad behavior stopped. Tony'd had something to do with it, as well.

Elaina stepped out on the porch. "Hello, Sabrina."

The tension in her shoulders relaxed. They didn't seem angry with her. She hadn't seen them since that day at the hospital. Before they found out about Levi.

"I'm ready." Levi bounded out the door with a bagful of chocolate chip cookies.

"What's that?" Sabrina stared at his hand.

"Your favorite." Abuela gave Sabrina a hug. "Levi and I made them special for you."

"Thank you."

"I told you they weren't mad at you," Tony

whispered in her ear as he walked her and Levi to her car. He opened the door for her. "It looks like Levi's not, either."

"Mom, can we go with Tony to the barbeque next weekend? They're even having fireworks." Levi fastened his seat belt.

Sabrina shot Tony a look. "Are you volunteering at the barbeque?"

The annual Little Mountain Barbeque had been the topic of the town for a week. Held at the regional park, the children set up a booth to sell handmade arts and crafts and the money raised from the barbeque made it the biggest fundraiser of the year. The addition of a talent show, open to the public, was supposed to bring people in from all the neighboring counties.

"Yes." Tony leaned against the side of the car. "What did you get wrangled into doing?"

"Actually, nothing." She pushed a lock of hair back up into her bun. "I have a previous engagement that I couldn't get out of, so I'll be attending as a spectator only. By the way, Dad is plowing a new field tomorrow and won't be back after lunch. Can you babysit Levi all day tomorrow?"

Tony flinched. He leaned forward and spoke too low for Levi to hear. "He's my son.

It's not babysitting. And he comes first. Always."

She wasn't going to argue with him in his grandparents' driveway. "Except when duty calls," she said softly.

The muscles in his jaw twitched. He only gritted his teeth when he was upset. It seemed like he did that a lot around her. Maybe she should cut him some slack.

"Mom," Levi groaned from the passenger seat of the car as soon as they'd pulled out of the driveway. "I'm not a baby."

His face was red and she knew she'd embarrassed him in front of Tony. "No, but Grandpa is going to be out in the fields all day. You can't stay home alone."

"I'm big enough to stay by myself." He groaned.

"The last time I let you stay alone, I came home and you had a fat lip and a black eye."

Levi rolled his eyes. "That was a long time ago. Besides, that was in Houston. Who am I going to get in a fight with? The chickens?"

She smiled at his scowl. "I know you're big enough to stay by yourself. But you're not used to living in the country. Lots of things could happen and you won't know what to do."

"Like what?"

"One of Grandpa's cows could break through the fence and get stuck in the yard. The rooster might want to use you for a flogging post. You could wander out in the pasture and step in a prairie dog hole and break your ankle. You could get bit by a rattlesnake. You could—"

"All right, all right." Levi waved his hands at her. "I get it."

"Good." She nodded. "Because Tony is picking you up again in the morning."

CHAPTER SIXTEEN

IT WAS FRIDAY before the barbeque. Tony's time was almost up. Sabrina had tossed and turned all night, thinking about what Tony had said the week before. An undercover task force. Just the word *undercover* sent her heart into a frenzy. What if something happened to him? Levi was barely getting his emotions back under control. Levi would never be the same. She had to put a stop to this now.

As soon as got off work, she drove straight to the Montoya house.

"Sabrina, what a nice surprise." Elaina greeted her with a kiss to the cheek. "Tony and Levi are in the backyard building a rabbit hutch."

"Thanks. I know the way." She walked around to the back of the house.

Tony was helping Levi measure for a side wall of the hutch. He was the perfect teacher. Slow. Patient. He'd be the perfect father if he didn't like putting himself in a position to get shot all the time.

Could she blame him for wanting to return to a job he loved? No. She'd heard the pride in his voice when he talked to the kids at Little Mountain about boys who'd gotten out of gangs with his help. Not bragging, though. He never boasted or implied that he'd rescued them from gangs. In his stories, the boys were the heroes for being brave enough to want more from life.

If only he wanted to stay in Salt Creek. But there was nothing for him here and it was selfish of her to want him to stay.

"Hi, Mom." Levi saw her watching from the corner.

"Hi, Levi. You better run inside and get your stuff."

Tony watched her with narrowed eyes. "I know that tone. What's wrong?"

As soon as Levi left, she pasted on her best smile. "I'm sorry, Tony. But Levi won't be able to go with you to the fireworks tonight."

He frowned. "Why?"

"I have some friends from Houston who are coming down for the barbeque." She held her breath.

Tony's eyes narrowed. "That's okay. I'll

take Levi so you can spend time with your friends."

The word *friends* dripped with sarcasm. "You don't understand. They want to see Levi, too."

Tony's jaw clenched, but he nodded. "Fine. I'll pick him up in the morning."

She wrinkled her nose. "Actually, Levi won't be available until Monday. I'm sorry."

"I'm getting some pretty intense vibes from you. Did I do something wrong?"

"No." Sabrina's stomach flipped. "You've spent every day with Levi, but when we get visitation set up, you're both going to have to adjust to seeing each other occasionally."

"Visitation?" Tony snapped to attention. "I thought we were doing okay. Since when do we need to establish visitation?"

"I think it's past time we do. That way Levi will always know what to expect."

"Is that really what you want?" Tony stood rigid.

Crossing her arms, she looked him in the eye. "Yes. It is."

"Fine. I'll see Levi Monday morning." She went out to the car to wait for Levi. He jumped in the car. "Tony said I couldn't go to the fireworks with him tonight. Why not?"

"Julie and Craig will be here this afternoon. They wanted to take us to dinner and to the fireworks. You don't mind, do you?"

Levi's eyes lit up. "No, it's okay. I see Tony all the time. What time will they be here?"

Sabrina backed out of the driveway and headed for home. How could she tell him that he wouldn't be seeing Tony as often? Would his anger return?

TONY SLAMMED HIS palm against the rabbit hutch. His frustration turned to anger. What had he done to cause Sabrina to threaten him with visitation? *Visitation.* The word left a sour taste in his mouth. He didn't need a judge to tell him when he could and couldn't see his son.

The rancor in her voice had surprised him. Had he been fooling himself into thinking they might have a chance? And who were these friends who had come to visit?

His phone chimed. I need an extra set of eyes at the fireworks tonight. You in? Don't let me down.

After a quick text conversation, Tony discovered that Jarrod had received a tip that something was going down at the fireworks tonight. Tony really hoped it was more than a gut feeling and rumors overheard by his teen-age son. Jarrod would be tailing Nick Johnson all night and was counting on Tony to keep an eye on Martin.

In the mood he was in, he didn't want to be around anyone. He'd rather sit at home and wallow in self-pity. The realization hit him hard. When did he start hiding from his problems? Maybe an evening with the boys was exactly what he needed to remind him of what he needed.

He stared at the screen, and before he could change his mind, he typed, I'll be there.

THE PARKING LOT of Little Mountain was a whirl of activity. Three vans with the home's logo on the side were parked together. Tony pulled his SUV in behind them. He inhaled deeply, waiting for the tightening in his chest to disappear.

A bang made him jump. Kyle leaned over the hood of his vehicle, his hands tapping the metal like a drum.

Tony opened the door and got out, forcing a smile onto his face. "Hey, Kyle. Trying to give me a heart attack?"

"Tony!" Kyle jogged around to his door and

bumped fists with him. "I didn't know you were going with us tonight."

"Ready for some fireworks?" *Pretend everything is okay.* He could do this. After all, he'd had plenty of practice pretending everything was fine. For years, he'd managed to convince his teachers that his home life was as normal as the next kid's.

Kyle shook his head. "The girls are gonna make us late. Why do they have to take so long?"

"Might as well get used to it." Out of the corner of his eye, Tony saw Martin watching him.

The kid hung back from the others, a look of trepidation on his face. Tony approached him. "Hey, man. You okay?"

Martin's dark eyes dropped to the ground. "Yeah." He leaned against the van with his arms crossed over his chest. There was a wall around him screaming "Keep away."

Tony walked on to the next kid, stopping and chatting with all of them, but never letting Martin out of his sight. Something was going on with him. Tony would keep a close eye on him tonight.

Once they made it to the park, Tony and the other chaperones ambled through the park with four teenagers each. Music blared from the outdoor stage and the smells of popcorn, cotton candy and caramel apples bombarded his senses. He couldn't believe how many people had showed up to support the children's home. People jostled everywhere, trying to get a good seat for the talent show.

The constant push of the crowd had Tony on high alert. Crowds provided cover for activities that would seem suspicious elsewhere. The boys ahead of him joked and punched each other. Except for Martin, who hung back searching the crowd.

Up ahead, Tony caught a glimpse of Nick. Martin hurried to join the boys in front of him, suddenly eager to get in on the festivities. What was he up to? Tony recognized a distraction when he saw it. The boys stopped to check out a sunglasses booth and Tony stood back so he could keep an eye on all of them.

Nick stood at the booth closest to them, closely examining a leather belt. Martin's shoulder brushed against Nick's, but the two boys ignored each other. Tony's eyes narrowed. He didn't miss the exchange of a small plastic bag between them. Now, for the distraction.

It didn't take long. Martin popped a goofy pair of sunglasses on his head. "How do these look on me?" His loud voice drew attention while Nick slipped away.

Tony pulled his cell phone out of his pocket and sent Jarrod a text. You're right. Package delivered.

Seconds later his phone buzzed. Thanks. I'll take it from here.

The boys continued perusing the booths as they made their way through the park. Patriotic music blasted through speakers, signaling that the fireworks were about to begin so Tony and the boys found an empty area in the grass and sat down.

Tony continued to scan the area. Dozens of couples were scattered around the grass, cuddling together to watch the night sky, but one couple at the far end of the park drew his attention. Something about the woman, as she wrapped her arms around a man and hugged him.

He directed the teens through the crowd, closer to the couple. The man said something in her ear and her musical laugh drifted above the noise of the crowd. Sabrina's laughter.

Tony's blood ran cold. Her shoulders were missing the tension he'd become accustomed to seeing. Who was the man she was so completely relaxed with? Was this Craig?

Levi sat cross-legged by their feet, munching on popcorn and watching the fireworks. He turned and said something to the man. Tony couldn't hear what was said over the pounding in his ears. His breath came in short gasps. The temper he'd been able to control for years flared and he'd never wanted so badly to punch something.

He turned his attention back to the boys.

"You okay, man?" Kyle held out a bag of popcorn.

Tony took a handful. "Fine."

The sky lit up with a dazzling display of colors, but Tony wasn't able to appreciate it. His eyes kept drifting to Sabrina.

Halfway through the show, she got up and strolled down the pathway toward the portable bathrooms. He got the attention of another chaperone. "I'll be right back. Watch the kids for me." Before he could talk himself out of it, Tony jumped up and followed her. Surprise flickered across her face when she saw him. "Tony. Hi."

"You neglected to mention that your friend from Houston was a man. Is he your boyfriend?"

Her head whipped around. "He's not my boyfriend."

"So you get that cozy with every man you hang around with?" As soon as the words were out of his mouth, he regretted them.

Her nostrils flared. "What I do and who I do it with are my own business." Tossing her long hair over her shoulder, she pushed her way through the crowd.

Tony clenched his fist and walked in circles. His pulse thundering in his ears was louder than the fireworks.

"Excuse me," a voice behind him said. "Are you Tony?"

The woman standing in front of him smiled. Dark brown hair hung in curls around her face. "Yes. I'm sorry, do I know you?"

Her mouth, a tad too wide for her narrow face, grinned. "I knew it had to be you. I've heard so much about you."

"Who are you?" The woman seemed friendly enough, but she wasn't very good at answering questions.

"I'm Julie," she said, like he should know who she was.

"Have we met?"

"Oh, no. Never." Julie waved her hand at

him. "I'm a friend of Sabrina's. Levi looks just like you, so I knew it had to be you."

"Are you from Houston, too? Did you come down with her boyfriend?"

"Boyfriend?" Julie broke into a fit of laughter. "She and Craig may be best friends, but I can assure you, the only woman he goes home with is me."

So what was the display of affection he'd just seen on the grass? "But they were just hugging…"

"Oh, that scamp." She stomped her foot. "I knew better than to leave him alone. Craig probably spilled the beans." She rubbed her tummy. "After seven years of trying, we're finally having a baby. I knew Craig couldn't keep it a secret."

Tony felt a little numb. Now what was he supposed to think?

Julie linked her arm through his. "I'm afraid I'll get lost. Walk me back and I'll tell you all kinds of juicy secrets about our Sabrina."

THE SHAKINESS SHE'D felt when she first saw Tony was replaced with numbness. Then anger. How dare he accuse her of something? Who did he think he was?

Craig stood up. "You look like you're about to fall down. You okay?"

She sank onto the blanket they'd spread on the grass. "I'm just glad y'all are here."

His eyes tightened. "You just saw him, didn't you?"

Biting her bottom lip, she nodded.

"Where is he?" He tried to stand up, but she caught him.

"No. Please. Don't make a scene."

"There is something you aren't telling me," he finally said. "What is it?"

Sabrina laughed nervously. "You know me too well."

"Years of practice," he said. "Now, what is it? Get it off your chest."

She buried her face in her hands while the erratic beat of her heart spoke the truth. She took a deep breath and looked Craig straight in the eye. "I still love him."

Saying the words out loud released the weight from her chest and she was able to breathe in deeply. "I know it sounds crazy, but you don't know what he's been through in his life. By all accounts, he should be jail. Anyone else who'd been in his shoes would've been. The fact that he's here now…"

She stopped and shook her head. "That just

shows how determined he was to make something of his life. It's really amazing." She was proud of him.

"Have you told Tony how you feel?" Craig wrapped an arm around her and pulled her closer to him.

She didn't have to tell him. He knew. Still, speaking the words out loud wouldn't change anything. She shook her head. "I didn't tell him I was pregnant because I didn't want to force him to come back. He had an opportunity to get out of Salt Creek and make something of his life. I won't tell him I love him now because he's finally achieved everything he's ever wanted. I won't make him give it up for me. Or Levi."

Craig squeezed her hand. He leaned in close, his forehead touching hers. "Despite your tough exterior, you're a hopeless romantic. You want the real deal. You want him to proclaim his undying devotion to you in song. I get it."

She rolled her eyes. "You are so corny. How does Julie ever put up with you?"

Craig wrinkled his nose at her. "Because she's a hopeless romantic, too."

"Honey, look who I found," Julie called from behind them.

Sabrina turned and saw Tony standing with Julie and her heart dropped. Of all the people for Tony to meet, why did it have to be Julie?

"Tony!" Levi stood up and ran over to him.

Craig stood up. "You must be the hero cop."

"I don't know about hero, but I'm a police officer." He shook hands with Craig.

"Sabrina tells us you got promoted to undercover detective. You must be very excited."

Tony looked at Sabrina out of the corner of his eye. "I am. If you'll excuse me, I'm chaperoning some teenagers. I don't want the other chaperones to get overwhelmed."

Sabrina fielded question after question from Julie and Craig for the rest of the fireworks.

"Uh... Mom." Levi stood next to her.

She glanced around. People were folding up their blankets and gathering their stuff. The fireworks show was over. She hadn't even noticed. "You ready?"

They walked in silence back to the parking lot. She scanned the crowd, wondering if she'd see Tony again. If he was close by, he was giving her a wide berth.

When they arrived at Craig's car, Levi paused. He stared down at his feet for a minute before giving her a hug.

The gesture took her by surprise. After weeks of his bristly attitude, his sudden show of emotion brought a lump to her throat. She hugged him tight.

"Mom, are you sure you're going to be okay until Monday?" Levi climbed into the backseat. "I don't have to go camping with Craig and Julie."

"Nonsense. You love camping with them." She ruffled his hair. "I can take care of myself, you know."

"Maybe you and Dad can do something. I think he may be lonely without me, too."

Her heart leaped to her throat. *Dad.* She'd wanted him to accept Tony, but now he had. Just one week before Tony went back to San Antonio. Was Levi old enough to understand, or would he think Tony was abandoning him?

CHAPTER SEVENTEEN

TONY FOLLOWED THE teens back to their van, but his heart was no longer in the conversation. Was Julie right? Was it fear of his job that kept Sabrina from being able to make a commitment to him?

"Ain't that right, Tony?"

"What?" His eyes flew to boys in front of him.

"You got arrested a few times when you were a kid, and they still let you be a cop." Kyle leaned on the van.

Tony nodded. "They were all minor charges and most of them were purged from my record when I turned eighteen."

"I got arrested for shoplifting. Would that keep me from becoming a cop?"

Tony shook his head. "What did you steal and why?" There was a big difference in a kid who stole food because there wasn't any in the house and the kids who stole for the thrill. A good judge knew that.

Kyle popped his knuckles. "I stole a bag of apples."

Tony's tension melted. "Are you interested in being a police officer?"

"I don't know. Maybe. If I could be a cop like you."

Martin snorted. "He won't be around much longer, anyway."

"What do you mean? Why not?" Kyle shot Tony an accusing glance.

Tony took a deep breath. "I'm only here on medical leave. I report back to work at the end of next week."

Kyle was quiet the rest of the ride back to Salt Creek.

Tony kept his eyes focused on the road. Until that moment, he hadn't realized how much he wanted to stay. Was it possible? Was there a way?

Travis Anderson met the boys at the vans and checked them all in. A flicker of surprise crossed his face when he saw Tony. "I didn't know you were supervising tonight." He shook Tony's hand.

"I wasn't. My plans changed last-minute and I decided to lend an extra hand."

Daniel, one of the cabin parents, began rounding up the boys to take them to their cabins. Martin volunteered to stay behind to help clean out the fans.

Travis waited until the large group had left, then he stepped close to Tony. "I wanted to let you know that Karen has announced her retirement. We'll be looking for a new associate supervisor. Interested?"

The man was offering him a job? It could be the perfect solution. There was a possibility he could transfer to the Lampasas County Sheriff's Department. But not for another year. Being a cop was all he'd wanted to do. He was good at it. Could he be happy doing anything else? Even if it was just for a year. "I'm very tempted, Travis. Let me think about it for a few days."

"I can't pay nearly what they pay in San Antonio, but you're welcome here as long as you want to stay." Travis shook his hand and turned to go. "The position won't officially open until the end of the month, but we can start on the paperwork whenever you're ready."

A heavy weight pressed on his chest. Maybe things could work out after all. If he wasn't a cop, could he convince Sabrina to give him a second chance?

His phone vibrated. Jarrod. Still at the home?

Just leaving. He sat in the driver's seat, but didn't start the SUV.

He didn't have to wait long. Meet me in town? Behind the gas station.

Be there in five.

A flash of light blinded him. He squinted. Headlights glared from down the street. The car was parked on the wrong side of the road, angled right at the parking lot. The headlights flashed off, then back on again. One of the vans from Little Mountain flashed their lights back. The green car turned around and sped away.

Something came up. Give me fifteen minutes. He sent the message to Jarrod and kept on eye on the van. From here, he couldn't tell who the driver was.

Tony parked across the street from Little Mountain and watched the other vans unload. A tall, skinny woman climbed out of the driver's seat of the van he was watching. When all the kids headed inside, she waved Martin over. The two of them walked into the house together. Just before they got inside, she handed something to Martin.

The streets were deserted as Tony drove

through town. Jarrod's patrol car was parked behind a gas station on the edge of town. Unless someone was looking, they'd never see the vehicle hiding in the shadows. Tony parked next to the car and rolled down his window.

Jarrod's elbow was in the open window of his car. "How'd things go at the home? Anyone give you any trouble?"

"I know where they're getting it."

"Where?"

Tony told him about the flashing lights and the girl. "They left it in the van. I'd be willing to bet Martin will sneak back out to get it. You should put surveillance on him."

"Hmm…" Jarrod scratched the stubble darkening his chin. "Do we bust them now, or try to find out who the supplier is? Was the girl Rachel Johnson?"

"It could be, but I'm not sure. She usually comes to work after I leave. I'll find out."

The truth was, he'd been so wrapped up in watching Sabrina, someone very well could've talked to Martin. It was just dumb luck that he happened to catch the two vehicles signaling each other.

How could he have made such a stupid mistake? He knew better than to let emotions get in the way of his job. It might not be an official job, but Jarrod was counting on him.

Jarrod pulled out a notepad and went over all the people he'd seen Nick talk to after leaving the sunglass booth. "But if he made a drop-off, he's sneakier than anyone else I've ever watched. I didn't catch it."

"Maybe he was just picking it up tonight. Or maybe it was for him. Maybe Martin is selling and Nick is just a buyer."

"Are you volunteering tomorrow?" Jarrod tapped his fingers on the side of the patrol car. "I'll work on getting a search warrant for Martin's room and you keep an eye on him."

"Not a problem." The adrenaline that had been rushing though his system all evening began to ebb, leaving him feeling a little drained.

"Didn't you say you did mostly street duty in San Antonio?" Jarrod waited for Tony's affirmative nod. "They're wasting your talent. You should look into undercover work."

"I am. Captain Rodriguez called to tell me, not only did I get the promotion to detective, I'll be running my own undercover task force."

"That's fantastic." Jarrod's freckled face broke out in a wide grin.

"Thanks." Shouldn't he be more excited? It was the culmination of everything he'd worked for over the last seven years. Most of his colleagues would kill for this chance. Stakeouts, undercover operations to bust the bad guys. It was everything a cop could dream of.

"It's a shame Sheriff Cameron couldn't swing the transfer. It'd be great to work with you."

Tony shrugged. "A year isn't that long. Maybe I'll still be around."

SABRINA PARKED HER car behind her dad's truck, feeling the first signs of a tension headache. It was after midnight and she was dead tired. Thank goodness tomorrow was Saturday and she could sleep in.

She'd only taken one step toward the house when her father appeared at the door.

"The group home called. They have an emergency and need you to get there right away."

She turned around and got back in her car. Hadn't she just been wishing for a distraction? Not like this, though. She hoped everyone was okay.

As soon as she arrived, she saw a little girl on the steps.

"Mia, where's everyone at? And why aren't you in bed?"

Mia nodded to the staircase. "Ms. Karen told me to wait down here for you. Lacey is bleeding again, so Ms. Karen is with her."

"Bleeding? Take me to her."

The little girl ran up the stairs and Sabrina took them two at a time to keep up. They went through an open door to a large dormitory-style room and Sabrina stopped short. Pandemonium had erupted. Girls of all ages were running around the room. Several jumped on the beds while four more engaged in a pillow fight. In the corner of the room, Karen sat with her arms and legs wrapped around a struggling girl. Blood poured from the girl's arms and the frazzled woman was trying to apply pressure to the wound and yell at the girls running amok in the room.

Instinct kicked in. "KNOCK. IT. OFF!" Sabrina's voice was so loud that most of the girls stopped running in surprise. "You." She pointed to one of the older girls. "Go get me a large bowl of water. And you, take these little ones to the recreation room and play a game."

Another one of the older girls tried to slip through the door. "Not so fast, Keisha." Sabrina twirled around to her. "You start cleaning this mess up."

Keisha crossed her arms. "What if I don't?"

Sabrina took two steps to the girl and looked her straight in the eye. "I suggest you don't try to find out."

The girl dropped her defiant gaze and bent down to pick up sheets scattered around the floor. Once again, the room erupted into chaos, but this time it was organized chaos. With a sigh of relief, she hurried to the woman and child in the corner.

"What happened? Where is your help?" She pulled the pillowcase off a pillow on the floor. With quick rips, she tore it into strips.

Karen was talking in a low, soft tone to the girl in her arms. When the girl had calmed down some, she gave Sabrina a soft laugh. "Lacey got cut and she panics at the sight of blood."

Got cut? She raised one eyebrow, but didn't correct her. Sabrina recognized a cutter when she saw one. Scars from previous episodes crisscrossed the girl's forearms.

The girl hadn't panicked. She'd been fighting Karen's attempts to help. Her eyes pleaded with Sabrina not to reveal the girl's secret, so Sabrina nodded and began to wrap the tiny arms with the makeshift bandages. "I'm sorry that you've had an accident, Lacey. But it doesn't look too bad. I think we can have you fixed up in no time."

Lacey raised her face to look at Sabrina. "I'm sorry. I didn't mean to."

The pain in Lacey's eyes was heartbreaking. She smoothed the girl's stringy hair back and patted her cheek. "There, there. Accidents happen. Let's get you fixed up."

Together, she and Karen walked Lacey to the medical office where they could get her cleaned up. "Where is the rest of the staff?" she whispered over Lacey's head.

Karen frowned. "Rachel is the weekend supervisor. She got a phone call a little while ago and said she had a family emergency and took off."

"You don't believe her?"

"No. She'll be back by morning and put on a big show. You just wait and see." Karen laid the girl on a cot and tucked a blanket in around her.

Sabrina reached out to squeeze Karen's hand. "I'm really going to miss you when you retire. Are you sure you don't want to stay on a few more years?"

"Nonsense," Karen laughed. "I'm not worried. With Tony coming on staff, I can rest easy knowing these kids will have someone they can count on."

Sabrina almost dropped the box of bandages she was holding. "That's impossible. Tony's going back to San Antonio."

Karen shook her head. "Travis told me this morning that he was going to offer the job to Tony."

Sabrina's throat went dry. Had she jumped to the wrong conclusion? Was Tony giving up the job he loved to stay in Salt Creek? "But what about his promotion in San Antonio?"

"I don't know. I'm just repeating what I heard. Now, if you'll excuse me, it's one in the morning and I need to get those little girls back in bed."

Sabrina nodded. "We'll be fine." She sank into the chair next to the cot. In all the excitement, her headache had disappeared. Now it returned with full force. Standing up, she rolled her head in a circle and dug through the cabinet for some ibuprofen.

A tall woman with bright pink hair stuck her head into the room.

"Can I help you?" Sabrina asked.

The woman's eyes narrowed. "I'm the night

supervisor for the girls' dormitory. Who are you? Where's Karen?"

"I'm the medical assistant, Sabrina Davis." She held out her hand.

"Rachel Johnson."

Johnson? Sabrina stepped back. "Are you kin to Allen?"

The woman gave her a saccharine sweet smile. "I'm his sister-in-law. Kurt's my husband."

Her mouth fell open. Kurt was married? The Kurt she remembered had been a hateful, arrogant bully. He derived great pleasure from making other people miserable. She couldn't imagine him being nice enough to anyone to win their heart.

She'd grown up with Allen. He'd been a sweet guy, right up until high school. Then he'd spent his time trying to live up to his older brother's bully reputation.

"We had a little bit of excitement. Karen's upstairs trying to get the girls back into bed."

Rachel walked away without a word. "You're welcome," Sabrina said to the empty door.

After documenting the incident, Sabrina put the file away and straightened up the office. Lacey was sleeping and there was still no sign of Karen. She'd better call Dad and let him know she might be here a while. But as soon as she picked up the receiver, voices on the line caused her to freeze.

"I need it delivered tonight." Urgency marked the woman's voice.

A man answered. "You haven't paid me for the last package. No more shipments until I get my money."

"Fine," the woman huffed. "I'll have one of the boys meet you at the old roundhouse at midnight. But I want my package."

The line went dead and Sabrina replaced the receiver in the cradle as quietly as she could. The light next to the recreation room extension blinked and then went off. She tiptoed down the hall to the rec room.

Rachel pushed past her and took a few steps before stopping. "Did you pick up the phone just now?"

Sabrina swallowed the panic. "No. Why?"

Rachel shook her head. "I thought I heard the line click."

Sabrina forced a laugh. "Sorry. I was busy cleaning up blood."

"Of course you were." Rachel tossed her stringy pink hair over her shoulder and coasted down the hall.

A shudder ran through her. Looked like Kurt had finally found someone who could match up to him.

Tony yawned. He'd barely gotten to sleep when Jarrod called. He'd received a tip that something was going down at the roundhouse. Eager to get his mind off his problems, Tony volunteered to watch the rundown building out of town while Jarrod waited farther down the road.

Once a train repair shop for the railroad, the building was large enough to house three locomotives. It hadn't been used in decades, but had seen its share of high school parties. Empty beer cans and remnants of bonfires littered the interior.

Jarrod's tip was perfect. At exactly 3 a.m., the same green Chevy Nova Tony'd seen at the park pulled up to the building. The heavy wooden door creaked and the driver entered. A few minutes later, he exited with a large duffel bag, followed by two boys.

Tony focused his binoculars on them. Thanks to the full moon and headlights, Nick and Martin were easy to spot. The driver pulled another bag from the trunk of his car and handed it to them. Fifteen minutes later, the Nova sped off.

Jarrod spoke into his radio. "I've got a deputy trailing the Nova. Hang tight. I'm on my way. We'll bust the kids before they leave."

Tony stopped him. "Wait. Follow Nick. Find out who they're taking it to."

Nick's truck didn't follow the dirt road back to the main road. Instead, it bounced down the rutted out road that once ran alongside the railroad tracks.

Tony stayed crouched in the brush until all the vehicles had left. "Jarrod, you better move. Nick went the back way. I repeat. He's not headed to you."

"I'll be there in two minutes." Jarrod blazed a path to the roundhouse. He signaled for Tony to come out.

"Good thing I had an officer waiting on the back roads, just in case. My patrol car would never make it where Nick's going." Jarrod pulled out his flashlight. "The officer was told not to stop him. Just keep an eye on him."

"How many officers does this little town have?" Tony was impressed. In San Antonio, calling for backup was easy, but in this little town, the resources were limited. "Aren't most of them in Lampasas?"

"I called in a couple of officers to help tonight. We've been waiting for this for a while."

The officer tailing Nick's truck informed Jarrod he'd lost sight of the boys. "Sorry, Butler," the voice on the radio crackled. "I lost him somewhere around the school. He's probably halfway down Old Lampasas Road by now."

"They aren't taking it back to Lampasas," Tony said. "They wouldn't have brought it here to begin with. This is a drop-off for someplace else."

"Where do you think they went?" Jarrod's eyes darted up and down the side roads of town. "You grew up here. Where would you stash drugs?"

"I never touched the stuff or associated with anyone who did." Tony tapped his fingers on the dash. "Wait a minute. The first night I saw the kids, Nick waited for Kyle on top of Little Mountain. I bet that's where it is."

Jarrod nodded. "Right in plain sight. They'll probably lay low until later. I'll get a drug-sniffing K9 unit out there."

Despite the fact that it was almost four o'clock in the morning, Tony was nowhere near sleeping. The night's adventure had convinced him of one thing. He couldn't quit being a cop. It was in his blood. But what was he going to do about Levi? About Sabrina? Could he convince her to go to San Antonio with him?

When the sun came up, he was sitting on his grandparents' front porch, still trying to think of ways to prove to Sabrina his job wasn't too dangerous.

Clangs from the kitchen told him Abuela was up, too. He stood and stretched. He trudged into the house. Coffee. He needed coffee.

Abuela smiled at him. "Good morning, *mijo*. Were you out all night? Did you get supper?"

He poured a cup of coffee, sat at the table and bit into a piece of the toast that Abuela had stacked on a plate. "I just grabbed a hot dog at the park last night."

Tony looked at the mail on the table. His letter from the SAPD was on top. "Did you read this?"

"It's not addressed to me." Abuela reached out and took his hand. "I've kept my mouth shut long enough. I think you're making a huge mistake."

"How?"

"You can't go back to San Antonio. Your son is here. Your life is here."

Tony reached across the table to hold her hand. "I'm working on it, Abuela."

"We all have choices to make. Choose wisely."

Easier said than done. A job with the sheriff's department wouldn't open for at least a year. In the meantime, he could take over the hardware store and help Papa. Or he could accept Travis's job offer and work at the children's home. But neither of those would make him happy. His dream job waited for him in San Antonio. But how happy could it make him if it meant leaving everyone else behind?

By 9 a.m. he was going stir-crazy. He sent Jarrod several text messages to see if the dogs had found anything yet.

Not yet. Hold tight.

He needed to do something to expend some energy. Papa was already at the hardware store and Abuela had gone shopping in Lampasas.

He picked up his phone. Going nuts. Will be at the hardware store.

Twenty minutes later, he was stocking shelves at the store. This was what he needed. A mindless chore to keep his body busy. The back door opened and Kyle peered around the corner. "Hi, Tony."

"Hi, Kyle." He stepped off the ladder. "Did you call Chris about that job?"

The teen shook his head. "Why bother? If you go back to San Antonio, I won't have a sponsor anymore."

Papa came around the corner. "I'll sponsor you, *mijo*."

Kyle's eyes opened wide. "Really? You will?"

"You do real good work. Chris needs a mechanic like you. If Tony is not here, I'll be happy to sponsor you."

Tony followed him to the back room. Kyle had started a variety of new projects since finishing up the car. Currently he was fixing a lawn mower for Mrs. Whitaker.

"Uh…Tony?"

Tony glanced up. "Yeah?"

Kyle toyed with a wrench he'd removed from the toolbox. "Why do you want to leave Salt Creek?"

"I don't. I want to be here with my son. But I can't walk away from my job."

The door between the storage room and the main building opened and Jarrod stood in the doorway. "Tony? Are you in here?"

"Back here."

"Whoa." Jarrod's eyes widened when he

spotted the old car in the middle of the room. "Nice car."

Tony nodded toward Kyle. "He did all the work."

Kyle sidled by them and bent over the lawn mower.

Jarrod pulled up a stool and sat next to Tony. He nodded.

Tony sat up straight. The dogs must've found what they were looking for. Had they found who else was involved?

Jarrod eyed Kyle and Tony knew he couldn't say much in front of the kid. "By the way, the sheriff wants to talk to you later this week."

He probably wanted a statement on what he'd observed at the home over the last few weeks. "Sure."

CHAPTER EIGHTEEN

SABRINA NEVER LEFT Little Mountain during her lunch hour, but Karen's words rang in her ears all morning. She clocked out and ran to her car, dialing Tony's number. No answer. Where was he?

No one was at his grandparents' house. It was Saturday. Maybe he was at the hardware store. She drove slowly through town, and her heart caught in her throat when she saw his Durango parked outside the hardware store.

The Closed sign was on the door. For as long as she could remember, Antonio closed the store for lunch. Sometimes he reopened at one. Sometimes not until two.

Sabrina pressed a hand to her jittery stomach and pushed the door open, anyway. The store was dark and silent.

Her shoes didn't make a sound as she searched the aisles. Maybe he was in the back storage room.

A light peeked from under the crack of the

door. She took a breath and reached for the handle, just as the door flew open.

Tony stood in front of her, his back rigid and straight. "What are you doing here?" His voice was stilted.

She swallowed. "You didn't answer your phone. I've been looking for you."

"Is Levi okay?"

"Levi's fine. I wanted…" Her throat felt like sandpaper. "I wanted to apologize."

"Apologize?" He frowned. He didn't move.

Oh, good grief. He wasn't going to make this easy for her. She took a deep breath. "Yes. For misleading you at the fireworks. And to tell you not to do it."

In two steps he pushed her back into the store and closed the door behind them. "Not to do what?"

"Karen told me you were going to quit your job to work at the group home." Her voice was shaky. "You love being a cop. You can't give it up. Especially for me."

Tony took her hands in his. "As long as I have you, I'd be happy being a pooper scooper."

She shook her head. "No, you wouldn't."

A knock on the wall behind them pulled them apart. Jarrod held up his phone. "I really hate to interrupt, but Tony, we have a meeting we need to get to."

"Now?"

Sabrina dropped her arms to her sides. "What's going on? Does this have anything to do with Rachel Johnson?"

"Rachel?" Tony and Jarrod spoke in unison.

Jarrod crossed the room. "What do you know about Rachel Johnson?"

His tone of voice alarmed her. "Nothing. I just heard her on the phone last night. That's why I sent you that text."

"You sent me the text? Why did you block your number?"

Jarrod's gaze was intense and she stiffened. Tony traced circles on the back of her hand with his thumb, absorbing some of the stress. She swallowed. "I didn't want Rachel to find out it was me. So I blocked my number and deleted the text as soon as I sent it. Did I do something wrong?"

Tony grinned. "You know what this means?"

Again, they spoke in unison. "Kurt Johnson."

Sabrina's eyes darted back and forth between the two men. "Someone want to tell me what's going on here?"

Tony took her by the hand and led her to

the door. "I'll explain it later. Go home and wait for me. I'll be out there as soon as I get finished."

"I'm on my lunch break. I have to get back to Little Mountain."

Both men exchanged worried glances and Tony shook his head. "Call in and tell them you got sick or something. Don't go back there today."

"You're scaring me, Tony. What's going on?"

Tony walked her to her car. "I'm not at liberty to say right now. But something is about to go down, and if it spills over to Little Mountain, I don't want you anywhere around there."

"What about the kids? If it's too dangerous for me, it's too dangerous for the kids." She couldn't just walk away knowing the children might not be safe.

"It's not like that." Tony opened the car door for her. A battle raged in his eyes.

"Don't lie to me," Sabrina said. "Not after all this time."

He let out a long slow breath. "We think Kurt and Rachel Johnson are using some of the teenagers at the children's home to smuggle drugs. People do desperate things when they know they're about to get caught and I don't want you in the way."

Her heart lodged in her throat. "You think Kurt might try to hurt me?" Thank God Levi was still camping.

"I'm not willing to risk it, so I'd rather not tempt him. He knows the best way to get to me is through you." He ran the back of his hand along her jawline. "Levi's still out of town with your friends, right?"

Her mouth was too dry to speak. She nodded.

Jarrod said, "We need to roll, partner."

Tony pressed a kiss against her forehead. "Go home. Promise me."

She nodded. Did she have any other choice? Her hands shook so much she could barely start the car. Finally, the engine roared to life. At the intersection, instead of turning toward Little Mountain, she went straight. In her rearview mirror, she could see that Tony watched until she was safely through the intersection.

It took a moment to locate the cell phone in her purse while she was driving. She hit the speed dial button and waited for Karen to answer the phone. "Karen, I'm going to take the afternoon off. I think I ate something bad at lunch and I'm not feeling too well."

"Don't you worry. You go home and get some rest. We'll manage without you."

She ended the call and waves of hysteria washed through her. Had Jarrod recruited Tony for some type of undercover sting operation? He hadn't even gone back to San Antonio yet and she was already living out her worst nightmare. If he made it back to her, she was never speaking to him again.

JARROD AND TONY stood in the parking lot of Little Mountain. A search warrant for Martin's cabin had already been served and they were waiting for a drug-sniffing K9 unit to arrive.

All the residents and staff were being escorted into the recreation room. Tony followed a uniformed officer there and scanned the room for Martin.

He raised his hand to quiet everyone. "Good afternoon, ladies and gentlemen. I've been asked to speak to all of you and inform you of what's going on. The county sheriff's office suspects that there may be drugs on campus. They are waiting for a K9 unit to arrive from Lampasas. So if anyone has something to admit, now is the time to do it. Before the dogs find it. And they will find it."

Martin shifted in his chair, his eyes darting around the room.

Karen walked to the front of the room and smiled. "We're going to be here awhile, so we might as well get comfortable. Pizza's been ordered and will be here soon. Until then, let's watch a movie."

The room was buzzing with action as chairs were stacked and pushed to the side. The younger students plopped on the rug in front of the projector screen.

All the while, Tony kept an eye on Martin. The chaos in the room seemed to be exactly what Martin needed. He slipped out the back door. He quickly texted Jarrod: Headed your way.

"What's going on here?" A loud voice caused everyone to stop what they were doing.

Tony slid over to Allen Johnson. "Didn't an officer brief you outside?"

"No. They just told me to come in here and that no one was allowed to leave." Allen straightened the tie of his three-piece suit.

Tony pulled a flash drive out of his pocket. "This is video footage from a security camera behind Montoya Hardware. You'll see two boys, Nick Johnson and Martin Burton, sneaking around in the alley."

Allen's mouth twitched. It was video footage from the same camera that had proved Tony innocent of the robbery Kurt and Allen had set him up for.

The other man frowned. "That's impossible. The boys here have a curfew. And why would my nephew be hanging out with them?"

Tony shook his head. "You'll have to ask him. All I was told is that the police caught Nick with a bunch of drugs and he implicated some staff and students here at Little Mountain."

Allen cursed under his breath. "It's Rachel, isn't it? I should've known better than to let Travis hire her."

Jarrod walked through the door and nodded. Tony pointed him out. "I think that officer wants to speak to you and Travis."

They all went to Travis's office.

Jarrod closed the door. "Last night, one of your employees made contact with a known drug dealer. She helped Martin sneak out of the residence where he and Nick exchanged money for drugs. The boys hid four hundred pounds of marijuana on top of Little Mountain where it was recovered this morning by Nick."

"What does this mean for Little Mountain?" A note of panic laced Travis's voice.

"It's been determined that the employee was acting without the knowledge of other members of the staff and the county sheriff's office has decided not to pursue a charge against the home. Rachel Johnson has already been taken into custody and booked on a variety of charges. Officers are now looking for Kurt."

Allen's shoulders slumped. "I thought he was doing better. He just got out of rehab."

Tony felt sorry for him. Allen clearly loved his brother and didn't have anything to do with the drugs. "Don't ever give up."

Allen nodded sadly. "Tony, can I speak privately with you?"

"Yes." He stiffened. Didn't Allen know he'd been volunteering at the home? Would he try to stop Travis from hiring him? If he decided to stay, that is.

Both men waited in silence while the others left the room. Allen walked slowly over to Tony and pulled him into a bear hug.

"I always wondered what happened to you. And I've waited a long time to apologize."

Until that moment, Tony had never thought he needed an apology. But the words meant more to him than he'd ever imagined. "Thanks. I appreciate that."

"Excuse me," Allen said. "I need to go talk to Travis."

Stepping into the hallway, he caught Jarrod's attention. "I need to go. I promised Sabrina I'd fill her in."

Tony reached the entrance when he heard someone calling his name. He turned around to see Kyle running toward him.

"Police arrested Martin a few minutes ago. Did you have something to do with that?"

"I did, Kyle. Remember when I told you that doing nothing is as bad as helping the drug dealers?"

Kyle nodded. "I know that. I've been sending Scott's dad tips for weeks."

"That was you?" Jarrod asked.

"Yes. But I didn't know someone here was involved. What's going to happen now? To the home, I mean."

Tony nodded to the closed doors. "Nothing. The home wasn't at fault. I'm proud of you and I want you to know that I'll never give up on you. Or any of the kids here. I'll do everything I can to make sure you have a home."

"We want that, too." Travis stood in the open door.

Allen stepped around Travis and extended his hand. "Travis told me he offered you a job, but I have the feeling the sheriff's department is going to be keeping you pretty busy."

Tony clasped Kyle's shoulder and grinned. "Don't worry, I'll always make time for Little Mountain."

CHAPTER NINETEEN

SHE PACED AROUND the house all afternoon. Tony had said he'd come over later. Where was he? She'd already swept and mopped, dusted everything twice and scrubbed out the refrigerator. What more could she do? She wandered through the house.

The dirty clothes hamper was only half full, but she carried it across the backyard to the laundry shed. The old house was too small for a washer and dryer, so her father had added a laundry room to the back of his workshop. Her mother had been so excited the day Dad installed the appliances. It hadn't taken much to make Mom happy. And making Mom happy was what had made Dad happy.

She stuffed clothes into the top of the old machine. All she'd ever wanted was to have someone look at her the way her mom and dad used to look at each other. No. Scratch that. She wanted Tony to look at her that way.

She turned to go back into the house and ran into Tony.

"Whoa." He caught her arms when she almost bounced off him.

"Sorry. I didn't see you there." She'd been too busy wishing for something that she'd never have. "Is everything okay? What happened?"

"Drug dogs found a stash of marijuana hidden on top of Little Mountain. They hid in the bushes until Kurt showed up to recover it. Turns out, Nick would pick up a message from the supplier and pass it off to Martin, who in turn helped Rachel hide the drugs. Then Kurt would wait for the coast to clear and he'd pick it up."

Martin was one of the few teens at the home that she hadn't connected with. Something about the way he stared at her had given her the creeps, so unless he came to the medical office, she steered clear of him. "So it's over?"

"For the most part." He lifted her chin to look at him. "It's my turn to apologize for snapping at you at the fireworks. I was jealous and there's no excuse for my behavior."

Maybe because she'd just been dreaming about Tony looking at her, it was easy to imagine that his eyes were filled with love, not remorse. "It's okay. I could've set you straight, but I didn't."

Tony tucked a loose strand of hair behind her ear, sending shock waves down her neck. "I wanted to talk to you about something."

The whir of the washing machine faded as the thumping of her heart increased. "What?"

The warmth in the stuffy shed was mild compared to the heat radiating from his body. Sabrina tried to step back and give them both some air, but Tony refused to let her move. He brushed his lips across hers, softly at first, then with more demand. She was only too willing to respond.

Her fingers tangled in his hair, pulling him closer. She knew she should break away, but she couldn't. Just for a moment, she wanted to remember what it was like to be loved. She wanted to be engulfed by feeling and forget about all the responsibilities that had weighed her down for so long.

Pulling away, she pressed her fingers to her trembling lips. "What did you want to talk to me about?"

"This." He nuzzled her ear, sending chills down her neck.

She tried to push away from him. "You don't make any sense."

He rubbed her shoulders. "I needed to know if your friend Julie was right."

Julie. She rolled her eyes. Julie was convinced that everyone would find their knight in shining armor. When she brought Levi home tomorrow, Sabrina was going to give her a piece of her mind. "Whatever she said, don't believe it."

"Tell me the truth. Is it me you don't love? Or my job?"

Sabrina let out a heavy sigh. "It doesn't matter, does it? They go together."

"Growing up, I didn't have a home. I rarely slept in the same place for more than a month. Everywhere I went, I was looked down on. No one expected me to succeed at anything. Teachers expected me to fail so they gave me failing grades. When I became a police officer all that changed. It gave me a purpose and a sense of identity. Being a cop is as much a part of my blood as this farm is of yours."

"Yes." Sabrina put one hand on his cheek. "I understand. I've seen the look in your eyes when you talk about your job. I know how much you love it. Which is why I won't let you throw it away for me."

He covered her hand with his where it rested on his cheek. His intense gaze sent heat through her. "For ten years I tried to move on. Something was always missing. I didn't know what it was until I saw you again. You and Levi make me whole. Come to San Antonio with me."

"I'm proud of the man you've become. Of the father that you are. Levi will be here whenever you can get away, but I can't share that life with you." She felt like her heart was breaking all over again. Why couldn't he have asked her to go with him a decade ago? She would've followed him all over the world, if only he'd asked.

She couldn't let herself love him. She'd never survive losing him again.

"I'm not giving up. I needed to see for myself if you still loved me." He caught her face in his hands. "And now I know. You can't kiss me like that and tell me you don't love me, too."

She took advantage of his confusion and stepped out of his grip. "I can't let you give up your job for me and Levi. Sooner or later, you'd resent us for it."

"So you want me to leave?" His eyes were cold.

"Yes. There's nothing for you here." She walked back out into the sunshine and rushed into the house.

"Bree," he called from the porch, a smug look on his face. "You still love me. And I'll make you admit it."

If her hands weren't shaking so badly, she'd have thrown something at him.

TONY COULDN'T KEEP from grinning all the way to town. He was making progress. With her in his arms, he felt...complete. Like there was nothing he couldn't do. She'd built a wall around her heart and he was determined to knock it down. Was this how Sabrina felt when they first met?

From the very beginning, she'd pursued him and he'd pushed her away. It didn't matter how many people warned her about him, she was convinced that he was worth it. All his life people had let him down. By the time he went to live with his grandparents, the wall he'd built around his heart was thick and solid. She'd chipped away at it until he let her in.

He was too wired to sit around his grandparents' house, so he drove up and down the back roads of town. Some things never changed. The high schoolers still sat in the bank parking lot on Friday and Saturday nights. Farmers and ranchers had coffee at

The Eagle's Nest every morning and solved the world's problems several times over. Women still sat around the beauty shops and gossiped about everything that happened in town.

Everywhere he looked, things seemed the same. On the surface. But the very fact that a county deputy had sought him out when he got to town was evidence enough of change. Or was he the one who'd changed? Had he been so blinded by his own biases that he'd failed to see the community for what it was? Good people who were willing to help out their neighbor, even if they sometimes were a little hesitant to let outsiders in.

A manila envelope on the passenger seat, stamped and ready to go. His application for the county sheriff's office. He didn't need a new job. He had a great one in San Antonio, one that appreciated him. He had the letter of promotion on the kitchen table to prove it. If he was smart, he'd send his acceptance letter to his captain.

A picture of Sabrina and Levi flashed in his mind. His stomach clenched. How could he abandon his son?

Was it abandoning him if he lived just two and half hours away? He'd still see Levi every weekend and he'd be close enough to attend some of his soccer games. Some. Except when he was on an undercover assignment. Or a drug bust was set to go down too close to the weekend. He gulped. That wasn't good enough. He'd already missed ten years with Levi and he didn't want to miss out on anything else.

He loved being a cop. But he loved his family more. His family. Sabrina and Levi. Didn't they count more than a paycheck? The job Travis offered at Little Mountain was as far from police work as it could be, but he enjoyed working with the kids. They needed someone to believe in them. Someone who'd give them a second chance. His heart began to pound. Someone like him.

If he really wanted to make a difference in the lives of kids who'd been affected by drugs, Little Mountain was the perfect place for him. A peace settled over his heart and a weight he didn't even realize he carried lifted.

He was suddenly anxious to get home and tell them about his decision. They'd be thrilled, even if Sabrina wasn't. Her words contradicted the emotion in her eyes and the passion in her kiss. Why couldn't she just ask him to stay?

It wasn't late and he knew his grandparents would be up. He jumped onto the porch, ignoring the stairs and burst into the living room. "What's with all the racket?" Papa frowned from his recliner, the remote in his hand.

Tony pulled his shoulders back. "I need to talk to you."

Abuela set down her needlework. "Last time you said that, you gave us a great-grandchild. You didn't find another one, did you?" Only the twinkle in her eye betrayed the sense of humor under the surface.

"Not this time." He grinned and sat on the couch beside her. "I think you should know that I've decided to stay in Salt Creek permanently."

"Oh, *mijo*!" Abuela grabbed his face and kissed him on each cheek. "You've made me so happy."

Papa folded the footstool of his recliner. "Why would you do that? There's nothing here for you. You're going to give up your promotion to move here and do what?"

"I love being a cop. Eventually, I'd like to work for the county sheriff's department. They don't have any openings right now, but

Travis offered me a job at Little Mountain. I could work there until something opens up."

His grandfather took his glasses off. "You would give up being a cop to work with the children at Little Mountain?"

He moved to kneel beside the old man's chair. "You saved me, Papa. I want to help others the way you helped me. I can do that at Little Mountain."

"Yes, you can. But you're a cop and you can't do both. What happens to the children at Little Mountain when you leave them to work at the Sheriff's Department?"

"I'm still working that out."

Papa shook his head sternly. "I want you to do what makes you happy, but don't start something at Little Mountain that you can't finish."

Finish what you start. One of Papa's rules. Under his watchful eyes, Tony hadn't gotten away with anything. He'd spent the first six months in the town trying to prove just how much he hated it. But no matter what he did, his grandparents hadn't given up on him. And they'd held him responsible for his actions.

How many hours had it taken him to whitewash an old barn he'd defaced with spray paint? Or worked after school to pay for damages he'd caused? The worst part was having to stand in front of someone and apologize. It was easy to throw a rock through a window or decorate a building with graffiti, but understanding the impact his actions had on others was a difficult pill to swallow.

His grandparents had never talked about his mother. He always suspected it was too painful for them. "I don't know why Mama left you. I don't know why she never told me about you. But maybe it happened for a reason. Maybe I grew up the way I did so that I could help others."

"I know why she left," Abuela said quietly. "She was a daddy's girl from the moment she could talk. She followed him everywhere. I could scold her and she'd just glare at me. But Antonio…" she sighed. "Antonio could look at her and she would burst into tears.

"I think she decided she'd rather run away from home and live on her own than to tell her father she was pregnant. That was her way. She never faced her problems. It was much easier to hide from them."

A knot settled in his stomach. He was just like that. It was always easier to run away from his problems than discuss them. Was that what Sabrina was doing, too? Was she pushing him away because she thought he was leaving anyway?

Abuela stood up from the sofa. She stepped close and took his face in her hands, pressing another kiss to his cheek. "You used to be like that, *mijo*, but no more. You're strong. You face your problems. I'm proud of you."

Guilt weighed on his chest like a boulder. His cheeks flamed hot, and he was too ashamed to tell his grandmother that was exactly what he'd been doing.

"GOOD MORNING, ROBERT." Tony waited for him to open the door. "I need to talk to Sabrina."

"She's not here."

He knew that. Her car was gone. Where was she? "Will she be back soon?"

Robert's face twisted. "No."

Tony waited, but it was obvious Robert wasn't going to offer any more information. "I know you don't like me, but please, I need to speak with her."

"We should talk, first." Robert held open the door and waited for Tony to enter. "I want to know what your intentions are."

"My intentions are to marry her and love her every day for the rest of her life." Tony pulled his shoulders back. "I'd like to have your blessing, but honestly, it won't stop me if you don't give it."

Robert laughed. "I don't reckon it would stop her, either. But maybe you should tell me what you did that's got her all in a tizzy."

"Sabrina is afraid I'm going to regret quitting my job in San Antonio."

"You quit your job in the city? That's a big step." Robert leaned back in his chair. "How're you gonna support Levi with no job?"

"I've been offered a position at Little Mountain, but I also have my application in with the Lampasas County Sheriff's Department. If they don't hire me, I'll apply with San Saba, Goldthwaite and every little town in a fifty-mile radius."

"So you're not going to quit being a cop?"

"I can't quit being a cop any more than you can quit being a farmer." Tony shook his head.

If he could get Robert to believe in him, why couldn't he get Sabrina to?

Robert scratched his head. "She's in Lampasas trying to apply for a grant. She got accepted into the nursing program and needs it for tuition."

"No offense, Robert," Tony said, "but didn't she get an inheritance when her mother died?"

"She used most of it for her prerequisites. Once she starts the program, she won't be able to work full-time anymore. Little Mountain has agreed to use her part-time, but she says it won't be enough to cover it all. Darn girl won't let me pay for nothing, either."

"Do you know what grant she's applying for?" Sabrina might not want anyone's help, but she was about to get it.

Robert dug some papers out of a drawer in the kitchen. He pulled out a notepad with Sabrina's messy scrawl scribbled across it. "Here. That's all the information I can give you."

It took a few minutes to decipher the handwriting, but Tony managed to do it. His chest swelled. "Thank you, Robert. I won't let her down."

Tony jumped in his Durango and headed to Central Texas College as fast as he could go.

The clerk behind the desk was young, which was a plus. When she called Tony's number, he put on his most charming smile and sat across from her. It took him all of ten minutes to convince her to help him.

"I could probably lose my job if this goes badly." The young woman glanced over her shoulder.

Tony's knee bounced with energy. "I don't want you to do anything that will make you feel uncomfortable. All I need is a letter on college stationary and a college stamp."

She shrugged. "It's okay. This job stinks anyway and I love a grand gesture. It's so romantic. What do you want the letter to say?"

He rattled off the information to her. Her fingers flew across the keyboard. "I changed the wording a little to make it sound more believable."

With an official stamp across the bottom, no one would know that it was a bogus letter. He should feel guilty for deceiving Sabrina, but he didn't. Not at all. "This looks so great I could kiss you right now!"

She turned purple and grinned. "Good luck. I wish I could find a guy willing to create a fake grant to pay my way through school."

Tony winked and floated down the hallway. He dropped the envelope in a mailbox outside. No use sending a letter from the college if the postmark didn't match up.

Now to go back to Salt Creek and let Sabrina know he was staying and there was nothing she could do about it.

Tony marched up to Sabrina's porch. Her

car was here and this time, she was going to listen to him. He pounded on the door.

"I'm right here," Sabrina yelled.

The brush of her body as he stepped inside sent electrical shocks through him. Was it any wonder he'd never been able to connect with anyone else in the last ten years? Just being in the same room with Sabrina now was enough to make him lose his train of thought.

She crossed her arms. "What is so important that you have to break down the door?"

Tony cleared his throat. "I think you may be under a false impression."

She frowned. "I don't think so."

"I was offered a promotion, but I never accepted it. I'm not taking it. I already turned in my resignation."

Her face remained neutral and Tony held his breath. Did she need more?

He stepped toward her. "Did you hear me? I'm not leaving."

"I heard you." Her voice was clipped. "You're making a mistake."

"Loving you could never be a mistake."

She blinked. "Are you sure? I mean, about staying?"

"Absolutely. I'll never make the same mistake I did ten years ago." He did what he'd been wanting to do since she opened the door. He pulled her into his arms and kissed her.

A loud moan came from the sofa. "Come on, guys. Gross. Are you going to be kissing all the time?"

Tony laughed. "You better get used to it. I plan to spend a lot of time kissing your mom."

CHAPTER TWENTY

A SCRATCHING NOISE woke Sabrina up. She lifted her head off the pillow and listened. Crickets chirped and somewhere near the barn, an owl hooted. *Scratch.*

She froze. Something was outside her window. Slowly, she turned her head. The pale moonlight cast shadows across the yard. A figure crouched by her window, messing with the screen. Her heart raced and she eased out from under the sheet.

The figure paused. It lifted its head and peered at her. "Hi, Bree."

She collapsed onto the bed. "What are you doing? You gave me a heart attack."

Tony grinned, mischief dancing across his face. "Got a minute?"

"Hang on." Tossing the covers off, she pulled on her robe and walked to the window next to the one he was fiddling with. "This is the window with the broken screen."

Within moments, the screen popped out

and Tony crawled through the window. He sat on the floor next to the bed, in the corner farthest from the door. That way, if her dad opened the door, he could duck down and hide. Just like in high school.

"You're crazy." She leaned against the bed next to him. "Why're you here?"

He shrugged. "I've spent a lot of time thinking about my future the last few days. Since it's your future, too, I thought we should discuss it."

Sabrina studied his face. He looked...drained. "Does this have something to do with the job at the children's home?"

Like so many nights before, he sat next to her on the floor but didn't touch her. "Yes. Are you still afraid that I'll regret leaving the force and resent you for it?"

Sabrina pressed her lips together and nodded. Despite the warm summer breeze coming through her window, she shivered. "I don't want you to be stuck in a job you hate because you feel like you have to stay."

"What if I told you that I'm not taking the job for you? I'm going to accept the job for me."

The urge to run her finger along the scar on his jaw had her gripping her hands together in her lap. "I don't understand. What do you mean?"

"I mean, the kids at Little Mountain need me. And I need them." The words were spoken lightly, but they rang with conviction.

The passion in his voice sent tingles up her arm. "I think you missed your calling. You should've been a counselor, not a policeman."

Tony chuckled softly. "The kind of kids I want to help would never go to a counselor of their own free will. The judge can order them to see one, but they'd never really open up. Everything stays locked up in here."

One hand came up to rest on his chest. Sabrina covered it with her hand. His heart pounded below her fingertips. "You used to be the same way. What changed?"

He took her hand in his and traced his finger over her palm. His voice was thick with emotion and heat rolled off his body in waves. "You know the answer to that."

Yes, she thought she did. But she needed to hear it, anyway. Shivers raced up her arm from the touch of his hand on hers. "Tell me. When did things change?"

"Ten years ago, I was sitting in a jail cell in Lampasas, mad at the world. I hated Salt Creek. I hated the fact that no matter what I did, all people saw was a troubled kid with no parents. And I didn't help things. I was belligerent and angry. It was too easy to believe that I'd been the one stealing things from stores in town.

"Then an officer unlocked the cell and said I was free to go. I had no idea you told the police I'd been with you all night." He squeezed her fingers in between his. "No one had ever stood up for me before. You put your reputation on the line for me."

"I couldn't stand by and let you go to jail for something you didn't do." Sabrina's heart caught in her throat. "And everyone would've known nine months later, anyway. That was the night Levi was conceived."

He shifted his body to face her. Brushing her hair from her face, he ran his finger along her jawline. "I'm sorry you had to go through all that alone."

She raised her chin. "I wasn't alone. You were there every time I looked at Levi. And I'm sorry I didn't tell you. You deserved to know. I was just too scared. We both left because we were too afraid of the consequences of our actions. You didn't want me to give up school and I didn't want you to feel obligated to marry me."

His eyes tightened. "Was the thought of marrying me that horrible?"

The pain in his eyes was visible, even in the dark, moonlit room. "No. But building a life with someone who didn't love me was."

"You don't still believe that, do you? Don't you know that sticking up for me that night, putting yourself on the line for me, changed the entire course of my life? I didn't deserve you, but I was going to do everything I could to become a man who did."

Her throat tightened. She wanted to believe him. She wanted to know that he loved her wholly. Fully. With no strings attached. "I'm not sure. In the back of my mind, I'll always wonder if you're only around for Levi."

He wrapped both arms around her and hugged her tight. "Then I'll do whatever I have to do to prove you wrong. I love you, Bree. I never stopped."

She shook her head. "I won't say it. As soon as you hear that word, you freak out and leave. You know how I feel. I don't have to say it."

"That's good enough for me."

The warmth of his body wrapped around her like a cocoon. Brushing her lips across his was natural instinct. His response was immediate and he captured her lips, deepening the kiss.

Her pulse exploded and she wrapped her arms around his neck to hold him close.

It was Tony who broke the kiss. "You look exhausted, so let's tuck you into bed. Then you can tell me about Houston."

She wanted to argue, but the yawn that watered her eyes was enough to convince her he was right. She crawled under the sheet on her bed and he snuggled beside her...on top of the covers.

POUNDING ON HER BEDROOM DOOR woke her up. She bolted up out of bed. What time was it? Her robe twisted around her. Why was she in her robe? Oh. Tony. Her gaze shot to the window. Sliding out of bed, she checked the window screen sitting neatly in its frame.

On the edge of the window sill perched three rocks. Three. Not two, like he'd leave when they were in high school. A smile broke out across her face.

"Mom," Levi called from the door. "We're hungry."

Straightening her robe, she danced to the kitchen to make breakfast.

Levi, dressed and ready for the day, peered

up at her from the table. He wrinkled his nose at her. "You look awful. Are you sick?"

"She probably had a hard time sleeping."

Sabrina jerked her head to the door frame separating the kitchen and living room. Tony's one-sided grin warmed her all the way to her toes. Her hand flew to her hair. It was a tangled mess.

He stepped forward and handed her a small paper bag. "I think you look beautiful."

"What's this?"

"Breakfast." He leaned against the counter. "I had the feeling you might oversleep today."

"Thanks." The rich aroma of fresh-baked blueberry muffins filled the room when she opened the bag. She inhaled deeply. "Mmm… your grandmother's muffins."

He jerked to attention. "I'll have you know, I made them myself."

Levi giggled. "No, you didn't. Abuela made them."

"Tattletale." Tony slid into the kitchen chair next to him.

Tony stared at her for a split second and her pulse raced. Her chest swelled as his gaze penetrated right through her. He sauntered across the room to her. "There's something

I need to know. And I need you to be completely honest with me."

"Okay."

"Was my being a police officer a problem because it was in San Antonio? Or would you be opposed to my being a policeman anywhere?"

"Don't ask me to decide your future, Tony. I don't want to stand in the way of what you want."

He rubbed his chin. "You're stuck with me, no matter what, but I have two job offers now and I need you to help me decide which one I should take."

Two job offers? She didn't know he'd been looking anywhere else. Was he already having second thoughts about working at Little Mountain? She let out a long, slow breath.

Tony sat down at the dining room table next to Levi. "This morning the sheriff's department offered me a job as a deputy."

Levi took a bite of his muffin. "Does that mean you'll be a cop again?"

"I still plan on being involved with Little Mountain, just not full-time." He pulled Sabrina down into his lap. "Unless you have any objections. The sheriff's department is better pay and better benefits. But I won't do it if it makes you nervous."

She ran one hand up his arm to rest on his shoulder. "Will you be working undercover?"

He shook his head.

"Will you be taking unnecessary risks?"

"Never."

The love shining in his eyes was enough to chase away her fears. "Okay, then. As long as you promise to come home to me every night, I think I can live with it."

"Sabrina," he whispered in her ear.

"Yes?"

"I need you to take a risk for me." His breath tickled her neck. "Ask me to stay. Please."

She pressed a kiss to his lips. "Stay. Forever."

EPILOGUE

TONY SEARCHED the room. Everywhere he looked he saw friends and family. Sabrina and Abuela set trays of food out for hungry teens while Levi, Kyle and Scott hung up mini graduation caps all around the recreation room.

"You look like the cat who ate the canary." Sabrina sidled up to Tony and wrapped her arms around his waist.

He laughed and pressed a kiss to the top of her head. "I feel like one."

"Dad, can you bring in the cake for Abuela?" Levi called from across the crowded room.

His heart swelled each time he heard that word. Dad. "I'll be right there. Do you mind?"

Sabrina laughed. "Why do you get to do the fun stuff and I get to referee Dad and Papa's checkers war?"

"Someone has to take care of those men. Now that you're a full-fledged nurse, that honor falls on you."

"I guess it does." She grinned and tapped the cap and tassel she hadn't taken off her head since the graduation ceremony at the college that morning. "Although Abuela is a little too anxious for me to start working."

Tony reached down to rub Sabrina's enlarged belly. "Can you blame her? She can't wait to take care of this little girl while you're at work."

"Thank goodness Little Mountain is okay with me continuing to work part-time." Sabrina sighed. "I couldn't stand being away for more than that."

He understood. After missing out on Levi's first ten years, he didn't plan to miss anything with this one. Even diapers.

Jarrod and Marissa meandered across the room. Marissa gave Tony a big hug. "You've done a great job organizing the graduation party."

Jarrod took a sip of his punch. "I see Kyle made it home from college for the special occasion."

"Yes. And it's taking everything I have to convince him to stay at school when the baby's born." Sabrina wrapped her arm around her husband.

Marissa patted Sabrina's stomach. "Can

you blame him? He's lived with y'all for the past two years. He sees her as his sister."

A few minutes later, the Butlers went to visit with another couple, leaving Sabrina and Tony alone.

"By the way." Sabrina wrapped her arms around his neck and kissed him. "Thank you."

"For what?"

"I called the school to find out the address of NGU Industries. I wanted to send them a thank-you letter for the grant they awarded me, the one that covered my tuition. I talked to a very sweet woman who kept telling me how lucky I was."

"Huh." Tony nodded. "That's weird."

She slapped his chest. "What does NGU stand for?"

"Never Give Up." Taking her face in his hands, he kissed the tip of her nose. "You've made all my dreams come true. I just want a chance to redeem myself by making yours come true."

"You're redeemed," she said, just before she kissed him.

* * * * *

*Look for the next Harlequin Heartwarming
romance from debut author
LeAnne Bristow, coming soon!*

*And if you love secret baby stories and
romances with rugged heroes, read
Tara Taylor Quinn's HER SOLDIER'S BABY,
Leigh Riker's THE RELUCTANT RANCHER
and Lee McKenzie's TO CATCH A WIFE.*

Available now from Harlequin.com!

Get 2 Free Books,
Plus 2 Free Gifts—
just for trying the Reader Service!

YES! Please send me 2 FREE Love Inspired® Romance novels and my 2 FREE mystery gifts (gifts are worth about $10 retail). After receiving them, if I don't wish to receive any more books, I can return the shipping statement marked "cancel." If I don't cancel, I will receive 6 brand-new novels every month and be billed just $5.24 for the regular-print edition or $5.74 each for the larger-print edition in the U.S., or $5.74 each for the regular-print edition or $6.24 each for the larger-print edition in Canada. That's a saving of at least 13% off the cover price. It's quite a bargain! Shipping and handling is just 50¢ per book in the U.S. and 75¢ per book in Canada.* I understand that accepting the 2 free books and gifts places me under no obligation to buy anything. I can always return a shipment and cancel at any time. Even if I never buy another book, the 2 free books and gifts are mine to keep forever.

Please check one:

☐ Love Inspired Romance Regular-Print   ☐ Love Inspired Romance Larger-Print
(105/305 IDN GLQC)   (122/322 IDN GLQD)

Name _____ (PLEASE PRINT)

Address _____ Apt. #

City _____ State/Province _____ Zip/Postal Code

Signature (if under 18, a parent or guardian must sign)

Mail to the **Reader Service:**
IN U.S.A.: P.O. Box 1867, Buffalo, NY 14240-1867
IN CANADA: P.O. Box 611, Fort Erie, Ontario L2A 9Z9

Want to try two free books from another line?
Call 1-800-873-8635 today or visit www.ReaderService.com.

*Terms and prices subject to change without notice. Prices do not include applicable taxes. Sales tax applicable in N.Y. Canadian residents will be charged applicable taxes. Offer not valid in Quebec. This offer is limited to one order per household. Books received may not be as shown. Not valid for current subscribers to Love Inspired Romance books. All orders subject to credit approval. Credit or debit balances in a customer's account(s) may be offset by any other outstanding balance owed by or to the customer. Please allow 4 to 6 weeks for delivery. Offer available while quantities last.

Your Privacy—The Reader Service is committed to protecting your privacy. Our Privacy Policy is available online at www.ReaderService.com or upon request from the Reader Service.

We make a portion of our mailing list available to reputable third parties that offer products we believe may interest you. If you prefer that we not exchange your name with third parties, or if you wish to clarify or modify your communication preferences, please visit us at www.ReaderService.com/consumerschoice or write to us at Reader Service Preference Service, P.O. Box 9062, Buffalo, NY 14240-9062. Include your complete name and address.

LI17R

HOMETOWN HEARTS ♥

YES! Please send me **The Hometown Hearts Collection** in Larger Print. This collection begins with 3 FREE books and 2 FREE gifts in the first shipment. Along with my 3 free books, I'll also get the next 4 books from the Hometown Hearts Collection, in LARGER PRINT, which I may either return and owe nothing, or keep for the low price of $4.99 U.S./ $5.89 CDN each plus $2.99 for shipping and handling per shipment*. If I decide to continue, about once a month for 8 months I will get 6 or 7 more books, but will only need to pay for 4. That means 2 or 3 books in every shipment will be FREE! If I decide to keep the entire collection, I'll have paid for only 32 books because 19 books are FREE! I understand that accepting the 3 free books and gifts places me under no obligation to buy anything. I can always return a shipment and cancel at any time. My free books and gifts are mine to keep no matter what I decide.

262 HCN 3432 462 HCN 3432

Name   (PLEASE PRINT)

Address   Apt. #

City   State/Prov.   Zip/Postal Code

Signature (if under 18, a parent or guardian must sign)

Mail to the **Reader Service:**

IN U.S.A.: P.O. Box 1867, Buffalo, NY. 14240-1867
IN CANADA: P.O. Box 609, Fort Erie, Ontario L2A 5X3

* Terms and prices subject to change without notice. Prices do not include applicable taxes. Sales tax applicable in NY. Canadian residents will be charged applicable taxes. This offer is limited to one order per household. All orders subject to approval. Credit or debit balances in a customer's account(s) may be offset by any other outstanding balance owed by or to the customer. Please allow 4 to 6 weeks for delivery. Offer available while quantities last. Offer not available to Quebec residents.